# She
# Who
# Dared

James Walker

and

Francesca Garratt

*She Who Dared*
Published by The Conrad Press Ltd. in the United Kingdom 2024

Tel: +44(0)1227 472 874
www.theconradpress.com
info@theconradpress.com

ISBN 978-1-916966-73-4

Copyright © James Walker, 2024

Typesetting and Cover Design by: Charlotte Mouncey, www.bookstyle.co.uk
The Conrad Press logo was designed by Maria Priestley.

Printed and bound in Great Britain by Clays Ltd, Elcograf S.p.A.

*To my wife, Jo, as ever, for her love, patience and support*

ISABELLA'S FAMILY:

Philip IV The Fair of France 1268-1314
*m*
Joan of Navarre 1274-1305

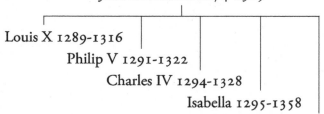

Louis X 1289-1316

Philip V 1291-1322

Charles IV 1294-1328

Isabella 1295-1358

and Robert 1297-1308

EDWARD'S FAMILY:

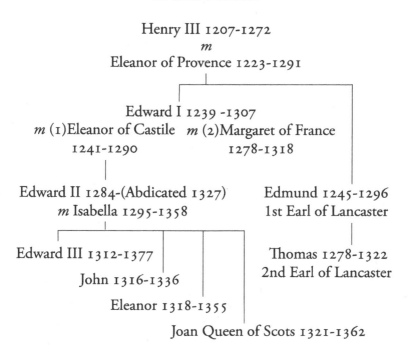

Henry III 1207-1272
*m*
Eleanor of Provence 1223-1291

Edward I 1239 -1307
*m* (1)Eleanor of Castile   *m* (2)Margaret of France
1241-1290                           1278-1318

Edward II 1284-(Abdicated 1327)        Edmund 1245-1296
*m* Isabella 1295-1358                          1st Earl of Lancaster

Edward III 1312-1377                              Thomas 1278-1322
John 1316-1336                              2nd Earl of Lancaster
Eleanor 1318-1355
Joan Queen of Scots 1321-1362

# PREFACE

*For rather than my Lord be oppressed (by) evil mutinies, I will endure a melancholy life and let him traffic with his minion.*

Words spoken by Queen Isabella in Christopher Marlowe's play, *Edward II*

In this play Queen Isabella of England 1295 - 1358 is portrayed as a submissive person who changes into one who is power-loving, unscrupulous and immoral. She is remembered in history as an essentially unworthy she-wolf and as a consequence has to an extent been ignored and largely forgotten, although, apart from Marlowe's play, some readers may recall her portrayal in the film *Braveheart* in 1995. Yet, this novel, in which she tells her own story, seeks to portray her as a strong, loyal and intelligent woman, who was forced by extreme circumstances to act against her husband for the good of the realm, and thereafter acted with personal integrity in what is a remarkable story.

# PART 1

# CHILD BRIDE

# PROLOGUE

## MY DESTINY

When I was but nine years old, my dearest mother, Queen Joan of France, died suddenly. I was left utterly bereft, whilst at a stroke deprived of all the innocent joy of childhood. I missed the loving arms of my mother along with the care and mentoring that only she could give me.

As I grew older, I remained in awe of my father, King Philip IV, of the House of Capet, known as the Fair, who in his looks and bearing appeared to me to be the very embodiment of Kingly virtue. Yet, I struggle to recall him ever bestowing any expressions of love upon me, or even an occasional smile.

Instead, I best remember him towering over me like some great statue, and when he spoke to me doing so in a stern voice that required me to do my duty as a Princess of France. I think he shied away from showing me too much affection, knowing, as he did, that I would need to grow up very quickly.

It was then that I became aware that I had been betrothed at the age of only three to the heir to the throne of England, Edward, Prince of Wales.

At first this meant little to me, but gradually I came to appreciate that my future lay in a foreign land as the wife of a man I had never even met and could not expect to meet until the very day of our marriage. I wondered, indeed, if I would even have to learn a new language, but was assured that the

English King and his court spoke French. In any case, I was determined to learn to speak the language of a country that was to become my new home.

I was filled with a mixture of fear, anticipation, and foreboding. I realised that once married I could not expect to ever see Paris again, or, for that matter, either my father or any of my four brothers. Of these, it was my younger brother, Robert, who I knew I would miss most, as we were so close in age, and spent so much time in each other's company.

All I could do was hope that when the time came, I would be brave and do my duty as befitted a Princess. I had to hope that I would find some happiness and that I would make my father proud. In my childish mind I could not give up on the notion that I would and should find some joy in my life. My mother would have wanted this for me, I was sure, as she had loved me so much.

# Chapter 1

## Boulogne-Sur-Mer Cathedral,
## 25th January 1308

The day of my wedding to Edward had arrived, making me so tense that my head began to throb, and I found that I had lost my appetite. I was thirsty, though, so sipped some watered-down wine, being at the still tender age of twelve too young to drink it neat.

I tried, as well, to relax as my ladies-in-waiting helped me don my wedding dress. I loved this; it was so beautiful, making me feel more grown-up than I had ever done before. It was made of silk, blue and gold in colour, and I had a lovely red-mantle cloak that was lined with fine, yellow-sindon cloth, which I have treasured ever since.

I felt so uncertain and nervous, but once I put on the crown that my father had given me, although this was heavy and uncomfortable, I felt like a true Queen about to fulfil my God-given destiny. Indeed, I was imbued with growing confidence.

Since the death of his father the previous July, Edward was now King of England, so I knew this day would be something of a rehearsal for a yet greater event, namely his coronation, when I would also be crowned Queen of England. More than ever, I now understood that my childhood had been but a preparation for these events, so I could but pray that I would not be found wanting. This was a ceremony that would mark the end of my childhood, and, in many ways, I was happy to let it go. I had experienced the sadness of losing my mother and the coldness of my father towards me. I hoped for better things to come on a personal level as well as in my role as queen.

Young as I still was, I also believed that I had one God given asset that was hugely to my advantage and that was my fair looks, which I had surely inherited from my father. I had often been complimented for being a pretty child and I was told that I was going to be a beautiful woman, not just by courtiers trying to please me, but by my ladies-in-waiting and the few childhood friends I had known.

As I looked at myself in the mirror on the wall in front of me, it was my blonde, curly hair, reaching down my back, of which I was most proud, but I liked as well, my plump, rosy cheeks, and well-shaped face, so I knew I had every reason to be at ease with my appearance.

'Princess, it's time!'

At these words I took a deep breath and turning around began the short walk to the Cathedral.

I was yet to set eyes on Edward but had already received an assurance from no less than my own father that he was a most handsome young man. This proved to be true.

When we came together at the great west door of the cathedral, to be met by the bishop who would perform our wedding service, what first struck me most of all was Edward's height. He towered over me, much like my father. I felt myself to still be no more than a tiny child in his presence, making me tremble a little. I felt overwhelmed by his authority and majesty, which again was a familiar feeling.

He was three months short of his twenty-fourth birthday, so almost twice my age, but still very much in the flush of youth, muscular, bearded, with unblemished skin and light-brown, curly hair, worn long enough to reach his shoulders. He was resplendent, too, in the surcoat and cloak he was wearing, the latter adorned with jewels that sparkled in the sunlight as it was an auspiciously fine day with high, broken cloud. As we turned our heads towards each other, I also thought his face was truly handsome, and I was set at ease by the bashful smile he bestowed on me.

Spontaneously, I returned his smile and then curtseyed to him. 'Your Majesty.'

In return he smiled before bowing to me.

'Your Grace.'

They were just two words, gently spoken, but enough to encourage me into believing that despite the age gap between us this might become a happy union.

I felt slightly lightheaded, and though, beneath my splendour, I was trembling, I tried to appear regal and dignified. I was afraid but proud. My mother had taught me how to carry myself as a princess and to be aware of my status. I took a deep breath and stood as tall and straight as I could manage.

Then the door was opened, and the bishop greeted us both. Looking behind him I could see that the cathedral's nave was full and knew that all eyes were upon us. I tensed slightly, determined to remain composed despite the continuing discomfort the weight of the crown on my head was causing me.

A courtier handed Edward my wedding ring, whereupon the bishop, speaking in Latin, blessed it with holy water along with my dowry with which Edward had already been presented by my father. Then Edward proceeded to place it, first on my thumb, saying as he did so, 'In nomine Patris', next on my index finger saying, 'et Filii', next on my middle finger, saying, 'et Spiritus Sancti,' and finally on my ring finger, saying, 'I marry you, wife.'

With these four words we were joined together as man and wife in the eyes of God. That I had not been expected to say anything during the ceremony, was a relief to me.

Then, holding hands, we processed down the nave behind the bishop until we reached the high altar, whereupon the mass began. In doing so we passed not just my father, who offered me the faintest of smiles, but also three other Kings, my brother Louis, King of Navarre, Albert of Habsburg, King of the Romans, and Charles the Second, King of Sicily, as well as three Queens, an Archduke, and a host of princes and nobles from across the whole of Europe. I believed that their presence was a tribute to my father's power as King of France so felt duly proud to be of his flesh. I made sure that I looked at them all, with my head held high, proud to be a queen and, I believed, their equal. I may not have had words to speak but I wanted to give a clear indication of my attitude and demeanour. I was not a child anymore; I was a queen!

At the same time, as the centre of attention of such an exalted gathering, I suddenly felt overwhelmingly self-conscious to the point of trembling so decided to keep my eyes focused on the bishop. The mass he then performed seemed torturously long as I became increasingly thirsty, which only served to intensify my feelings of discomfort under the weight of the crown I was wearing.

Eventually, though, this came to an end, so we processed out of the cathedral, once again passing the high and the mighty who had assembled to witness our marriage. I tried to smile but by now my mouth was so parched and my resulting discomfort so intense that I fear it was more of a grimace. As we left the cathedral I found the wind coming off the sea painfully cold, but at least the sun was still out, which I took to be a good omen for my future happiness.

There were to be a solid eight days of feasting and tournaments before our departure for England. My father spared no expense in providing these entertainments and, recalling those days, I suspect it was particularly the tournaments, which encouraged so many nobles to attend. They could show off their jousting skills as well as enjoy copious quantities of food and wine.

I cannot emphasise too strongly that at the tender age of twelve I was essentially an innocent child, entirely subject to the mercy of powerful men. I rejected the notion at the time, as I wanted to assert myself and appear to be more of an adult than I really was, but this was essentially bravado.

My progress into womanhood had begun, but not yet my courses, and as the day of my marriage approached what had filled me with the greatest trepidation was the prospect of being ceremonially bedded by King Edward on the first night of our marriage. I knew something, from my ladies, of what might be expected with regards to the wedding night and I had huge fears about this aspect of the marriage in the preceding weeks.

However, the day before the marriage, I had received an assurance from my nurse, Theophania de Saint-Pierre, Theo for short, to whom I confided the most intimate details about my person, that in the light of my youth I was to be spared this ceremony.

'Princess, you need have no fear on that account. I have been

14

assured that you will not be required to lie with your husband, the King, until your courses have begun.'

At this welcome news I had flung my arms around Theo; delighted, too, that I had already been told that she would be accompanying me to England as a member of my household. Twenty-five years old when I was born, she had been a constant presence in my life for as long as I could remember, and, especially since the death of my mother, she was always the person to whom I turned for emotional support. A patient, unflappable woman, with a kindly face and temperament to match, she would continue to fulfil that role in the years that lay ahead.

During this period of celebration, I inevitably spent a considerable amount of time in Edward's company, sitting at his right hand and I must say that my first impressions of him were entirely favourable. He was not only tall and handsome but also entirely chivalrous in his behaviour towards me. Furthermore, unlike my father, he had a ready smile and was easily given to gentle laughter. He also seemed kind and interested in my welfare, so I felt reassured that he would not force me into doing anything I was not comfortable with.

As Theo had promised me, nor did we lie together. Instead, at the end of each evening, he simply at me.

'I wish you goodnight, dear wife. Sweet dreams.'

Without making the slightest attempt to even kiss me, we then went our separate ways to bed in Boulogne's chateau.

The more chivalrously Edward behaved towards me, the more relaxed I became in his company and the more that I imagined that our union would be an untroubled one. Yet, as events were to prove, I was being naive, and I now believe my childhood sheltered me too much from life's harsher realities.

The first hint of darker days ahead came even before the festivities ended.

Three days after our marriage Edward reciprocated my father's generosity by entertaining my uncles, Louis of Evreux and Charles, Count of Valois, to a magnificent dinner, which I attended. It began as an entirely happy occasion but as Louis was about to depart, he handed a letter to Edward.

'It is from my brother, King Philip, concerning certain matters that trouble him relating to Gascony. He asked me to deliver it into your hands and would welcome the assurances his letter seeks from you before your departure for England. Kindly read it at your leisure. Now I thank you profusely for your hospitality and wish you a good night.'

With that he bowed to Edward as did Charles before they both walked away. They had barely left the hall before Edward broke the seal on the letter and I saw his face darken as he read its contents.

'God's teeth!' he exclaimed. 'This goes too far.'

'I am sorry if my father has written anything that offends you,' I offered.

Edward gave me a glum look. 'I do not take kindly to being threatened, but please do not trouble yourself. This is no concern of yours.'

I was soon to lose count of the number of times I was to hear those last six words. On this occasion I went to my bed none the wiser as to what the letter had threatened, although from what my uncle had said it clearly concerned Gascony. I had listened to my father talking with his courtiers and with my brothers, as they did not send me out of earshot when they discussed serious matters of state. I don't think that they thought I was listening, or that I would be interested , but how wrong they were. In fact I found these matters fascinating because it seemed natural to me to listen to and digest such important information.

I understood perfectly well that Gascony was a rich fiefdom, thanks to its many vineyards, in the Southwest of France, centred upon the city of Bordeaux. It had been in the possession of the English crown for more than a hundred and fifty years.

I had also heard enough to know that my father would have liked to rule over it, save that this would have involved a bloody war, which it was by no means certain he could win. Consequently, he was willing to tolerate a status quo, which had been in place since the days of my grandfather, King Louis IX, whereby the English crown accepted that Gascony was a vassal state of France. This gave my father the right to some say in its affairs. More importantly, from my own point of view, it was in exchange for this continued settlement, that I had been pledged in marriage to Edward.

By the time this took place I had learnt to play chess and come to enjoy it. As such, I understood that pawns could be sacrificed to a player's advantage and as the years have passed, I have come to believe that, for all my royal blood, as a Princess and a woman, I was no better than a pawn in the hands of my father. Certainly, if it was not for the English Crown's possession of Gascony, I might well have lived a very different life in some other realm, perhaps even in my homeland.

For the remaining three days of the festivities, I remained none the wiser as to what had so upset Edward, but I was alert enough to notice that my father and Edward were far less cordial to one another. Then, all too soon, the time came for me to say my farewells to my family. I must confess that I felt quite tearful, especially as I embraced Robert, whose face wore the saddest of expressions. My father's usual sternness was also replaced by a more tender gaze before he kissed me gently on both cheeks.

'I wish you every happiness, dear daughter. I'm sure you will acquit yourself well as Queen of England and be a credit to the House of Capet.'

'Thank you, father. I will endeavour to be so.'

On our journey to England, we were to set sail from the port of Wissant, accompanied by my two uncles, Louis and Charles. Given the time of year and having never set foot on any sea going vessel before, I was naturally apprehensive that conditions in the Channel would be rough, or even stormy. Indeed, for three days the weather was so poor that we had to delay our crossing.

Finally, on the fourth day, the weather calmed down. As a result, I enjoyed our crossing to Dover, on the Kent coast, far more than I had expected to, especially as we came closer to its white cliffs, on top of which I could make out its castle's great keep, where I was told we would be spending the next two nights. I felt great excitement as we travelled towards, what was to be, a new life for me.

# Chapter 2

# Rude awakening

Edward was on deck along with my uncles. We were together, but most of the time, to my disappointment, he ignored me. The closer we came to the shore the more he paced up and down in an agitated fashion. He was clearly impatient to disembark and the moment we were able to do so went ahead of me, even, to my surprise, breaking into a run, as he stepped on dry land. It was as though he found some kind of freedom, or relief in arriving on home ground. He seemed childlike and almost gleeful, which both surprised and mystified me.

A short distance away I could make out the figure of a young man, dressed in the attire of a nobleman with a red surcoat, fastened by a belt made of gold. He was smiling warmly and spread out his arms as Edward practically fell into them. The warmth of such an embrace caused me to ask an obvious question of those around me.

'Is this the King's brother?'

Even as I spoke Edward went so far as to plant a kiss on the man's cheek and seemed to answer my question as I was sure I heard him exclaim, 'dear brother.'

But then I recalled having been told that Edward only had one male sibling, a half-brother named Edmund, who was not yet seven.

'It's the King's favourite, I believe. His name is Piers Gaveston,' my uncle Louis informed me. I was left with a feeling of shock, almost dismay.

Even after almost fifty years that name still makes me shudder. Young and innocent as I was when I first set eyes on him, for Edward to throw himself into his arms in my presence when I had barely arrived in England, felt like an affront to both my position and my dignity. I had not yet received that kind of affection from my new husband, and I felt resentful. I was also aware of the young man's frosty glare towards me. He was handsome, no doubt, but haughty and superior in his demeanour. His attitude towards Edward seemed proprietorial and I felt excluded by them both. It was as though I was an unwelcome stranger, intruding on their intimacy. This caused me to dislike the man, almost instantly, and to this day I believe my judgement was well founded.

As the son of a Gascon knight his origins were quite humble, yet by the age of twenty-four, thanks to Edward's friendship, he had risen far above his natural station in life to be Earl of Cornwall and even Regent of England while Edward was marrying me in France. Certainly, I found him to be nothing better than a strutting peacock of a man with much too high an opinion of himself. Edward, clearly, had a quite different opinion.

In the meantime, much as I believed that Edward had behaved badly in my presence, it was not my place as a newly-wed twelve-year-old to remonstrate with him. I still had a lack of understanding, of the world of adults, not always knowing what to think about events that were happening around me. My powers of interpretation, after all, were still developing, but I knew how I felt.

Meanwhile, I was just swept along by fast moving events, although, I have to say that I found the attention that Edward paid Gaveston increasingly irksome. My uncles, too, more than shared my dislike of the man, and it was through them that I came to appreciate that he had a sizeable number of enemies amongst the English nobility. It was interesting to hear how much they resented, suspected, and felt irritated by Gaveston's closeness to the king.

—⁓—

I spent my first two nights on English soil in the great keep of Dover Castle. It was so imposing that I did not feel comfortable within its rather cold and dark confines. I was more than a little homesick, but I knew that I had to overcome this and behave in a dignified manner. I began to train myself not to reflect my innermost feelings, this 'act' becoming more real to me as time went by. Gradually, I was accessing a level of resourcefulness and forbearance that I had not previously known.

As for companions, my ladies-in-waiting, were, without exception, far older than I was. This was a disappointment to me, although I soon formed a firm friendship with my namesake, Isabella de Beaumont, widow of a certain Baron de Vesci, for all that she was thirty years my senior.

'Your Majesty, I am the King's cousin through her blessed Majesty, Eleanor of Castile, his late mother,' she told me with a smile, when we were introduced.

I was immediately drawn to her engaging disposition, as well as her pretty, open, and honest face, and she was to become something of a mentor to me in the months and years that lay ahead. I felt that I could trust her and confide in her, as I had done with my mother.

At the first opportunity she related how she had once been in a similar position to my own and could therefore fully understand what I was going through.

'Your Majesty, I was not much older than you are now when I married the Baron, whilst he was well into his thirties.'

'Did you have children by him?' I asked.

She grimaced a little. 'Alas, none that survived, but our marriage was not an unhappy one. He was a chivalrous man, and we came to love one another.'

'And is it many years since he died?'

'Twenty, or thereabouts. I still miss him.'

'Were you very afraid when you had just married him? I mean, afraid of your wifely duties, what might…what would happen between you in the bed chamber?'

I was nervous to ask her, but I needed to know. I was seeking reassurances to assuage my own very real fears.

'Forgive me, my Lady Beaumont, I do not mean to intrude.' I said, afraid that I had gone too far with my questions.

'Do not worry on my account your majesty, I understand, and I will gladly advise you, in the future, but for the time being, I do not believe the King will require you in his bedchamber quite yet, you are still so young.'

I found her words to be a great comfort and my fears were assuaged for the time being.

Whilst I was physically still quite small and slender, I was learning quickly, watching, listening, taking note of all that I was told and by whom. I knew that I must be careful and cautious in whom I placed my trust. I was aware that the court of a King was also a politically precarious place. I knew that not everyone would welcome me and not everyone had my best interests at heart. I had seen firsthand how the court of a king worked and I knew that courtiers could be duplicitous. Hidden jealousies, whispering behind doors, unexpected alliances, as well as grudges that were harboured over many years, were all things that my father had warned me about.

I was to become used to taking long journeys across the country. Some of my ladies felt that travelling was very dull, but I enjoyed watching the scenes that passed before my eyes. I was curious about the way that ordinary people lived in my new country, noticing their clothing, their dwellings, and sadly, their apparent poverty. I used these journeys as part of my education, and I found learning in this way was pleasurable.

After travelling through the Kent countryside, we arrived at Eltham Palace. With its great hall and deer park it is a place that I immediately fell in love with. Unfortunately, my sense of pleasure at my surroundings turned to anger when I saw that popinjay of a man, Gaveston, had the effrontery not only to wear the jewels and rings that my father had given Edward but also, he even dared to wear some of the jewellery I had brought with me as part of my dowry.

'This will not do,' I exclaimed to my uncles. 'This man has no right to be wearing any of these.'

'I agree,' my uncle Louis responded. 'The man is an upstart who seems to have cast a spell over the King. Yet, I believe his days as favourite may be numbered. I had a conversation last night in which I was told that plans are afoot to have him banished.'

'But surely only the King can do that?'

'True, but he's not yet crowned and the threat can be made to not take any part in the coronation unless he agrees. Charles and I are willing to add our voices to this demand.'

To compound my unhappiness at Gaveston's conduct, I discovered the income promised to me upon my marriage, was being withheld. Rather than complain to Edward about this, I decided to write a letter to my father explaining my predicament in the knowledge that he would act on my behalf. He did so very promptly, only to receive some feeble excuse from Edward along with assurances that the money would shortly be forthcoming.

The original intention had been for our coronation to take place on the nineteenth of February but once the demand, supported by my uncles, that Gaveston be banished was received by Edward, this led to its postponement as he temporised over the matter by offering to accede to the wishes of Parliament when it next met in March. This was agreed to and the decision made to proceed with the coronation on the twenty-fifth of February.

Everything that had happened since my arrival in England made me fearful for my future happiness and security, but I was once again swept along by events as we made a grand entry into London. I had heard that it was as fine a city as Paris and in this regard I was not disappointed. The streets of the city were also crowded with people as we entered as well as being brightly decorated with banners and pennants. There was much cheering, too, as we passed by.

'God bless you, good Queen Isabella! people called out.

When the time came for the Lord Mayor to follow the custom of handing over the keys to the city to Edward, I was impressed by the colourful livery that members of the city's guilds were wearing in our honour.

It was an altogether uplifting experience to be cheered so loudly so I responded by smiling broadly and waving my hand in acknowledgement. It was on this day, too, that I had my first real experience of England's mother tongue of which I knew nothing. Whilst I was aware that at court as well as amongst the higher echelons of the nobility there was no necessity for me to learn how to speak it, I nonetheless resolved to do so. In this regard I also received due encouragement from Edward who in conversing with the Lord Mayor and Alderman of the City, demonstrated that he had a fluent grasp of the language.

As he began to teach me a few words, I felt the beginnings of a bond between us, as he did so patiently and with a gentle smile. Furthermore, he continued to show me every courtesy, without any of the aloofness I had grown used to from my father. It was my hope that with time I would grow to love him. Yet, Gaveston's presence at our side continued to irritate me, and never more so than on the day of our coronation at Westminster Abbey.

Alas, Edward chose to give Gaveston responsibility for organising the occasion, something of which he took full advantage. When I first set eyes on him that day, he was so over-dressed that I was forced to put a hand to my mouth in order to suppress a giggle. Worse than this, he had the arrogance to wear purple, like some Roman Emperor of old, as if he was more powerful than Edward, who was about to become his God anointed King.

But more than even this, he chose to be the bearer of that most sacred relic, the crown of St Edward Confessor, a right normally only given to the highest born noble in the land, when he, of course, was very far from being any such thing. As I looked around me I could tell from the expressions on the faces of the many great men who had gathered for the ceremony that they were very far from pleased.

Indeed, I even heard one voice exclaim in anger. 'God's teeth, the impudence of the man. Has he no shame?!'

The coronation then proceeded and when the time came for my anointment as Queen, I knew with pride that I was fulfilling a destiny, which had been planned for me since I was but a small child. Yet, once we had processed out of the Abbey, before entering the Great Hall of Westminster, with the intention of enjoying the banquet that was being prepared for us, my sense of happiness turned to one of affronted dismay when Edward chose to desert my side and instead take his seat at the other end of the high table, next to Gaveston.

'This is nothing less than an insult to your dignity as Queen, 'Uncle Louis exclaimed.

'And look at this,' Uncle Charles added, pointing towards the tapestries that had been hung behind us in the hall to mark the occasion. They were beautifully made, using the brightest of colours, but what he was drawing our attention to was that the tapestries bore the coats of arms of the King and Gaveston.

'This is disgraceful!' Uncle Louis said angrily, banging his fist the table in front of us. 'It is your coat of arms as a Royal Princess and now Queen of England that should be entwined with the King's, not those of this upstart Earl.'

His words were surely said loudly enough for Gaveston and Edward to hear them. Yet, they chose to ignore him, which was just as well in the circumstances, as the last thing I would have wished for was an angry altercation.

A copious amount of wine was then served, and whilst I only sipped from my glass, many around me drank their fill, including my uncles, which inevitably loosened tongues, causing the volume of conversation in the hall to grow louder. My uncles also continued to grumble on about Gaveston and my ears pricked up when Uncle Charles asked a particular question. 'Do you think the rumours are true, then?'

My Uncle Louis shrugged. 'He's certainly besotted with the man to give him such attention, even though he must surely appreciate the offence it causes. From the evidence of our own eyes, I certainly think the rumours are very likely to be true.'

'Rumours, what rumours are these?' I asked.

Uncle Louis gave me a somewhat embarrassed look. 'My dear Isabella, forgive me, we should not have begun to talk about such a matter in your presence.'

'Why? I may still be very young, but I am nonetheless now Queen of England and it's my husband you speak of.'

'...Very well. You will know your bible and the injunction that man shall not lie with man. Need I say more?'

'No, no, uncle. I understand.' Or at least, being still but a child, I was beginning to. As part of that process my eyes were opened to the fact that Gaveston was essentially an effeminate individual who, as if he was a member of the female sex, took pleasure in dressing up in colourful clothing and wearing jewels. Furthermore, I began to appreciate why his fellow Earls held him in such contempt for he was not just an unduly favoured upstart but also a man who offended their strong sense of manhood.

Naturally, I also began to wonder what this meant for my future happiness with Edward. If he did indeed prefer lying with men, it seemed to me that I might never bear any children. Equally, I might never come to enjoy all the pleasures to be derived from a loving relationship. It was a prospect I found so awful that I even wondered if I might as well have been sent to a Nunnery for the remainder of my existence than made Queen of England at such a tender age.

Looking towards Edward as he conversed happily with Gaveston, I also decided that I needed to hear the truth about their relationship from his own lips. Yet, how was I to insist on such honesty when the matter was so intimately delicate, there was such a difference in age between us, and I had sworn to love, honour and obey him? It was a dilemma to which I really had no easy answer.

Nonetheless, I resolved to find a way, no matter how painful a process that might be. How I would then live with the answer I received was quite a different matter, but one way or another I knew I would have to come to terms with it as best I could. Of course, there was also the possibility that for all my endeavours, he would still decline to give me any answer. In that event, I would have to draw my own unhappy conclusions.

As I continued to sip on my wine, time began to drag, and those about me in the hall grew increasingly restless as the promised banquet failed to appear. Indeed, we must have sat there for more than an hour before I noticed Gaveston hastily making his leave with an anxious frown on his face. A few minutes later he returned and immediately spoke briefly to Edward before making an apology for the delay to the entire assembly, though I doubt if his voice was loud enough to carry the length of the hall.

'...I am assured that the food will be served soon. Thank you for your patience.'

In fact it must have been the best part of another hour before anything appeared, by which time restlessness had grown to anger, much of it directed at Gaveston, whom Edward had after all placed in charge of all the day's arrangements. He sat glum-faced as the light faded and candles were lit. Finally, to a collective sigh of relief, the food did begin to be served. Yet, to everyones dismay, it was so poorly cooked as to be virtually inedible, whereupon Edward decided to call a halt to the event by indicating that we should leave without further ado.

I must say that if ever there was an ill omen on a coronation day of far worse disasters to follow, this was surely it.

# CHAPTER 3

## FRUSTRATIONS

The day following the coronation both my uncles departed for France. As I stood waving them farewell, I felt sadness at the thought that I might never set eyes on either of them again as well as an even greater pang of sadness at my separation from my younger brother, Robert. In consolation, I had at least my beloved Theo for company as well as my ladies-in-waiting. Yet, in the continued absence of any money to pay for it, no greater household of my own, which I found increasingly annoying given that this flew in the face of everything to which I was entitled as Queen.

My home for these first few weeks as Queen was the newly refurbished Palace of Westminster, where, especially as I lacked a proper household of my own, I could reasonably have expected to see much of Edward. The reality, though, could not have been more different as he largely ignored my existence, preferring, so I was led to believe by more than one of my ladies-in-waiting, the company of Gaveston, which only served to fuel my sense of resentment.

I wanted to reproach him for his lack of attention to me when I was his newly-married bride, but he gave me so little opportunity that it was impossible to do so, whilst the fact of the matter is that we were never properly alone together. My frustration at this state of affairs also grew more intense with each passing day to the point that I would have given my jewels, which Gaveston had the temerity to be wearing, for twenty minutes entirely on our own so that I could question him about the true nature of his relationship with this upstart.

Meanwhile, it was my ladies-in-waiting, especially Isabella de Beaumont, who were my eyes and ears as to what was taking place beyond the confines of my apartments in the Palace. It was through them that I learnt that the campaign to have Gaveston banished was gaining momentum. At the same time I was free to continue my correspondence with my father, who assured me that he had raised a fortune through taxation for my dowry and that this had been paid to Edward. At this news I became really angry and resolved to confront him even if it meant falling on my knees and begging him to hear my complaint.

For several days I was denied even this opportunity as I was told that Edward was away hunting and would return when it pleased him to do so. I was mightily suspicious that he was also enjoying Gaveston's company rather than mine but there was nothing to do but wait, which I found increasingly tedious especially as the weather was cold and wet. Finally, after ten days Edward did return and deigned to send me an invitation to join him for dinner.

As I entered the beautifully decorated hall where this was to be served, accompanied by my ladies-in-waiting, I immediately noticed to my dismay that Gaveston was seated to Edward's left, still looking like the over-dressed popinjay he undoubtedly was. Worse than that, as if to spite me, he was still wearing some of my own jewellery, which made me very tight-lipped as I struggled to contain my anger.

As was my due, the assembled company of men including Edward and Gaveston rose to their feet and Edward smiled at me in greeting whilst motioning me to join him on his right side. I could not bring myself to return his smile and merely nodded my head.

'Are you well?' he asked me once I had taken my seat.

'As well as can be expected when you choose to desert me for so long,' I answered him, frostily.

'Forgive me, I have been otherwise engaged.'

'Hunting, you mean?'

'...Why, yes, partly that. I also have affairs of state to attend to. I am King, after all.'

I looked at him askance, wondering how honest an answer he had given me. I remained determined to complain about his treatment of me, but decided it was prudent to bide my time a little until I judged the moment was right. This arrived about an hour later, by which time we were enjoying our sweetmeats. The atmosphere in the hall had also grown relaxed, if noisy, thanks to the amount of wine which had been drunk.

In the meantime, Edward had offered me only a minimal amount of conversation, preferring instead to talk to Gaveston and other nobles seated close to us. As far as I was concerned it was mostly idle chatter about hounds and horses as well as passing references to men and women whose names meant little to me. There was some merriment, too, and not for the first time since we had met I realised that Edward had a gentle sense of humour and liked to laugh. This certainly appealed to me, though I was still too angry with him to give it much heed.

'Your Majesty...,' I said at last, speaking into his left ear as there was a lull in conversation and Gaveston had excused himself from the table, saying he had a call of nature.

'Call me, Edward, please.'

'Why yes, of course. Edward... I am concerned to have learnt from my father that you are in full possession of my valuable dowry and yet you have still failed to give me any funds for my personal expenses, let alone those of my household. Why is this?'

'All in good time, Isabella, all in good time.'

'But your Majesty..., Edward, we have now been married more than a month. How much more time do you need?'

'As I've told you before there are legal complications, but I expect all will be resolved in a few weeks. In the meantime, are you not well provided for in my household?'

'I have the basics of life, but nothing more. It galls me, too, to see your favourite wearing jewels that are rightfully mine. He overreaches himself. Surely, you see that?'

'Hum, yes, perhaps in this instance he does. I will speak to him on the subject.'

I could now see Gaveston returning and realised that for the time being at least there was nothing to be gained by pressing my case any further. All the same, I decided to allow Edward no more than another month to provide me with the funds to which I was entitled before speaking to him again on the matter.

To my delight it was then only a matter of days before I received my jewels in person from Edward, and though he was only handing me what was rightfully mine, I thought it tactful to be profusely grateful. In return, he smiled at me indulgently and even kissed me on the cheek before we parted.

'We shall be spending Easter at the royal castle of Windsor,' he told me. 'You should like it there. It stands close to the

Thames, in fine countryside. The hunting's usually good, too. It's also no more than a day's ride from here, although I've a mind to travel a little further afield first so I can show you the fine Abbey at Reading as well as the royal castle at Wallingford. Like Windsor, it also stands on the Thames.'

I did not dare to ask whether Gaveston would be joining us on our progress for fear of betraying the level of anger I still felt towards the man. In the event, when we set off without him I could not have been more delighted, and saw this as an ideal opportunity for Edward and me to gain a better acquaintance of one another without that hateful man being forever at Edward's shoulder.

The weather was also kind to us with signs of spring growth everywhere, whilst people gathered to wave us on our way in every hamlet and village we passed through.

I grew somewhat weary of the amount of smiling and waving that was required of me in response, but I could not begrudge it when we were greeted by so many smiling faces as well as a great deal of cheering. Edward also amply demonstrated that he had the common touch by the number of friendly conversations he entered into with even the lowliest of his subjects, not that I understood more than a few words of what was being said. It was a side to his character that I warmed to, whilst in Gaveston's absence he paid me more attention than at any time since our marriage.

Still, we were never totally alone together, so I was forced to put any hope of talking to him about his relationship with Gaveston to the back of my mind. Then, to my chagrin, we had not been at Windsor more than two days before the wretched man put in an appearance and Edward effectively ignored my existence once more, which only served to make me angrier than ever.

To lift my spirits somewhat, we were also joined by the Sir Roger Mortimer, who had been present at my wedding. Younger than Edward by some three years, he was tall and well built, and I thought him the most handsome of men with a courteous disposition and a ready smile. More than that, whereas I was finding some of the English nobility coarse and unlettered, with an apparent interest in nothing more than war, hunting, and the pursuit of their own ambitions, Roger pleased me greatly by demonstrating that in sharing Edward's love of literature, poetry and music, he was just as cultivated.

He also liked to dress well and in many respects he and Edward could have been brothers. Roger, though, had a far more martial spirit as well as a reputation as a good soldier, whereas I was coming to understand that to the annoyance of many of his Earls, Edward had no desire to fight anyone if it could possibly be avoided.

By the time we left Windsor to travel back to Westminster, we were well into April and yet I had still not received any of the income that was rightfully mine. Once again I therefore found an opportunity to gently reproach Edward about this only to have my just concerns shrugged to one side with the same lame excuse about unresolved legalities. I stamped my foot a little.

'But this is what you told me weeks ago. Surely, there can be no doubt as to the money to which I am entitled!'

His face darkened. 'Do not try my patience. I tell you, you will receive what's due to you when I see fit to bestow it upon you and not before.'

'Then you're treating me unjustly. I shall complain to my father.'

'Do as you please!' And with that he turned his back on me and stalked off.

I sighed, and then turned towards Isabella de Beaumont, who was standing in the background. 'Your Grace, I would advise you to beware his Majesty's temper,' she said.

'Really, it's my temper that he tries when he shows me such scant regard.'

'Even so, I have witnessed him fall into a rage when he thought his wishes had been crossed. His father was much the same.'

'Well, that's as may be, but so long as he continues to deny me what is rightfully mine, he leaves me with no choice but to risk his wrath.'

As I had threatened, I also immediately set about composing a letter to my father, in which I complained bitterly about Edward's behaviour towards me in withholding what was rightfully mine. Nor could I resist telling him of my dislike of Gaveston as well as relating the ongoing struggle between Edward and the majority of his barons over the upstart's future. By now, thanks to what I learnt from my ladies-in-waiting, I knew that the situation was becoming so serious that civil war was even a possibility, especially as Edward had deferred the meeting of Parliament in March that had been expected to settle Gaveston's fate.

# CHAPTER 4

# BECOMING A QUEEN

It was becoming clearer to me that Edward was by nature an indecisive procrastinator, who had been born to rule yet seemed to lack either the calibre or inclination to do so well. 'Never do today what can be put off until tomorrow' might as well have been his motto, but faced with a growing threat of armed conflict as well as a stern letter from my father admonishing him for his treatment of me, he finally agreed to a meeting of Parliament at Westminster at the end of April.

Yet even then, for all that it was made clear to Edward that Gaveston had taken advantage of his favouritism towards him by seizing funds to which he was not entitled and should thus face banishment, he still wouldn't agree to it. My predicament was also debated, leading a few days later to the King's own Council trying to make him see reason, but still he prevaricated.

By now, I was beside myself with frustration and prepared to personally berate Edward for his unjust treatment of me even it should test his patience beyond its breaking point. However, I was denied the opportunity as he would not show his face to me, no doubt preferring Gaveston's company to mine.

Once again I had no choice but to appeal to my father, saying in my letter that Edward's treatment of me showed that he had no sense of honour and was the worst of Kings. 'And as for Gaveston, his unnatural infatuation with that man, leaves me utterly humiliated. Help me father, I beg you, for I am in the most wretched of states!'

My father responded swiftly by sending envoys to Westminster bearing a stern warning that unless Gaveston was banished, he would regard anyone who supported him as a mortal enemy. At the same time the envoys made it clear that Edward's treatment of me was totally without justification and must be put right 'forthwith.' Furthermore, I learnt through these envoys that my father had gone so far as to offer financial support to those intent on ousting Gaveston from court.

Yet, for a few days Edward still appeared to ignore my father's stark warning, while at the same time continuing to keep his distance from me.

I was forced to the conclusion that civil war a real possibility, when finally Edward deigned to pay me a visit. He was as cordial as ever.

'I've decided to settle the revenue from two of Gascony's counties upon you with immediate effect. They'll provide you with an ample income, I'm sure, so more than enough to pay for all your personal needs along with those of your household.'

'Thank you, Edward, I am most grateful.' I was tempted to add that it was ridiculous that he had waited a full three months before making this settlement in my favour. Yet I was old enough to appreciate that this would have been tactless of me, so merely dropped him a deep curtsey to which he responded with a low bow.

Only a few days later he then finally agreed to banish Gaveston from the Kingdom by the end of June and at the same time deprive him of his Earldom. Nonetheless, as I was coming to understand was typical of Edward, he did not stop there, bestowing upon Gaveston a generous gift of land in Gascony as well as making him his Viceroy in Ireland with full royal powers. At the same time, he also remained determined to enjoy his favourite's company right up to the day of his departure to take up his new role.

Consequently, even when we left Westminster at the end of May to undertake the short journey to the Royal Manor of Langley near St Albans, Gaveston came with us and I continued to be largely ignored. Naturally, I still wondered about my resolve to question Edward about the nature of his relationship with his favourite, but apart from being denied any real opportunity, decided that once Gaveston had left the country there would be far less need to pursue the matter, anyway. All I could hope was that Edward would begin to forget the man and show me, if not affection, then at least a measure of attention, which up to now had been so sadly lacking.

Yet, for all my anger with Edward, I did not dislike him. After all, whenever he did deign to spend a little time in my company, he was perfectly courteous, whilst I still warmed to his easy sense of humour and gentle laugh. That he was such a cultured man with a particularly strong love of music also had a strong appeal, and when I thought how much we had in common it irritated me that we had not yet begun to create a proper relationship. I therefore found myself counting down the days to Gaveston's departure.

'It cannot come too soon,' I told both Theo and Isabella de Beaumont.

But, of course, I was naive to imagine that once Gaveston had finally departed everything would change for the better. Edward was thrown into a state of melancholy akin to how I had felt at the loss of my dear mother and worse besides, not just for a few days but several weeks. Indeed, as I grew heartily sick of his sullen indifference towards me, I began to wonder if he would ever recover. Finally, I could stand it no longer and even though it was in the presence of my ladies-in-waiting turned on Edward.

'In God's name, why are you still so mournful all the time? You're no pleasure to be with and in fact positively insult me with your constant state of melancholy. It's as if you had an unnatural love for Gaveston and cannot bear to live without him.'

Edward gave me an angry stare. 'How dare you talk to me in such a fashion! I am King. I do not have to justify my feelings for Piers to anyone, even you. And I'll grieve for his absence as much as I damn we'll choose. Do I make myself clear!'

His voice had now risen to a crescendo of rage, of which I had been warned he was capable, causing me to flinch in some alarm.

'I said, do I make myself clear?!' Edward reiterated.

'Yes, Edward, I'm sorry. It's just… '

'No, enough, not another word before I lose my temper completely.'

I was forced into silence, though not without shedding a few tears, whilst I still felt a sense of grievance at his obsession with Gaveston, a man for whom I had no respect whatsoever. In a mood of considerable despair, I then made an abrupt decision to go on pilgrimage to the shrine of St Thomas Becket in Canterbury. I had been told of the martyr's fame even as a child and upon our arrival in Dover in February had been disappointed that it had not been possible to visit the shrine during our journey to London. Now, I saw my decision as a way of asserting my growing sense of independence, given that at last I had my own income to do with as I pleased.

'As Edward refuses to forget his favourite and appears to have no regard for me, I can't wait to set off,' I asserted to Isabella de Beaumont.

'I take it you'll be seeking the King's permission?'

'I shall tell him what I have decided. I cannot see him raising any objection. I needn't be away for more than a week. Can you come with me?'

'I will be pleased to.'

In the event, I was right to think that Edward wouldn't object to my plan, but at the same time I was surprised by his contriteness.

'I apologise for being so angry. It is true I've been poor company. When you return from your pilgrimage, I promise to pay you more regard. I... I want us to be friends.' And with that he offered me a bashful smile.

'As do I, Edward, I assure you.'

This occasion proved to be a turning point in our relationship. I departed on my pilgrimage in a much better humour than I had anticipated after Edward came to see me depart and even kissed me on both cheeks. He had never previously offered me such a gesture of affection either in private or in public, so naturally, I believed this was real progress.

Despite his initial display of anger, it occurred to me that the spirit I had shown in questioning his behaviour had impressed him. What I also sensed was that I was beginning to blossom as a woman and that, whatever his proclivities, he was beginning to find me physically attractive. This was what I desired more than anything else, I wanted to become his queen in every sense of that word.

I was also growing used to admiring glances and enjoyed being the centre of so much favourable attention throughout my pilgrimage. I was beginning to realise that men looked at me in a way which made me feel proud and yet bashful at the same time. These new sensations must be part of my growing up. All of this helped to make me increasingly confident that I had inherited my father's good looks as well as his intelligence, which I now hoped to be able to put to beneficial use in Edward's favour.

I sensed that he was weak in certain respects, but with time, I believed that I might yet become his backbone, enabling him to rule with authority and wisdom. I wanted to have a role in my husband's life that was more than just providing him with children. I knew that I was expected to provide him with heirs and secure the royal lineage but I wanted to be more than a physical receptacle. I wanted indeed to add my intellect and abilities so as to be of service to his reign.

—⁂—

It was a few weeks after my return from Canterbury that Edward asked me for the first time to play a role for him as Queen by hosting, in his absence, a feast at the Great Hall at Westminster. I was delighted to be asked by him as this meant that he trusted me, having recognised that I was ready to assume the mantle of being his Queen at an important event.

'I should be there in person, I know, but I have had a splitting headache for the past two days and am not feeling at all well. I fear I have been drinking too much wine of late and I know it does me no favours.'

In the years that lay ahead I would frequently see Edward in an inebriated state, his breath stinking of alcohol, and although he was no worse in this regard then many of his nobles, it still increasingly irritated me. However, at this stage of our marriage

I was suitably sympathetic that he felt unwell. In fact, I was won over by his blue eyes, flecked with golden streaks, the little dimple in his chin, his strong slightly square jaw, and his clear, smooth complexion. I noticed, too, his good looks, which rendered me shy and yielding to the point I would have done anything for him, and looked forward to playing my role as Queen to the full. I wanted him, too, to be impressed and just possibly to begin to fall in love with me.

'I will be happy to do as you ask, Edward. I trust that the food will be better prepared than it was on our coronation day.'

He laughed. 'Oh, have no concern on that account. The number attending is much smaller.'

And it was, not that there wasn't still some delay in serving our courses, but the food when it arrived was still properly cooked and the event went well. Of all those present, it was Roger Mortimer who once again most caught my eye. As imposing as ever, he must have been the tallest man in attendance and exceedingly handsome. It even crossed my mind that, had I been free to marry any man I chose, he would have been the one. Yet, I knew this was no more than the idle fancy of a young girl, whereas I was now Queen of England, so I quickly set aside any such notion.

For all that I was now on far better terms with Edward, it still irritated me that he was continuing to try and negotiate Gaveston's return. I feared that so long as he lived, I would never supplant him in Edward's affections, so every day in my prayers I included one that he would never be permitted to return from exile. That way, whatever he might feel in his heart, Edward would have no choice but to continue to pay me the regard which was my due as his Queen.

# Chapter 5

# Arguments

I was beginning to take pleasure in my role as Queen, spending an increasing amount of time at Edward's side, and while doing so, getting to know and like him better. He was no longer the maudlin individual he had been for the first few weeks after Gaveston's departure and instead showed the friendly and often jovial side of his nature as well as frequently demonstrating his common touch with his subjects, regardless of their station in life. Sometimes, I thought he went too far in this regard, demeaning his dignity as King, but it undoubtedly made him more popular. I wanted that for myself, as well as being seen as his loyal and beautiful wife.

Above all, I came to realise how much we had in common, including a shared love of music, plays, and literature, especially poetry, helping me to believe that we could with time develop a real affection for one another.

I was now thirteen and, through my nurse, Theo, let it be known to Edward that my courses had begun so that we could, if he wished, begin to lie together as man and wife. The idea of this filled me with fear as I still retained some of my childlike qualities. However, I was also curious about how the physical relationship between a husband and wife was meant to be, I felt emotions that were strong in this regard, and I had an increasing physical desire for intimacy to begin. Yet, I waited in vain for him to share my bed and this filled me with all sorts of fears. Perhaps I was wrong to imagine that he found me attractive, perhaps he was still obsessed with his favourite, perhaps he was simply too shy, perhaps it was a combination of all of these? Furthermore, no matter how much time we spent in each other's company, it was always in the presence of others, making me long for the opportunity to be completely alone with him.

Days became weeks and still he did not come near me, I grew increasingly impatient, much as I had when he had denied me any income of my own. Finally, I could stand it no longer and even though we were not alone, decided to whisper into his ear.

'You know my courses have begun. Are we never to lie together as man and wife?' He tensed but said nothing. 'I would like an answer, please?'

'All in good time,' he whispered back. 'I will do my duty by you.'

'I like to think it could be more than that.'

'Um, perhaps.'

My heart sank and I felt a pang of self- doubt, it was not the most encouraging of responses, but I decided to take comfort in the fact that it had not been an outright rejection. I was, after all, still very young so perhaps he still wanted me to be more mature before sharing a bed with me. Then again, perhaps in his heart he was still obsessed with Gaveston. It was hard to be certain, either way. In any event, I decided that it was pointless worrying too much about where the truth lay. In every other respect my life was now everything I had hoped for, so for the time being at least I was content to make the most of that.

Now and then I gave myself over to girlish daydreams,

imagining the Edward was entirely in love with me and that he would court me as a lady in the tales of romance I had read in France as a young girl. I began to long for the courtly love described in the tales of King Arthur and his knights.

I also now had the means to bestow my patronage on worthy causes whilst Edward began to demonstrate that he was capable of being generous when he made me lavish grants of both money and land. The events surrounding Gaveston's banishment had also taught me that though Edward was King his power was far from being absolute. At all times he needed to earn the support of his Earls, especially those who possessed the greatest wealth. For his sake I was prepared to use my feminine charms to garner the support of these men, even though I considered most of them to be nothing better than ignorant philistines. I knew that I had charm aplenty and I wanted nothing more than to be a great source of help and of pride to my husband.

All his Earls were proud, as befitted their rank, and most of them arrogant, to boot, especially Thomas, Earl of Lancaster. I say that even though he was my maternal uncle. Of course, I showed him the respect, which was his due, but I really wasn't that sorry when he fell out with Edward until I learnt through my 'eyes and ears,' Isabella de Beaumont, the main reason for this happening.

'He believes the King is scheming to have Gaveston restored to his Earldom and will have none of it.'

On this at least I was in total sympathy with my uncle, and I felt a deep sense of hurt that Edward was still in thrall to that odious creature. Furthermore, on every occasion I ingratiated myself with Edward's Earls for his sake, the irony was not lost on me that I was doing so to help him achieve an ambition, which would very likely drive me into the shadows once more. I wanted what was best for Edward and I did not feel that Gaveston was included in that. As far as I was concerned he was a dreadful influence on my husband.

I was also disappointed when Roger Mortimer departed from court to take up a position in Ireland. This disappointment was then turned to deep grief and then devastation when I received news from France that my younger brother, Robert, had died. We had enjoyed so many happy hours together as children and I had always imagined him growing into a handsome young man. I felt his loss so deeply, I was empty and bereft. All I could do was pray for his soul, which I did so fervently every day for a month.

Once again Edward demonstrated the gentle side of his character by showing me every solicitude in my grief, even embracing me firmly with both arms as well as planting a kiss on my forehead. I was glad of his affection and felt somewhat consoled by his tenderness towards me at that time. If any good had come out of my brother's death, I thought this might be it, but still Edward did not come near my bed. Further, as we entered a new year it also became clearer to me than ever that he was doing everything he possibly could to restore Gaveston to his Earldom.

For all that I was still so young and, to a large extent, uninitiated in the ways of the world, their relationship never felt right to me. Certainly, the love Edward had for Gaveston went beyond the normal brotherly comradeship that many men shared with their friends, and was, to me, an unholy kind of love.

With the coming of spring, I learnt through my father, that Edward had even had the audacity to ask him to intercede with those nobles very much opposed to Gaveston's return. Of course, the very notion affronted him for all that Edward had gone out of his way to curry favour with him on several matters concerning Gascony.

Gaveston was also under threat of excommunication from the Archbishop of Canterbury, but Edward turned to the Pope with a request that he remove this threat. To my consternation the Pope duly obliged, towards the end of April, just before Parliament was due to meet once more at Westminster. Yet, to my relief, Edward's request for his favourite to be allowed to return was still roundly rejected.

This time, though, Edward refused to accept his nobles' decision and pressed on regardless with plans to enable Gaveston to return. When I then learnt that a summons was about to be sent to him in Ireland, I was frankly furious, and decided to tell Edward at the first opportunity how opposed I was to this, though, of course, finding the right moment when we could be sufficiently alone together was as hard as ever.

Eventually, when we were in company as usual and I could wait no longer, I resorted to asking Edward, if he would be willing to come to my apartments one evening to dine alone with me. I added that there were some personal matters I wanted us to talk about and I asked him if he could come soon. Of course, I knew that my servants would still be present but that didn't concern me as I could always order them to leave us.

'What is so important that we cannot discuss it now?'

Such a response was irritating, but I was prepared for it,

offering him a smile. 'We are man and wife. I thought you might welcome such an occasion.'

'Oh, very well. I will come to you tomorrow evening.'

'Thank you. I will look forward to it.'

I felt pleased with myself for having dared to pursue the need for a meeting and for refusing to accept Edward's attempt at a rebuttal. I would not be disregarded, nor spoken to as if I were a mere child, I was beginning to stand firm and live up to my status as his queen.

When he duly arrived, at first, he looked rather nervous, but I immediately offered him a glass of wine and, as I had hoped would be the case, this helped to put him at his ease. We then began to enjoy a delicious four course meal, prepared with the greatest of care by my cooks, upon my orders. It was only when we had eaten the second of these, by which time Edward had downed his third glass of wine, that I decided to come to the point.

'Edward, is it true that you've summoned Gaveston back from Ireland?'

'Um, yes. What of it?'

'But how can you possibly do such a thing when you must know how hated he is?'

'I am King and I have obtained the Pope's support. I just wish I hadn't agreed to Pier's banishment in the first place. I need him by my side.'

'So, what about me?'

'I'm sorry, I don't know what you mean.'

'Since Gaveston was banished last year, you have treated me with the respect, which is my due. It's helped us to grow closer, I believe, for which I'm grateful. What concerns me is that once Gaveston returns he will once again come first in your affections, in which case I will be ignored.'

'No, no, not at all. Have I not been generous in the gifts I have made you?'

'Yes, yes you have, but this man seems to have a hold on you. Where will that leave me once you are together again?'

'I will continue to honour you as my Queen. On that you have my word.'

'So, I will continue to be by your side and travel with you as I have since he was banished?'

Edward drew in his breath,'...Yes, though Piers will be with us...'

'Whatever hold he may have on you, I don't want that. I don't like him.'

'Well, be that as is it may, he is my dearest friend, and I am determined to have him by my side. In fact he's such a vital support to me that I cannot rule without him. I need him to return.'

'Even at the risk of more conflict with many of your Earls?' I was not just going to accept this as a reasonable reply.

'Why, of course. I am King and will not be dictated to by anyone, least of all you.'

This last remark upset me, so, for all that Edward was now clearly becoming angry with me, I retaliated.

'Oh yes, I know I'm just a slip of a girl whom you don't even want to share your bed with, but still I am your Queen with every right to expect to be treated with the respect that is my due.'

'You are, and you will be. Haven't I already made that plain?'

'Not if you insist on having that fop of a man by your side instead of me!'

'You will continue to be my side, I tell you?'

'Really? Shall I be on your right and Gaveston on your left, then?'

'Now you're trying my patience. I have given you my assurance, be satisfied with that.'

'Alright, if you insist.'

# Chapter 6

# A vital question

I realised that I needed to rein in my sense of despair. However, I also knew that this was not to be the end of my objections. I had a perfect right to demand that I should come first in Edward's affections, I was his wife after all.

Another course of food was now brought to the table and our conversation turned to more mundane matters; not that I was really at all satisfied with the assurance Edward had given me. There also remained the uncomfortable question of whether he preferred to lie with men rather than women, and, if that was indeed the case, what chance there was of his ever sharing his bed with me.

Servants were still serving us, but I suddenly made up my mind that the question needed to be put. I couldn't just leave things as they were. I felt a surge of courage coursing through my body, I had not felt so fearless and determined before.

'Leave us, please. I will call you when I want you to return,' I said.

They bowed their heads to me and quickly withdrew while Edward gave me a curious look.

'What's this about?'

'There is something else I need to ask you. Is the true reason why you have not come to my bed, because you prefer lying with men rather than women?

There it was, I had asked the question that no one else would have dared to ask. I knew that I had taken a huge risk and whilst I greatly feared the consequences, I needed an answer even more.

Edward, stared at me, a mixture of emotions seeming to cross his normally impassive face. First he looked taken aback that I should have dared to ask such a question, then he darkened with fury, lowering his brow. Finally, he appeared to collect himself in a regal manner, almost bemused, rather than affronted. I held my breath, fearful that I had gone too far, though at the same time quietly pleased with myself for having found the courage to finally ask this question.

'…I've said I'll do my duty by you, and I meant it,' he said, almost in a whisper.

'But when will that be?'

'When I judge the time is right. You're still very young.' Now his voice was louder and more forceful, the voice he used when he made a decree.

'But will you not answer my question?' I continued, with not a little trepidation.

'No damn you, I will not!' And with that Edward brought his fist down on the table with such force that his goblet of wine tipped over, spilling its contents. 'Christ!' he cried out. 'I'll not be questioned by you any further! Is that understood?'

His voice had now risen to an angry crescendo, causing me to shrink back, my emotions decidedly on edge.

'But as your wife and Queen I surely have every right to ask these questions.'

I felt my own voice rise to meet his.

'The hell you do! And with that he brought his fist down on the table a second time before rising to his feet. 'I've had enough of this. You only invited me to dine with you so you could interrogate me. Well, I'll have no more of it. I'm going.'

I stretched out a hand. 'No, please, Edward, don't do that. I really didn't intend to upset you, but I believe I have every reason to fear more humiliation if Gaveston returns and every right, too, to be upset at the thought that you have more regard for that man than you have for me.'

Edward drew in his breath. 'That may be so, but I'm tired and I've lost my appetite, so I wish you goodnight.'

He swept out, not looking back, the door closing behind him with a great thud.

I continued to just sit at the table for several minutes after he had left, seeking to absorb what had just happened. My heart was pounding in my chest, I was shaking.

'Your Majesty, would you like anything else to eat?' a servant respectfully enquired.

I shook my head, before waving him away, leaving me once more to my contemplations. I refused to feel any sense of regret for having angered Edward, firmly believing that I'd been fully entitled to ask the questions which I had.

I knew that Edward had been shocked by my grasp of the situation. In fact he seemed visibly shaken, not just angered. Perhaps he hadn't realised quite how much I had grown up over the last year and quite how much I had noticed.

What concerned me was that despite my entreaties, Edward was clearly hell bent on a course of action, which could well leave me humiliated once more. Further, after more than a year our marriage remained unconsummated, whilst his refusal to answer my question about the true nature of his physical inclinations left me thinking that it was probably true that he preferred to lie with men.

Worst of all, the implication of this left me doubting that he really meant it when he said, 'he would do his duty by me,' in which case I could well have been condemned to a marriage which would provide me with neither physical love or progeny. It was a grim prospect, which left me in tears.

I was left with only my ladies-in-waiting to console me, along with the tales of courtly love I so enjoyed. Otherwise, I had music to distract me as well as the pleasure I took in riding, but all the while I longed for Edward's love.

—⁂—

Towards the end of June Edward travelled north to Chester without me, saying that he expected to rendezvous there with Gaveston, who was by now apparently on his way back from Ireland.

'You are welcome to come with me,' he added, but I bluntly refused.

'Certainly not. Go to your favourite, if you must, but don't expect me to be complicit in this folly.'

He stamped his foot. 'Bah!' Then he turned his back on me and walked away. As I had feared, we were to see little of each other in the coming months as he devoted his time to Gaveston. Admittedly, I compounded this to an extent by declining some of his invitations to accompany him. Yet, I simply couldn't countenance the thought of being humiliated by that man, especially after it became clear that he was still as foppish and arrogant as ever. Indeed, the mere mention of his name left me bristling with fury.

My initial hope was that Parliament would decline to accept

his return from Ireland but when it sat at Stamford in early August, I was to be disappointed.

'It's the support of the Pope that seems to have made all the difference,' Isabella de Beaumont said to me.

'Um, that's certainly Edward's view. If only the Holy Father could meet Gaveston he'd surely realise what a foul creature he is.'

'I hear that in return for having his Earldom restored, he's promised to show his fellow Earls more respect.'

'I doubt if he's capable of doing that.' I said with feigned amusement.

Over the ensuing months my scepticism proved to be well founded as Gaveston, believing, I imagine, that he was invulnerable, behaved as insufferably as ever. Though he never did it in my presence, I also learnt that he was beginning to insult some of his fellow Earls, calling Lancaster a 'churn' and the Earl of Warwick 'a black dog.' I was then incensed when Isabella de Beaumont whispered to me one day he had been heard to call me, 'a little she-wolf.'

'On what possible grounds can he say any such thing?' I exclaimed, furiously.

It occurred to me, though, that Edward could well have told him about what had happened when we had dined alone together, but this only served to make me feel even angrier.

Worse than mere insults was to follow as Gaveston began to take full advantage of his new found favour by ensuring that some of the King's revenues found their way into his hands along with those of his Gascon relatives. When this went so far as to reduce my own income I was utterly incensed, leaving me with no choice but to complain to Edward.

I invited him to dine with me alone, as I had done before, but this time he said flatly that he was too busy.

'What, too busy cavorting with your favourite?' My voice was loud and sarcastic.

He glared at me. 'No, just too busy. If you've something important to say to me, say it now.'

We were in the presence of both servants and my ladies-in-waiting, but I was not to be deterred. 'I fear your favourite is cuckolding you by taking revenue to which he's not entitled. What's more some of that revenue is rightly mine. Put this right or you'll force me to write to my father, once more.'

'I've no knowledge of this.'

'We'll, I assure you it's true...' I proceeded to give him particulars of the income I was losing.

'Alright, I will speak to Piers about this,' he replied in a reluctant tone.

'Thank you.'

I did not feel any confidence in Edward doing what he had promised, and in the event there was no improvement at all in my financial situation. Indeed, if anything it grew worse, so I decided to carry out my threat without further ado. In the meantime, hostility towards Gaveston was on the rise again. In a matter of weeks, it became so intense that there was once again talk of civil war. I sensed that Edward was nervous.

Then he announced that he wanted to take the court to York, a city I had not previously visited.

'The royal apartments are situated in a Franciscan Priory. You should find them more than adequate,' he assured me.

Autumn rains turned the roads to mud, which slowed our progress. Worse, I had to endure Gaveston's presence in circumstances where despite his assurances to the contrary, Edward chose to give him most of his attention, whilst I was largely ignored.

By now I realised that remonstrating with Edward was pointless, it just made him angry, so I held my tongue. Inwardly I still seethed with resentment towards Gaveston. When I was forced to share his company, I struggled to contain myself, making as little eye contact with him as possible. Furthermore, I never offered him even the hint of a smile.

By Christmas we had come south again to stay at Langley. This was Edward's favourite residence and given its attractive setting I could understand why. Any pleasure I felt at the prospect of the festivities was however tempered by having to continue to endure Gaveston's presence. I couldn't overcome my feelings of hatred towards that man.

We returned to Westminster to begin the new year. Gaveston, at Edward's side; proud, foppish and barbed tongued as ever. He must have possessed the wits to realise how much this inflamed people's dislike of him. He simply couldn't help himself; it was as if he enjoyed his notoriety.

Edward summoned Parliament again but it was increasingly plain how much hostility Gaveston was generating. Finally, and to my huge relief, Edward sent him north for his own safety. He then apparently fell into a melancholy state, but none was happier than I to see the wretched man gone.

# CHAPTER 7

# FIGHTING THE SCOTS

I had never seen Edward so angry before. His fist, descended on the table at which we were seated for dinner with such force that a goblet, full of the finest Gascony wine, tipped over, spilling its contents in my direction. I quickly moved back in my chair, but some of the wine still splattered my fine, silk dress, causing me to cry out.

'How dare they do this to me?' Edward shouted with the full force of his lungs, totally disregarding my discomfort.

'What are you talking about?' I asked, tremulously.

He responded by flinging a letter at me. It had just been delivered into his hands.

'See for yourself,' he barked and brought his fist down on the table again, this time causing a plate of sweetmeats to fall to the ground with a resounding clatter. Only moments ago, the hall we were in had resounded to the noise of conversation and laughter. Now there was just a stunned silence.

What I read was a demand to which many of Edward's Earls had put their names, that he accept the appointment of twenty-one 'Lords Ordainers,' who would have the power to put an end to what were called abuses of power within the government of the realm, as well as the royal household.

I experienced conflicting emotions about this development. On one hand, I was fully able to sympathise with Edward's fury at having such a restraint placed upon his right to rule as King. On the other, it was plain to me that the purpose behind this was to bring an end to Gaveston's excesses once and for all.

As I put the letter down, Edward snatched it from the table, before proceeding to tear it to pieces. Then he turned to the young squire who had brought it to him.

'You can tell their Lordships, that I'll have none of this. I am King and have the God given right to rule as I please.'

The squire, looking understandably nervous, made his obeisance and then withdrew, leaving Edward to slump back in his chair. 'Wine, bring more wine,' he shouted, looking in the direction of one of his servants. I suspected that he could be about to drink himself into a stupor.

Almost as night follows day, our relationship had improved since Gaveston's departure, so notwithstanding my mixed emotions I decided to be sympathetic, placing a hand on his arm and leaning my head close to his.

'Edward, I'm so sorry it has come to this.'

Our eyes met. 'Hm, I'll be damned before I give in to this outrageous demand.'

Yet, give in he did, after an overwhelming majority of his Earls made it abundantly clear to him that, if he didn't agree to their demand, they would no longer recognise him as King. He then did his best to regain his authority and Gaveston even returned to court, though thankfully, not for very long.

Edward made it clear to me that he could not abide remaining in Westminster once these Lord Ordainers had been appointed.

'I must confessed that many of my Earls are also annoyed with me because of my lack of enthusiasm for war, especially when it comes to Scotland. I just wish my father hadn't been so determined to conquer it. I'll surprise them, though, by announcing that I intend to lead a campaign against the Scots. If it goes well this may persuade some of them at least to look upon me more favourably. Piers has also agreed to participate in the campaign, and he'll be leaving shortly to prepare for it. We'll follow on in a few weeks.'

For all my dislike of Gaveston and the adverse effect he had on my marriage to Edward, it was not my place to disagree, so in August we once more travelled north until we reached the border town of Berwick. Here, Edward was reunited with his favourite. I felt as though I had been returned to the shadows. Admittedly, Edward had begun to be more generous towards me of late, but still, after more than two and a half years, our marriage remained unconsummated. I feared this would never change so long as Gaveston was on the scene.

Having reached my fifteenth birthday, I was also becoming increasingly impatient with Edward. I even pondered the possibility of seeking to have my marriage annulled, before dismissing this as too extreme and emotionally painful a step to seek to undertake. I knew that this would not be politically expedient, but I was riven with impatience and torment. The situation could not continue indefinitely and even Edward knew that. I had begun to grow out of feelings of needing to be loved and cared for. Instead, I was more aware of political survival and the power I might acquire if I were to produce Edward's heir. This was something that my rival could never do.

For now, I would have to make do with continuing to remind Edward of the obvious, namely that I was no longer a child and that he was yet, as he had chosen to call it, 'do his duty by me.' Inwardly, I mourned for the romantic dreams I had once held, of being happily married to a loving husband and king, of having a family and being a good and much-loved queen.

Finding an opportunity to speak to Edward alone proved impossible when he and Gaveston commenced their campaign against the Scots. I did not set eyes on either of them for several weeks. When they finally returned to Berwick in November, Edward's mood was disconsolate. He spoke of the Scottish army as being frustratingly elusive.

'We could not bring them to battle and then they even burnt the crops in the fields before moving their livestock out of our reach. Of course, it soon proved impossible to feed our army, so I was left with no option but to order a retreat.'

'They are nothing but low-born cowards,' Gaveston added, in his typically haughty fashion.

I knew nothing of war. Yet, I still reflected that the tactic the Scots had adopted had been highly effective in circumstances where they probably judged that their forces were too small to give them any chance of victory in battle. I admired their resilience, something that I had begun to develop myself in the face of the now omnipresent Gaveston.

Near the mouth of the river Tweed, looking out towards the sea, I had already discovered that Berwick could be a cold, wet and windy place, so I looked forward to travelling south once more. Instead, Edward shocked me.

'I intend to see out the winter here.'

'Must we?' I asked, plaintively, pulling a long face.

He gave me a stern look. 'Yes, I insist. The Scottish campaign must be resumed in the spring so there's no point travelling the length of the country just to come back again within a short while.'

'No, I suppose not.' I yielded, suspecting the true reason was that he and Gaveston could be as close to one another as possible without raising the ire of too many of the country's nobility. The thought of having to spend an entire winter in Gaveston's company was also a prospect I dreaded.

'...Your favourite will remain with us, I assume?' I asked.

'Um, yes, but I've made it clear to him that he must show you every courtesy. I've added, too, that if I hear him uttering one disrespectful word about you, I'll be extremely angry.'

I thanked him for this but remained sceptical that Gaveston's behaviour would really change. Yet, against my expectations, I did see a marked improvement. Early in the new year this culminated in Gaveston even making a gift to me of a valuable wardship that Edward had previously bestowed upon him.

I duly expressed my gratitude for this, wondering even as I did so what motivation lay behind such a generous act. Perhaps it was no more than a desire to please Edward, whilst behind his polite words he still saw me as no more than a 'she-wolf'? On the other hand, it was possible that he was now revealing a better side to his character than I had previously thought he possessed.

I also thought that he must realise how isolated his position was, despite his bravado. After all, everything he had, he owed to Edward's favour. Without it he was nothing. Furthermore, I was no longer a mere child, and God willing, would continue to reign as Queen for many years, so he had nothing to gain by continuing to make an enemy of me.

It was evident to me, too, from the way he looked at me, that whatever the true nature of his relationship with Edward, he still found me attractive. I had only to catch a glance of my own reflection to know that I was becoming increasingly beautiful. Also, I knew that he was married and the father of at least two children.

Moreover, in mitigation of his arrogance and sharp tongue, the months we spent in, often close company, demonstrated that he shared Edward's appreciation of music, and poetry. Nor was he lacking in a sense of humour, so particularly when he deigned to smile at me, the resentment I felt towards him gradually began to soften a little. I became accustomed to his presence and less worried by him.

It proved to be a long winter with snow lying on the ground until well into March, by which time I had grown dissatisfied with the comparatively cramped accommodation available to us, longing instead for the greater luxury available at either Langley or Westminster. Yet, with the coming of spring, Edward insisted on embarking on another fruitless campaign against the Scots. Scotland was like a thorn in his side. He would not rest until he had subdued this enemy through victory in battle and cured the mental pain it caused him.

Left to my own resources, I was able to venture outside on an almost daily basis, and always accompanied by some of my ladies-in-waiting and squires, started to go for long rides along the coast to the south of Berwick. More than anything else these helped to keep my growing sense of isolation and boredom at bay until Edward and Gaveston returned in June as disconsolate as they had been the previous autumn.

'We've been led another merry dance,' Edward confessed to me. 'I doubt we'll ever be able to bring the Scots to battle.'

'Then can we go south at last?' I asked.

'Aye, soon enough. The so-called Lords Ordainers are

demanding my presence in London, so I intend to summon another sitting of Parliament there.'

'As a God anointed King you should be free to ignore their demands. In France my father would never tolerate such a restraint on his right to rule as he alone pleases.'

'No, I'm sure he wouldn't, but this is England, and we do things differently here. I can seek to persuade, I can cajole, I can even threaten, but their noble Lords are powerful enough to plunge the country into a state of civil war if they choose to. Nor do I have sufficient support to give me any hope of winning such a conflict.'

'You should be able to strip them of such power,' I responded, still thinking him weaker than my father would ever have been.

'I only wish I could but that would only be achievable through force of arms so is impossible given how little support I have amongst the nobility. To make matters worse, trying to wage war against the Scots has proved expensive so I'm heavily in debt.'

What we didn't discuss was the likelihood of the Lords Ordainers insisting on Gaveston once more being sent into exile, but this distinct possibility must surely have been on Edward's mind as we prepared to leave Berwick. For certain, it was also on his favourite's as much as it was on mine. Since we had been forced to be in each other's company on a regular basis my dislike of him had certainly softened somewhat, but the fact remained that I still saw him as an impediment to my future happiness.

As it then transpired, I'm sure out of dread at the prospect of what awaited him in London, Edward continued to tarry in Berwick until late July. Finally, he accepted that we could delay our departure no longer. It was then that I had to bear witness to another display of deep affection between him and Gaveston in which he embraced him fondly before planting kisses on both his cheeks.

'I do wish you could come with us Piers, but I need you to continue to pursue our cause against the Scots.'

'I am yours to command, your Majesty.'

As we then set off, Gaveston, standing his ground, raised an arm in farewell to Edward and then swept me a bow to which I responded with a faint smile and a wave. It was in the forefront of my mind that if the Lord Ordainers insisted on his exile, it might well be a long time, if ever, before I set eyes on him again, and in that event, for all his recent courtesy towards me, I would not be sorry.

Within a couple of days Edward then decided that he couldn't afford to travel at the pace of our carriages if he was to reach London before the sitting of Parliament commenced, so went on ahead of me by horse. By the time I reached Westminster he had been there for some ten days and the Lords Ordainers supported by Parliament had already begun to do their worst. Edward was all too predictably downcast.

'Damn them to hell, they're determined that I must send Piers into exile once more.'

He was so downcast that I felt the need to sound like a supportive wife, whatever my true feelings.

'I'm sorry.'

'Are you really? I know you've never liked him.'

'I have never liked the fact that he has always come first in your affections.'

There was more I would have liked to add about our still

unconsummated marriage. As ever, though, we were not alone so such an intimate matter would have to wait for another occasion, not that I was prepared for that to be too long.

Pondering the state of our marriage as I had travelled south, I had decided that whether Gaveston was to be exiled or not, I would have to give Edward an ultimatum to consummate our marriage or force me to seek an annulment. Certainly, with Piers gone, perhaps forever, Edward would no longer have any excuse for failing to put me first, especially as I had by now passed my sixteenth birthday.

Edward went on to bemoan the fact that the Lords Ordainers had not merely demanded Gaveston's banishment but also insisted on curtailing a wide range of his powers as a king, including the rights to grant land and go to war.

'They treat me as if I'm an incompetent child. It makes me so angry!'

When he made these complaints, I felt that he sounded like a thwarted child. I wished that he appeared to be stronger, more determined, and that he commanded more respect. Sometimes I thought that I would show greater strength were I in his position, but I kept this to myself.

Like it or not, Edward's position remained as weak as ever, so by the end of September all the demands made against him had been proclaimed with Gaveston being required to leave the Kingdom for ever and to do so within a month. By this time, he had also travelled south from Scotland, so Edward made it clear that he intended to spend the next few weeks in his company.

I found it deeply frustrating, so decided to go on another pilgrimage to the shrine of St Becket at Canterbury, an experience which I found uplifting, particularly as I was coming to love the gentle Kent countryside. I needed to get away to a place where I could reflect, consider, and form my own plans. From there, I then travelled back to the royal palace of Eltham, where Edward and I had stayed when he had first brought me to England as his Queen.

# Chapter 8

# Consummation

I remembered Eltham as a place which had impressed me because of its attractive position with views towards the river Thames, and immediately upon my arrival sent Edward a message suggesting that he might care to visit me there. I had also made up my mind that once he did so I would absolutely insist on a strictly private audience with him. After a wait of more than a week he finally appeared.

'So, have you said your final farewells to your favourite?'

'Yes, sadly I have. He will sail for France in the next few days. I beg you to write promptly to your father requesting that he allow him safe conduct to the domain of Ponthieu, which I granted you.'

'I'll gladly do so, of course.'

He then coughed, giving me a sombre look. 'I'm afraid I've also some news for you that I know you won't welcome.'

'Oh, what is that.'

'The Lords Ordainers have turned against Isabella de Beaumont as well as her brother, demanding they be dismissed from court.'

'But why?'

'They're accused of giving me evil counsel, which is nonsense, of course.'

'...Isabella has been a good friend to me. I will miss her.'

'I'm truly sorry. I tried to get them to change their minds but, as in everything else, they were implacable.'

Now we both had good reason to feel downcast and hoping that this brought us closer together emotionally, I decided to seize the moment by whispering into his ear.

'Edward, I need to talk to you in private. Please, it's most important.'

His immediate response was to say nothing, but at least he turned his head towards mine, so I was able to look him in the eye. 'Please, it is surely not too much to ask of you?'

'No, of course it's not. Let us dine together in my chambers. It can be just the two of us and once we've done so, I will dismiss the servants.'

'Thank you, Edward.' And with that I spontaneously kissed him on the cheek. He flinched slightly, I imagined in surprise at such a rare display of affection between us in the presence of others, but still managed to offer me a limp smile.

It was still disappointing that he did not seem to relish any sign of affection from me, I felt a sense of shame and rejection, too. Yet, I continued to hope for improvements in our relationship.

The last time we had dined alone together the outcome had been so disappointing that I was understandably nervous at what might happen this time. Nonetheless, I was more determined than ever to make it clear to Edward what the consequences would be if he continued to decline to consummate our marriage. It was heartbreaking to me that I had to insist on this delicate matter, especially as I now understood that there were others in court who found me attractive and would be only too pleased to take his place, if it weren't for the risk.

I was also now very much a young woman, not just the pretty slip of a girl he had married more than three years previously. Furthermore, I knew myself to be beautiful so decided to deploy all my feminine charms in the hope of achieving my aim.

Once I had bathed, I dressed in my finest silk gown which was embroidered with lace. I applied scent of lavender to my neck and wrists, and as was my custom wore my hair under a crespine so that it was largely visible. Finally, Theo helped me put on my most splendid gold necklace before declaring that I looked parfaite. I hoped that Edward would think so, too.

Edward rose from his chair as I entered the hall where we were to eat, with an expression on his face which suggested to me that he was suitably impressed by my appearance, before showing me to my chair in a suitably chivalrous fashion. We then ate well, but inevitably our conversation was dominated by his complaints against the Lords Ordainers for their lack of respect for his kingly prerogative.

I was suitably sympathetic as I had been many times before, reinforced by my sense of indignation at the Lord Ordainers treatment of Isabella de Beaumont and her brother. Yet, all the while, I was longing for our meal to end so that Edward would dismiss the servants from our presence. Eventually, after I had grown increasingly frustrated, that moment came.

'So, what is it you are so anxious to talk to me about in private?' Edward asked.

I tutted a little. 'Surely, you must know that full well?'

Edward raised his right hand. 'Um, I know I have not yet done my duty by you.'

'Your duty indeed, but can it not be more than just that?'

Am I not pleasing to your eye? Have you no feelings for me at all? I tell you, Edward, that I crave your affection. Is that so remiss of me?'

Again, he raised his right hand. 'No, no, not at all. I have waited too long, I admit. You are a woman now, I see that, and most fair.'

'Then will you take me to your bed tonight?'

He looked at me hesitantly. 'I don't know. I'm tired, I haven't bathed.'

It was more than I could take. I banged my fist on the table in front of us. 'You are just making excuses, Edward. It's what I've always feared; that you care only for your favourite.'

He looked at me contritely, 'No, no, that's not so. I know you're beautiful and I'm sorry that I have not always shown you the affection which is your due. I will try and make up for it, I promise.'

'So, I may join you in your bed tonight?'

'Yes, if that is what you want.'

'Of course, it is.'

Though it might have been forward of me to do so, I then came and sat on his knee, and with an enticing smile brought my lips towards his. At last, we kissed, and I sensed a kindling of desire on his part as he held me close.

I was relieved to have achieved my objective without having to threaten him with an annulment of our marriage. Edward was not greatly skilled in the art of lovemaking; I knew very little myself, but I could sense that he was nervous, and he seemed to be uncertain about my body. It was neither a romantic, or even affectionate act. Rather, our love making was fumbling and imperfect.

Although I felt a sense of disappointment and hurt, at least we achieved a consummation. This helped me believe that we might yet find greater happiness in each other's arms. I wanted to believe that this was just the beginning and that he might become more familiar with my body and more enthusiastic. I wanted him to find pleasure in being with me; pleasure indeed in my being a woman.

# PART 2

# WIFE AND MOTHER

# Chapter 9

# Calamity

Having finally lost my virginity, I began to enjoy a greater intimacy with Edward. This was, unfortunately, short lived as within a few weeks and to my great frustration, Edward ignored the powers that the Lords Ordainers had taken unto themselves, by contriving to bring Gaveston back to England.

He justified it to me by asserting his determination to throw off the yoke that the Lords Ordainers had imposed on him. He knew this was an objective with which I continued to have every sympathy, whilst being fully aware of my objections to the return of his favourite.

When Gaveston returned to court at Westminster at Christmas time, I decided to receive him with all due courtesy, choosing to believe that since the consummation of my marriage I had far more control over my relationship with Edward than I had ever enjoyed before. Perhaps this was just wishful thinking on my part, but it was what I wanted to believe.

I was impressed, too, by the resolution that Edward was beginning to show in his struggle to regain his authority as King. This made me slightly more amenable to his having Gaveston by his side, as he saw it as a necessary part of that process. The steps he then took to regain control of the Great Seal so that he could once again do what he saw fit as King also convinced me that he was more capable of acting decisively than I had previously imagined. Even so, I was not best pleased when he took Gaveston off to Windsor without me. It was as though he gave into my disquiet with one hand, then undid this 'yielding' to my wishes with the other. I was often perplexed by Edward.

I also felt a keen sense of sympathy with Gaveston's wife, Margaret de Clare, a pleasant enough young woman, not much older than myself, whom I had met briefly on a couple of occasions, and I imagined could well be as ill at ease with her husband's relationship with Edward as I was. A few weeks previously I had learnt she was pregnant, so to demonstrate my goodwill towards her, I sent her a new year present of fruit, spices and sweetmeats.

Then, though I had received no message from Edward to join him there, I decided to travel to Windsor. I was not going to continue to be fobbed off and left behind anymore. It was not something I would have dreamed of doing when we first married, but having now been Queen for nearly four years I was becoming far more self-confident.

'I have every right to be with my husband,' I said to Theo. 'I don't care if he and his favourite don't like it.'

Even so, the day before I left Westminster, I sent a message to inform Edward that he could shortly expect my arrival. When I reached Windsor, I was pleased that he was not at all angry with me. However, he also had news for me, which I did not entirely welcome, and which explained his acceptance of my arrival.

'Piers and I cannot tarry here for more than another couple of the days as I believe our enemies are prepared to try and take him by force of arms. We shall head to York where I believe he'll be far safer.'

'And may I come, too?' I blurted out, with not a little annoyance.

'I think not. We will have to make haste, riding on the fastest horses available to us, but follow on at your leisure, as and when you are ready to do so, along with your household as I intend to make York my seat of government for as long as is necessary.'

I was suspicious that such a decision was just an excuse to enable him and Gaveston to be alone together. Also, I was anything but enthusiastic at the prospect of travelling north during winter when there was an expectation of having to endure heavy snowfalls and icy winds. Taking my entire household as far as York would not be a cheap exercise, either, but Edward assured me that he would pay for my expenses, so I had to be content with that.

Once Edward and Gaveston had left, I saw no great purpose in hastening my departure, especially when I developed a heavy cold. It was more than three weeks before I finally set off. Then, a combination of poor weather and terrible roads contrived to make my journey north take all of three weeks, by which time the month of February was ending.

I was pleased to discover that Gaveston's wife, Margaret, was with him at court, and upon being informed that she had given birth to a daughter at the end of January, I went as soon as I could to her chambers to offer her my respects. I arrived during the morning and was immediately struck by how well she looked. She seemed genuinely pleased to receive me, and naturally the centre of our attention was her child, whom she had named Joan in honour of her own mother.

'It was not too long or hard a labour,' she assured me, 'and Joan is a healthy baby.'

As we smiled at each other and I cooed over her child, I wondered if we might be destined to form a close friendship so long as circumstances continued to keep us together. Certainly, we had much in common, and had we been alone together, it would have intrigued me to talk to her of our husbands and what her opinion was of their relationship. That, though, would have to wait for another day when I had more time at my disposal, so before leaving I asked if I might call on her again.

'Of course, your Majesty, it would be an honour.'

I smiled at her again. 'I hope we can be friends, in which case you must address me as Isabella.'

There was also something else that we might have in common if my suspicions were to be confirmed. I had been feeling a little nauseous and had missed two of my, normally regular, courses. Within a few days, I became certain that I was with child; a piece of news that I didn't hesitate to bring to Edward's attention. It would surely elevate me in his esteem. My own feelings were of delight and excitement, as well as a little trepidation. A baby would be a source of great joy and hope.

It appeared to make Edward genuinely happy, for he immediately embraced me before planting kisses on both my cheeks. There was, however, little else to offer him any comfort at this time, news having reached us only a few days prior to my announcement that no less than five of his most powerful Earls had taken up arms against the crown, with every one of them swearing that they would execute Gaveston should they be able to apprehend him. Edward was both angered and yet very downcast by this turn of events.

I was now less resentful of Gaveston's role in Edward's life than at any time since becoming Queen. During our prolonged co-existence in Berwick, he had demonstrated that there was a side to his character that was both courteous and cultured. I had also grown more tolerant of his sharp tongue as I came to appreciate that much of what he said about his many enemies was perfectly true. Certainly, whilst he was ostentatious and often arrogant, many of them were even more so, as well as being both belligerent and boorish. Whilst I still resented his place in my husband's affections, I could appreciate his wit and intelligence.

In any event, Edward now did his best to protect Gaveston by giving him the Lordship of Scarborough castle; the hope being that this fortress was not just capable of withstanding a long siege but given its position on the coast a place from which it might well be possible to escape by sea. Yet, when my uncle, the Earl of Lancaster, by far the most powerful of their enemies, threatened to capture York, Edward and Gaveston, as inseparable as ever, decided to withdraw as far as Newcastle, leaving me to follow on behind at a more leisurely pace. I felt that I was constantly following in their slip stream, and that they were becoming moving targets, remaining only a few paces ahead of the enemy.

It was not the life I had expected when I arrived in England as a girl queen, I felt desperately unsettled, undervalued, and almost abandoned. I was an afterthought to him, never central in his affections, never first in his concerns. I was also afraid that his enemies might be tempted to use me as a target against my husband. Would he be concerned enough to pay a ransom for me if they held me captive? These thoughts often entered my head. I felt that he might only be goaded into action on my behalf because of my more powerful family connections in France.

'Scarborough is in need of much repair,' Edward had told me before departing, 'so we've no choice but to try and keep as far away from Lancaster as possible until I can gather sufficient forces to be able to resist him.'

What followed became an increasingly unhappy experience for me in which I became even more fearful that Lancaster might seek to make me his prisoner. My fears were, of course, compounded by my impending motherhood, I was nearing my time and I was frightened. I needed support and reassurance. My travails began when shortly after reaching Newcastle Edward insisted that I take up residence in Tynemouth Castle.

'I fear that it cannot be long before Lancaster pursues us here in which case we'll again have to flee, and in your present condition I cannot expect you to keep following us. You should be safe there behind its walls, but, if necessary, you ought to be able to escape from it by sea.'

'But as your Queen, I would far rather be by your side.'

'Of course, I appreciate that, but I'm thinking of what's in the best interests of our child.'

I hoped that was indeed his only motive so did not argue with him any further, though when I arrived at the castle, I wish I had, for it was a miserably damp place in a thoroughly neglected state, made worse by the fact it was also a cold, wet spring. This was no place for me to spend my confinement, but my ladies did the best that they could to make me more comfortable.

As Edward had predicted it wasn't long before Lancaster's army reached Newcastle, and the first I knew of this was when Edward and Gaveston along with their retinue arrived at Tynemouth. I had never seen Gaveston look so downcast before, when he confessed that there had been no time to bring his wife, Margaret and their daughter, Joan, with them, so it was more than likely that they were both now Lancaster's prisoners.

'We do not intend to stay long,' Edward said. 'As soon as we can locate a suitable ship, we shall set sail for Scarborough…'

'And can I come with you?'

'No, I think not. You will be safer here, I'm sure.'

'But this place is in a sorry state. Nor can it withstand a siege.'

'I do not believe Lancaster means you any harm.'

'How do you know that?'

'His quarrel is entirely with Piers.'

'But you cannot continue to be a fugitive in your own Kingdom like this indefinitely. Is it not humiliating?'

'As I've told you, I need time to gather my forces.'

'That may be so, but at this of all times, when I am about to bear our first child, I would value your presence by my side.'

This caused him to look at me somewhat contritely. 'Hum… And how are you feeling today?'

'I could be better. I still feel nauseous at times.'

'Then, all the more reason for you not to travel by sea. Look, once Piers is safely ensconced at Scarborough I intend to head back to York. I should be there in no more than a week and will send you word once I arrive.'

'Very well,' I said far more tearfully than I had ever intended. I had never been a lachrymose creature. Indeed, I don't believe I had ever allowed Edward to see me in such a state before. It was just that my pregnancy, exacerbated by the growing threat from Lancaster, was making me far more emotional.

# CHAPTER 10

# A MOTHER AT LAST

Once Edward and Gaveston had boarded a ship and left for Scarborough, I became increasingly anxious and after a few days I could stand it no longer, deciding to immediately head for York. To my immense relief, I saw nothing of Lancaster's army and was soon safely reunited with Edward. Even so, I still felt that we were the hunted rather than the hunter, and that this undignified experience could not continue for very much longer.

Within another few days we learnt that Gaveston had surrendered himself to the Earl of Pembroke after he had put Scarborough Castle under siege. Edward was horrified by this news, though the messenger who brought this to him explained that Gaveston had surrendered on favourable terms after the castle had run low on provisions. I was mildly amused, knowing that Gaveston was not a man to put up with privations for long. I kept these thoughts to myself, however.

'He's to be held under house arrest at his own castle at Wallingford. My Lord Pembroke also swore on the Holy Bible that if the Lords Ordainers have not decided his fate by the 1st August, or he disputes their decision, he's to be free to return to Scarborough along with supplies.'

'I still fear that he's in grave danger,' Edward said to me. 'It's all very well for Pembroke to have sworn an oath, but that's not binding on the likes of Lancaster or Warwick.' And nor indeed was it.

On his way to Wallingford Gaveston passed through York, so Edward was able to visit him for a short while before his journey continued. When he returned, he told me that Gaveston remained in good spirits but that for his part he would not rest easy in his bed until his favourite was safe from all his enemies.

My feelings were mixed, I knew that Gaveston's presence made Edward a happier man and yet, if he were to be off the scene on a permanent basis, it wouldn't cause me any unhappiness. Indeed, there was a time when I would have celebrated his removal. However, I had become more mellow, as I had matured, and could see the impact on my husband of any threats to their relationship. Most of all, given my condition, I wanted a period of calm.

In early June I was sick two or three times, making Edward concerned for my health and that of my child. The weather had also turned quite dry and warm.

'I think you need the fresher air of the countryside,' he declared so I agreed to travel some fifty miles to the royal lodge of Burstwick near Beverley Minster. Consequently, I learnt nothing of Gaveston's fate until I received a message from Edward telling me that his favourite was now the Earl of Warwick's prisoner and had been consigned to a dungeon.

'I fear for Gaveston's life more than ever so have sent letters to your father and to the Holy Father begging them to intercede with his enemies.'

Upon reading this it did not take me long to decide to return to York. If Gaveston's days on this earth were indeed numbered, then I knew Edward would be devastated and in need of my support. Further, I was beginning to feel perfectly well again and though the lodge was not as dire as Tynemouth, it was not especially comfortable either.

When I reached the city after a two-day journey I was then informed that Edward had already departed with the intention of travelling to Westminster, upon learning that Gaveston had been put to death by order of the Lords Ordainers. This news came as a total shock to me, and I felt shaken. Perhaps it was due to my condition that I was so moved as my senses and emotions were in a state of high alert. Much as I had resented Gaveston's existence, I did not believe that he had done anything to deserve such a dreadful fate, so I immediately set about writing a letter to Edward expressing my deepest sympathies at his loss.

I ended the letter by asking if he would be content for me to follow him to Westminster before giving instructions to one of my squires to deliver it into the hands of the King with all due speed. In his reply, which I received a few days later, Edward made it clear that what had happened to Gaveston might yet lead to war and that it would be safer for me to remain in York until he could provide me with an armed escort.

'Though Piers was a fool to have surrendered himself, I am grief stricken by his murder, for that is what it was, and have vowed to avenge myself on those who perpetrated it.'

It was to be almost a month before that escort arrived and though I set out in the expectation of reaching Westminster quite quickly, I was now some six months pregnant, which slowed our progress considerably.

The journey was arduous for me, as I was now so much less mobile than was normally the case. I also felt very tired and cumbersome, as well as in need of more refreshment and sleep. Consequently, it was a week and more into September before I finally arrived.

In the meantime, while I had been travelling, Warwick and Lancaster had brought an army south towards London. They would have captured it, too, if the Lord Mayor had not closed its gates against them, whereupon they had halted their advance to the north of the city.

'Curse them, as if murdering Piers was not enough, they are still intent on treating me like a puppet and ruling the country in all but name,' Edward told me. 'But as God is my witness, I'll not give them that satisfaction.'

Though Edward looked understandably careworn, I was pleased to see him so resolved to defend his rightful position as King. At the same time, I wanted to afford him as much solace as I could, so, when we were alone together, I expressed my deepest sympathy for Gaveston's death.

'I thank you for that though I know full well you never liked him.'

'At first, it was difficult for me to come to terms with the place he had in your affections, but I came to see that he had qualities that were not initially apparent to me. Above all else, he did not deserve such a cruel fate.'

'No, he most certainly did not. What Lancaster and Warwick did was unforgivable.'

'So, will there be war between you?'

'Only if I am confident that I will be victorious, so I have sent Pembroke on a mission to your father to ask for his help. I am hopeful that now you are with child he will look favourably on this request.'

He then laid his hand gently on my now expanded abdomen and kept it there for a moment. This gave me great pleasure as I was always grateful to him for even the smallest sign of affection.

In the event, my father's response was to send my uncle Louis to England with the purpose of acting as a mediator. I was delighted to see him again and within a day of his arrival at court we were able to dine together and talk of a world that was now but a receding memory to me after more than four and a half years as Queen of England. I told him, too, that despite the travails I had suffered, I had fallen in love with England's beautiful countryside, if not its often wet and unpredictable weather, and was also now able to speak English, though I was by no means fluent.

As negotiations got underway with the hope of achieving a peaceful outcome, my time for giving birth drew closer, so in preparation for this I soon retired to Windsor where Edward, accompanied by my uncle, joined me after a short while.

It was also a comfort to me to be joined by my aunt, Margaret, who had been Queen to Edward's father following the death of Queen Eleanor, Edward's mother, and borne him children, for all that he was forty years her senior. Even now she was only in her mid-thirties and our relationship was entirely amicable, so the intention was for her to remain by my side until the birth took place. She provided me with much needed reassurance.

I hoped and prayed that I might be blessed with a son as I so much wanted to provide Edward with an heir, which would make him proud of me. Above all, I believed that once I had done this my position in his life would be unassailable.

Naturally, I was also anxious, having no idea what to expect of childbirth, whilst just thinking about the physical act terrified me. After all, I knew of many whose lives had ended in the giving of life. It was also hard to imagine the disappointment I might have to endure if I were to give birth to a girl as my first born.

I greatly appreciated Margaret's support, and she was present when my son was safely delivered in the early hours of the thirteenth of November. For all the pain I had to endure, when he was placed on my breast, I had never felt happier or more fulfilled. I felt a huge surge of happiness and relief. Furthermore, after everything that I had experienced since marrying Edward, I believed that I had gained a degree of maturity well beyond my seventeen years on this earth.

My prayer, too, was that with Gaveston's demise, Edward would finally come to place me first in his affections, his quarrels with his troublesome Earls could be amicably resolved, and that with much of my life still ahead of me we could begin to enjoy a long and prosperous reign. I had, after all, given him a son and heir. However, as the daughter of a king, I knew that no reign was that straightforward and that there would always be difficulties to overcome. I hoped we could do so together.

# Chapter 11

# Return to France

By the grace of God, our son, whom Edward was insistent should be named after him, gave every indication of being a strong and healthy infant. For my part, I must confess that his birth left me quite exhausted so that I needed all of six weeks further confinement to feel sufficiently recovered for my churching ceremony to take place.

By then, much to my relief, just a few days previously, thanks largely to the efforts of my dear uncle, Louis, a so-called 'final peace' had been achieved between Edward and Gaveston's murderers. Under the terms of this they humbly begged the King's pardon for their deed whilst in return for him granting this they handed back the treasure they had seized from Gaveston.

Nonetheless, beneath the outward displays of reconciliation, during which we even dined with my uncle, Lancaster, much antipathy remained, which I'm sure was mutual. I knew that Edward was inwardly seething, as he was not inclined to forgive. Indeed, I suspected that he would try to make Lancaster pay the price for what Edward saw as his 'vile act,' in the not too distant future.

'God's teeth, how I still abhor that man,' Edward exclaimed to me once the meal with him had ended. 'His arrogance knows no bounds. He murdered my best friend yet shows no real contrition.'

'Yet a reconciliation between you was surely better than war,' I responded.

'Yes, yes, I grant you that, of course. One day, though, when the time is right, I may yet have my revenge on that man.'

'Dear Edward, do not let your desire for that eat away at your soul. We have a son, after all, and with the Kingdom now at peace, much to look forward to.'

He smiled at me. 'I agree. The birth of a son has certainly helped to compensate me for Piers' loss, much as I still grieve for him and will always do so.'

Much to my annoyance, we had barely entered the year of our Lord, thirteen hundred and thirteen, when Lancaster and Warwick sought to renege on the agreement which they had solemnly undertaken only a few weeks previously. Understandably, this made Edward even more furious.

'Damn both of them,' he swore. 'How dare they suggest that I recognise Piers as a common felon when he was nothing of the kind. Whatever the consequences, I'll do no such thing.'

Negotiations resumed and this time the Earl of Hereford led these on Edward's behalf. In the meantime, we travelled to the city of London to attend a pageant in my honour, to celebrate the birth of our son. Despite the cold weather it was a joyous occasion which I very much appreciated. We then retired to Eltham Palace where I hoped we would be able to enjoy as much time as possible in each other's company, but to my frustration it was not to be as Edward spent most of the daylight hours hunting and still preferred his own bed to mine.

Though I had engaged the services of a wet nurse for my son, I still wanted to give him my full attention and to be fair to Edward he was happy to join me in his nursery. For up to half an hour, once a day, we were therefore a family together, which afforded me a small measure of happiness. Above all else, I wanted our son to know us well and to have a real love for us both.

I was growing impatient, too, for Edward to love me more. On one occasion I therefore decided to dismiss the wet nurse from our presence. Then I placed a hand on Edward's and looked into his eyes.

'Dearest, will you join me in my bed tonight. I would make you most welcome.'

He gave me a wary look. 'I'm not sure…perhaps.'

'I know you still grieve for your favourite, but I want to offer you some solace.'

'You have provided that already by giving me a son.'

'Thank you, but allow me to provide some physical comfort, too.'

With that I held his gaze for but a second or two before he looked away. 'I will think about it. And now I really must beg my leave of you.'

This felt like rejection. I knew I had become a beautiful young woman, yet to my deep frustration neither my body nor my feminine charms seemed to hold out any allure to him, leaving me to again believe that he much preferred to lie with men. That night I still waited for him to come to my bed but did so in vain.

Edward had upset me so often since our marriage, that I was beginning to despair of ever enjoying a loving and intimate relationship with him. Yet, if only for the sake of my son, I remained determined to make the best I could of the situation I found myself in.

The following morning, I resolved to make a pilgrimage to Canterbury again, to give thanks at St Thomas Becket's shrine for the safe delivery of my son, whom I decided it was best to leave in the care of his wet nurse. Throughout my pregnancy, and most especially whilst in labour, I had prayed to St Thomas and believed that my prayers had been answered by him. Despite everything, I would not allow my faith to waiver. Indeed, it was my rock.

Even in winter, I took great pleasure in travelling through the gentle Kent countryside, but once we arrived in Canterbury, where I was well received, the weather became exceedingly wintry with considerable falls of snow, which delayed my return. To my great relief, by the time I was able to leave the city, I had received word from Edward that he was now in Windsor and that, thanks to Hereford's efforts, he had finally received the promised treasure.

Lancaster and Warwick were still demanding that Gaveston be regarded as a common felon, but by the time I reached Windsor it was becoming clear that tensions had eased again. For this I gave thanks to God.

'Hell will frost over before I agree to this demand, and they know that perfectly well,' Edward told me. 'But at worst we have an impasse between us. Since Pier's murder and the birth of our son there is no appetite in the country for civil war, so I believe the peace we've both been hoping for is assured in all but name.'

I was pleased, too, to see that Roger Mortimer had returned from Ireland. I still thought him such a handsome man, the physical attraction I had towards him being as strong as ever. I felt that my attraction to him was returned and that we both enjoyed being in each other's company when the occasion arose. Whenever we were in the same room, I felt his eyes upon me and whilst this delighted me, it also caused me to feel flushed, I felt my cheeks burning and a strange shyness overcame me. I found myself daydreaming about him, in quieter moments, and I thought of him when I was alone in bed. My thoughts were distinctly immodest, especially for a married woman and a queen no less. Perhaps I would not have noticed him so keenly if Edward had deigned to show more interest in me, dare I say more desire for me.

With the coming of spring, I had reason to feel happier when an invitation arrived from my father, inviting us to attend a special ceremony in Paris when he would bestow knighthoods on my three brothers, Louis, Philip, and Charles, along with several other young noblemen. This would provide a joyous distraction.

I was delighted at the prospect of a reunion with my father and brothers, who I had not seen in five years, so urged Edward to accept. He was happy to do so, and despite mutterings that this was a bad time to leave the Kingdom when the Scots were carrying out raids into England and the dispute with Lancaster was still unresolved, we set out for France towards the end of May.

I had also not given up hope of forging a more loving relationship with Edward so above all else saw this visit as a further opportunity to try and do so. Certainly, as the first anniversary of Gaveston's death grew closer, there had been signs in Edward's behaviour that he was beginning to overcome his grief. I had seen him start to smile and laugh more often, whilst he had been generally more relaxed in my company to the point of my believing that we were on the verge of achieving a proper friendship at last.

Then, just a few days before we were due to leave for France he even came to my bed, taking me completely by surprise.

'I feel ready to accept the comfort you said you'd be happy to offer me,' he declared.

Of course, I welcomed him with open arms though our love making was brief. I derived little of the physical pleasure that I had been told by my confidantes that I could expect. The nature of our love making was, as it had been before, perfunctory. I felt saddened to admit to myself that Edward did not greatly enjoy the physical act with me. I imagined that he had felt much greater pleasure with other lovers, particularly, when he was alive, with his favourite, Gaveston. I decided that I must try to stop torturing myself with these thoughts. I must find the strength to fend them off. I must see our coming together as the start of something better.

My one reservation about returning to France was that it meant being away from our son. Yet, I knew he was in capable hands, and that so long as he continued to thrive no harm should come to him in my absence. I had become a doting and protective mother, it was in my nature, and gave me great pleasure.

After crossing the channel from Dover, we headed first for our lands in Gascony, where we were warmly received, before heading for Paris. Edward remained good humoured, and was even, occasionally affectionate in his manner towards me, taking my hand and planting kisses on my cheeks, which was encouraging, whilst I felt a growing sense of anticipation at the thought of being reunited with my family.

Once we arrived, it was a joy to be amongst my older brothers again, though I felt a renewed sense of sadness at the thought of my brother Robert's demise. I felt the warmth and strength of the family bonds with my brothers were undiminished. My father also seemed to my eyes to have changed little in appearance apart from a certain greying of his hair. I Remembered his often stern and aloof personality, so it was a relief that he greeted me with a smile as well as a fond embrace.

'You have grown most beautiful, dear daughter.'

'Thank you, father. I owe my looks to you.'

'…As well as your dear departed mother. When you first entered my presence, I imagined she had risen from the grave.'

'I always remember her in my prayers, father.'

'Good. So do I.'

After that initial display of affection, he largely relapsed into the taciturn introspection with which I had been all too familiar as a child. This disappointed me and it undermined my confidence as an adult and a queen, I had hoped for more respect. I felt that it was due to me for having shown my mettle successfully in a new country, becoming a mother, wife and queen. Then, something so awful occurred that I could very easily have been killed.

# CHAPTER 12

# FIRE

It was a few days after the ceremony to which we had been invited. This had been a splendid event followed by much feasting and merry making as well as the presentation of expensive gifts, of which I was the principal beneficiary thanks to my father's generosity. In truth far too much wine was drunk by many who were present and herein lay our downfall.

Edward and I were sharing a bed in a silken pavilion, which had been erected for the purpose of the celebrations outside the city walls. It was after midnight, and I was on the point of falling asleep when I became aware of a crackling noise as well as an acrid smell. Feeling alarmed I sat bolt upright, opened my eyes and screamed, for we seemed to be surrounded by fire.

Edward then seized my right hand. 'Quick, we must run for our lives.'

'But where?'

'Just come with me. Now!'

With that he pulled me from the bed and together we ran towards the entrance of the pavilion.

To reach safety we had to pass through what seemed like a wall of flame and smoke and as we did so I was conscious of one of the arms of my nightdress catching fire. I screamed again in both pain and horror but by now we were at least clear of the blaze.

I could see men running towards us to assist and one of them was quick-witted enough to throw a coat over my arm to smother the flame. My arm and hand were both still quite badly burnt but nevertheless without his prompt intervention as well as the courage Edward had displayed in leading us both through the blaze, I knew I could easily have died.

I admit to being concerned that my arm might bear some significant damage. I became frightened that I might even be scared for the rest of my life, making me repulsive to Edward. This was no mere vanity on my part as he did not need any further reasons to be reticent in relation to our love making.

It later emerged that some drunken merrymaker, who was late to bed, had collapsed while passing the pavilion and in so doing lost his grip on an oil lamp he was carrying so that it fell against it. My father, upon seeing how badly I had been burnt, was full of rage, declaring that he would have the unfortunate individual thrown into one of his darkest dungeons, but I successfully interceded on his behalf.

'Dear father, it was nothing more than an unfortunate accident. I expect I'll recover soon enough. Spare him, I beg of you.'

'You have a kind heart, daughter, so like your mother.'

'I hope I have.'

'Very well, I will do as you ask... And allow me to also say this...'

'...Of course.'

'I know that I have never been good at showing my emotions and that you may think me cold and aloof...'

'...No...'

'Well, I still think you've every right to think that. Nonetheless, I want to assure you of my deepest love. What's more, you have made me very proud. Indeed, I do not believe that any father could wish for a finer daughter.'

My father's kind words had a deep and lasting effect on me. He had never expressed his love for me before, and though I could not know it at the time, never would again, for in barely eighteen months at the age of only forty-six, he would be dead.

It would be several days before I felt well enough to travel, and many weeks after we returned home before my burns were, thankfully, fully healed. In the meantime, our shared experience in a blaze that could easily have cost us our lives, along with Edward's heroism, brought us closer than ever before. I began to feel a renewed optimism for the future of our marriage as well as stirrings of genuine affection for Edward, which I believed were reciprocated as he treated me with great tenderness.

Despite the continuing discomfort of my burned arm and hand, the remainder of that summer was a happy one for me. I was able to spend a good deal of time with my son in his nursery and was delighted when he began to crawl about. Edward also continued to be attentive, whenever he wasn't preoccupied with affairs of state, thus strengthening the bond between us.

At the same time the news from the north of punishing raids by the Scots was disturbing. Edward's dispute with the likes of Lancaster and Warwick seemed to be no closer to resolution. Negotiations, in which my uncle Louis was once again involved, dragged on into the autumn until one day Louis came to see me in the Palace of Westminster.

'I've been thinking that an intercession by you as Queen might resolve the impasse.'

'Uncle, I think you flatter me, if you imagine a mere woman can make any difference in this matter.'

'No, not at all. Do not underestimate your powers. It's also clear that the King now has a high regard for you, which gives you a crucial measure of influence that even Lancaster and Warwick should respect. All that's required to bring about peace is that they abide by what was originally agreed…'

'You mean, by begging the King's forgiveness, for their murdering Gaveston.'

'Quite so, though I suggest it would not be wise to use the word, 'begging,' in their presence.'

'Nor would I, but they both know what is at issue here, yet every effort at persuasion has so far failed.'

'…Which is precisely why I say that your intervention might make a difference.'

'Very well, but I need to speak with the King to ensure that he is comfortable with my interceding on his behalf.'

'Of course.'

'And assuming he is, how do you suggest I should go about this task? Do I write to Lancaster and Warwick setting out what is required of them, or just summons them to my presence?'

'I would suggest the latter. They are all lodging nearby, and I believe they are far more likely to do as you ask if you speak to them in person. They already know full well what is required here but getting them to do what is right requires tact and gentle persuasion. The King is far too angry to countenance either of them and, though God knows I have tried, I lack the authority that you have as Queen.'

I agreed and was able to speak to Edward that very evening. Despite my uncertainty about how he would respond to my uncle's proposal, in the event he welcomed it.

'Every other effort to bring them to their senses has failed so use your charms. It might just work.'

Next morning, I then duly had a message sent to Lancaster, Warwick and Hereford, requesting that they attend on me the following day at noon on a matter of great importance. I deliberately failed to specify what that might be and was pleased to receive acknowledgements from each of them that they would be willing to do so.

As the hour then approached for their arrival I grew more anxious about what exactly I would say to them. I considered it beneath my dignity as Queen to plead, especially as I shared Edward's view that Gaveston had been murdered. Equally, being censorious would be bound to be counter-productive. I derived some comfort from my uncle Louis having agreed to be present, but still had every intention of leading the discourse with the three Earls.

Above all, I was conscious of the fact that this was my first real opportunity to play an important role in affairs of state so was determined not to be found wanting.

They all appeared punctually, although Lancaster, now in his mid-thirties, the tallest as well as the most powerful of the three by far, was the last to be announced. As was typical of him, he was colourfully attired in a bold, red surcoat and walked with an arrogant swagger, which always irritated me.

Though he was my uncle through my grandmother, Blanche of Artois' marriage to Edmund, younger brother of Edward's father, I had never developed much, if any regard for him. He was too cold with rarely a hint of a smile on his face. By reputation he was exceedingly lecherous, which, given the lascivious way he had of looking at women, me included, was probably well deserved.

I decided to come straight to the point. 'My noble Lords, I have asked you to attend on me today so that I might enquire what it is that still prevents you from reaching an accommodation with my dread Lord, the King, over the matter of the late Piers Gaveston?

Lancaster gave me a thoroughly patronising look. 'Your Majesty is surely aware that he was nothing but a common felon.'

'My Lord uncle, I am naturally aware that this is your opinion…'

'Aye, and mine, too,' Warwick declared, though I noted that Hereford said nothing.

'Quite so, but is it not the case that only last December a 'final peace' was proclaimed on the basis that your Lordships were willing to seek the forgiveness of the King for Gaveston's death at your hands?'

'We swore no oath to that effect,' Lancaster responded testily.

'No, but nonetheless that was the clear understanding that was reached, surely? Forgive me, my noble Lords, but I thought you men of your word.'

Lancaster now began to look rather uncomfortable. 'And so we are, but having sworn no oath we reflected further upon the matter… We've nothing to seek forgiveness for. That man deserved his fate.'

'Yet, surely when you had him killed you must have known how much this would offend the King?'

'Perhaps so, but we'd lost all patience with that low born cur.'

'Yet, how are we now to achieve a peace, if you continue to refuse to ask for the King's forgiveness?'

'The King should concede that we are right in this matter.'

'But that he will never do. You know that perfectly well, the consequence being that we live constantly under the threat of conflict, which would tear the Kingdom apart to the advantage of no one save the King of Scots. For the greater good I humbly urge you to swallow your pride and be satisfied with what you have already achieved. After all, for better or worse, Gaveston is dead so can no longer be a thorn in your side. That fact alone surely gave you the victory you so desired.'

Lancaster frowned at me. 'I take it this was your only reason for requesting we attend here today?'

'Yes, and I thank you for listening to my plea. I seek only concord between you and the King, nothing more.'

Hereford responded. 'Your Majesty, we thank you for your words and will give them every consideration.'

'Is that a promise from you all?'

The three Earls eyed each other. 'Aye, it is,' they then all said as one.

'Excellent! Will you attend on me again at this hour tomorrow with your answer?'

After some momentary hesitation they also agreed to this, and I decided that I could not let them leave without raising one other matter with them.

'My noble Lords, if a final peace can be achieved, I would also hope that you can all agree that the Beaumonts can return to court? Isabella has given me loyal service in the past and I count her as a friend.'

'Your Majesty, we will also consider this,' Hereford responded, whereupon they all withdrew.

My uncle Louis gave me a warm smile. 'That was very well done.'

'I do hope so.'

# CHAPTER 13

# THE CURSE

Much to my delight, my intercession was successful. Others, including my dear uncle, Louis, had no doubt played their part, but I still had good reason to believe that my words had been crucial in bringing about an agreement. Apart from boosting my self-confidence, this made me feel that as Queen I had finally come of age. It was with great pride that I attended a ceremony in Westminster Hall in which Lancaster, Warwick and Hereford all begged Edward's forgiveness for their cruel deed. I knew that there was still a great deal of enmity between Edward and Lancaster and that fine words would not eradicate that. Nonetheless, I was greatly relieved that they'd finally been willing to set aside their differences.

The only thing that darkened my mood that day was the amount of pain I was still in because of my burnt arm and hand. Despite the soothing balms that had been applied by my apothecaries the burns had not healed, whilst the pain and discomfort they caused me were particularly distressing at night so that I was tired for want of sleep.

After a while I began to fear that the burns would never properly heal, which would leave me with a permanent measure of disfigurement and place a limitation in the use of my hand. Even worse, was a slight worry that this lack of healing might lead to my developing a dangerous fever. I tried to set aside any such notion by sending an offering to St Thomas's shrine in Canterbury in the hope that the saint would grant me relief from my sufferings.

Demonstrating his confidence in my powers of persuasion, Edward soon asked me to make another visit to France to present some petitions to my father concerning Gascony's affairs. Initially, my poor health prevented me from undertaking this mission, but by the turn of the year I was sufficiently recovered to be able to prepare to depart. I was greatly cheered by the affirmation my husband had shown me, fully trusting in my skills of diplomacy.

I was accompanied by the Earl of Gloucester as well as Isabella de Beaumont and her brother, Henry. We set sail from Sandwich at the end of February, in calm seas and accompanied by an armada of other ships as well as barges, all of which reached France in safety. I was naturally pleased to be returning to the land of my birth so soon, but had I known what lay ahead of me I might well have preferred to turn back.

Our journey to Paris via Amiens was undertaken at a leisurely pace, taking us about two weeks, and it was what I learnt upon our arrival that served as a warning of future difficulties. Only the day beforehand, my Godfather, Jaques de Molay, last Grandmaster of the Knights Templars, had been burnt at the stake.

I was horrified to hear that he had suffered such an end, regardless of what he might have done to deserve it. Although this was not a relationship that had ever meant much to me and the Templars order had fallen out of favour both with father and the Pope even before I became Queen of England, such a fate was still a shock.

When we met, it was my father who told me what had happened. He spoke brusquely of my Godfather having deserved his fate as a relapsed heretic. It was another few days before I learnt, through Isabella de Beaumont, what my Godfather had declared just before he was put to death.

'It is said that when the flame was lit he cursed your father and his descendants to the thirteenth generation. He then added that a calamity would soon occur to those who had condemned him to death.'

At the time I was inclined to dismiss these words as being of no consequence. Yet, in the light of the events that subsequently unfolded, I am left wondering if my Godfather was in fact in league with the devil when he uttered this curse.

My father graciously granted most of the petitions that I presented to him on Edward's behalf, for which I was duly grateful. Feeling closer to him than I ever had as a child, it was then that I made a fateful decision about something that had been troubling me for some while.

'My dear father, there is a delicate matter that I need to speak to you about in private, if I may?'

'Why, of course.' And with that he dismissed everyone else from our presence with a wave of his hand, before turning his gaze on me. 'Does this concern Edward?'

'No, no, not at all.' I then took a deep breath.

'...Last year shortly before Edward and I returned to England I gave silk purses, which I myself had embroidered, to my sisters-in-law, Marguerite and Blanche of Burgundy...'

'Yes, what of it?'

'They gratefully accepted these gifts, yet only a few weeks later, we gave a feast at Westminster, which was attended by several knights of your court. It was then that I noticed that two of these men were wearing the very same purses from their belts...'

'What! Who in the devil's name were they?'

'Philip and Gautier d'Aulnay. There might be some innocent explanation...'

My father looked at me sternly. 'Such as?'

'Knightly favours, merely to demonstrate that Marguerite and Blanche admire their skills at tournaments. Mind you, that they should pass on to others so quickly what were intended as personal gifts, still makes me angry.'

'So have you sought to inform Blanche and Jeanne of what you saw and asked for an explanation?'

'No, father. I cannot imagine that either of them would ever admit to any treasonous misconduct, and, should this still be continuing, I did not want to make allegations that might put them on their guard.'

'You suggest then that I should have them watched?'

'I think it might be a wise step to take, father.'

'You have been right to tell me what you saw. I only wish that you had done so sooner.'

'Forgive me for that, father. You know how unwell I have been because of my burns, and..., and, it has not been easy for me to come to terms with the implications of accusing either of my sisters-in-law on such a grave matter. I do not wish them any harm.'

'That I can understand, but if as royal princesses they are carrying on adulterous affairs they deserve the gravest of punishments.'

I felt a shudder of fear and a little regret at what I may have started but...I had no choice; my loyalty would always be to my father.

'Would you have them executed then?'

'That might well be the sentence imposed by the court, but having regard to their sex and titles, I would be prepared to commute this to life imprisonment. Even so, they would then be thrown into the darkest of dungeons to survive on nothing more than bread and water. As for the d'Aulnay brothers, they could expect nothing less than execution.'

It was everything I had feared my father would say in response to my revelation. Within the hour he also followed my advice, and though I believed that I had acted out of a sense of duty to him, I found myself praying that placing a watch on my sisters-in-law would not reveal any adulterous conduct.

Without delay, I then sent a letter to Edward, happily informing him of the success of my mission. I wanted to keep myself in his thoughts as well as gain his approval for my good works, being always anxious to improve our relationship. I did this before setting off on a pilgrimage that I had been planning to make to the basilica at Clery-St-Andre in the Loire valley where I made offerings to the blessed Virgin Mary. I was away from Paris for some twelve days by which time there were signs of spring everywhere.

I was dreading what I might learn upon my return but at first my father merely said just a few words to me in confidence.

'My dearest daughter, all necessary steps have been put in place. If anything untoward is occurring, I expect to be immediately informed.'

I stayed at my father's favourite hunting lodge in the forest of St Germain, enjoying the spring sunshine and resting my burnt arm and hand, which were still troubling me. It is a delightfully peaceful place that I had known all my life, where I was able to take my ease, but I still made frequent visits to my father in Paris. Ten days passed before I received the news I had been dreading.

As soon as I entered my father's presence and saw the grim expression on his face, I could tell that something was amiss.

'Only this morning, I have received irrefutable evidence of a love nest at the Tour de Nesle, no distance from here. The princesses, along with the d'Aulnay brothers, have all been spotted coming and going from the place. What's more, they've all remained under the same roof overnight. I shall have their servants questioned and as needs must, tortured, until I have the full truth of the matter. In the meantime, the princesses, along with the brothers, will be arrested forthwith.'

I felt an involuntary shiver run down my spine as well as fear, horror and a scintilla of regret, all at once.

'Have you yet informed my brothers of what has happened?'

'I have sent word to them. Their marriages will need to be annulled, of course.'

I was distressed that my worst suspicions had been confirmed. I also struggled to comprehend how Marguerite and Blanche could have behaved with such wanton stupidity, surely knowing the inevitable consequences if they were caught. I had some inkling that Marguerite's marriage to my brother, Louis, was not a particularly happy one, but that could still not excuse her conduct. I knew I must steel myself for what was to come.

With my health once again improving, it was my intention to visit the lands which had been bestowed on me in Gascony before returning to England, but before the time came for my departure, news arrived from Avignon that deeply shocked me. The Pope, who had set up residence there, was dead, barely a month after my Godfather had uttered his terrible curse against both him and my father.

I felt that the forces of evil and the occult were somehow to blame. Just as I believed in divine goodness, I knew there to be malevolence at large in the world.

This event made me especially fearful for my father's well-being and as I made my obeisance to him on the day I left Paris, I wondered if I would ever set eyes on him again in this world. Meanwhile, as I made my way home, my foolish sisters-in-law were put on trial along with d'Aulnay brothers.

Confessions having been extracted from them, their punishments were as terrible as I had feared and expected. The brothers were castrated before being executed, I shuddered at the thought of it, yet their crime had been terrible. Marguerite and Blanche were thrown into prison; their heads having been shaved. At least their lives had been spared. My father was capable of mercy.

I felt sorry for them, but my conscience was clear that I had done my duty, both to my father and the integrity of the Capetian dynasty, which had ruled France for more than three hundred years. Above all, I understood how vital it was that our bloodline should not be tainted by low-born bastards, which was always the attendant risk of unpunished adulteries.

Even so, for years after I experienced nightmares in which I found myself in the presence of either Marguerite or Blanche in some dank dungeon. They were wearing nothing but rags, their heads were shaved, and they had anguished looks on their faces.

'Sister, sister, we beg you, release us from our confinement!'

With increasing desperation, they continued to beg until I invariable woke up in a cold sweat. Within ten years both women were dead but even then, the nightmares continued although they gradually became less frequent.

# CHAPTER 14

# ANOTHER DISASTER

Upon reaching Dover, I made straight for St Thomas's shrine in Canterbury to make an offering in thanks for the success of my mission to France. Mindful, too, of the Pope's recent demise, I also offered a fervent prayer to the saint to keep my father safe.

When I returned to court I was warmly greeted by Edward who was effusive in expressing his gratitude to me for the success of my mission. By now I could also barely contain my impatience to be reunited with our son, who I had not set eyes on in almost two months. I longed to see him, thinking how much he must have changed, as babies do, even in short periods of time.

Edward assured me that he was in good health and together we promptly made our way to his nursery where we both played with him and delighted in his company. I was filled with happiness and joy. Maternal instincts leaping to the fore, I felt that I never wanted to let him out of my arms.

After six years of marriage, we were at last a couple together enjoying each other's company and that of our infant son. That night Edward even came to my bed, and I felt a real sense of fulfilment. This was the stuff of my dreams, everything I had imagined my life to be, married to a king and mother of his heir. My sense of joy was overwhelming, but alas, it was short-lived. Looking back, I realise, with much regret, that it was in fact a high point in our relationship.

Plans were now well advanced to invade Scotland in order to relieve Stirling Castle, which had been under siege for many years and whose governor had finally undertaken to surrender it to the Scottish King by the 24th June. Edward was confident that he would be able to achieve a great victory, but when he told me that the likes of Lancaster and Warwick were declining to give their support, I was perturbed that he might lack the overwhelming strength required to guarantee that.

When I gently questioned the wisdom of mounting an invasion at this time Edward reassured me.

'Our army will still be a large one; in fact, more than sufficient to defeat the Scots. Furthermore, if Lancaster joined us, he would simply claim the credit for our success. Far better that I win without him and enhance only my own prestige.'

I felt a pang of uncertainty and was dubious about his unerring confidence that victory would be so simple. Sometimes I wondered if I had a better grasp of strategy in warfare than he did. I would never have dared to question his decisions in an overt way, but inwardly I was unconvinced.

In May Edward travelled North to Wark in Northumberland where it had been agreed the invasion force should assemble. I followed on at a gentler rate and we reunited in mid-June in Berwick, where we had spent so long in Gaveston's company. We spent a cordial three days after which Edward said his farewells to me before riding forth at the head of an army that had twenty thousand men in its ranks.

I watched from the battlements of Berwick castle, mightily impressed by the sight of so many fine banners as well as knights in their armour and colourful livery, riding their splendid warhorses. I no longer doubted that such an overwhelming strength in numbers would prove victorious, so then waited in the pleasantly warm and dry weather for Edward's return.

—⁓—

'It was an utter disaster,' Edward told me through clenched teeth. There was a look of misery on his weary face, the likes of which I had not seen since he was in a state of abject grief following Gaveston's murder. 'Instead of the great victory I expected, I have been totally humiliated. Gloucester is dead, Hereford captured, my entire army either slaughtered or put to flight. I even had to abandon my great seal.'

'But how is this possible? Was the Scottish army far larger in numbers than you expected?'

Edward shook his head. 'No, we must have outnumbered it by nearly three to one.'

'Then I don't understand… '

'We were lured into a trap on ground that was unfavourable to our cavalry and then taken by surprise when despite their inferior numbers, the Scots still attacked us. Our archers might have saved the day, but they were soon overrun by the Scots cavalry. I tried to rally my army but Aymer de Valence and Giles d'Argentan insisted that the battle was lost and seized the reins of my horse. What galls me most of all is that Lancaster and Warwick will say they were right not to participate in the invasion and insist that I'm not fit to rule.'

I offered Edward as much comfort as I could for which he was grateful, bringing us closer together than ever. Nevertheless, his prediction that his defeat would empower his enemies proved to be well-founded. When a Parliament assembled in September in York, Lancaster duly attended, more arrogant than ever.

To my chagrin and Edward's dismay, he was quick to allege that Edward only had himself to blame for the dreadful defeat by the Scots, so should face the consequences.

'Had my Lord the King paid proper heed to the Ordinances that required him to have the consent of the Lords Ordainers before seeking to wage any war, this dreadful debacle in Scotland could have been entirely avoided. The invasion was therefore wrong in principle and now Scotland is completely lost to us. What's more, the Scots are free to raid our northern counties as never before. Worse still, the royal coffers are now empty to no one's benefit, save the King of Scots. Is it not therefore vital for the well-being of the Kingdom that my Lord, the King, now abides fully with the Ordinances?'

Edward, understandably incensed by this attack, sprung to his feet. 'Does my noble Lord seriously argue that I was wrong to go to the aid of the garrison of Stirling Castle? Not to have done so would have not only been cowardly but also besmirched the memory of my late father's endeavours against the Scots.'

'My Lord King, it is not your purpose I criticise, but rather your failure to seek the consent of Parliament for your venture, or to abide by the Ordinances.'

'I say that as King I was fully entitled to decide when to go to war. I also ask that Parliament now gives me the means to avenge our defeat?'

Unfortunately, Edward's plea fell on deaf ears. Gloucester's death had robbed him of a powerful ally, whereas Lancaster and Warwick also enjoyed the support of two other influential figures, namely the Earls of Arundel and Surrey. As a result, Parliament agreed to place a severe limit on the amount of money available to Edward and myself.

# CHAPTER 15

# MORE SADNESS

Throughout the sitting of Parliament, it was unseasonably wet and continued to be so well into the autumn, so the harvest was ruined. I learnt that it had been much the same in France and the Low Countries, causing widespread famine.

Then in late November, I received the dreadful news that my father was dead, after falling from his saddle whilst hunting. I immediately thought again of my Godfather's curse, which was surely now being fulfilled. Of course, this had not just been made against my father and the Pope but also our entire dynasty to the thirteenth generation, making me fearful for my brother Louis, who now succeeded to the throne.

I had never felt close to my father as a child, but I had come to both love and respect him more as I had grown older, especially following my two recent visits to France when he had treated me as an equal and behaved towards me with great tenderness. He had also always been as supportive of me as he possibly could during the difficult, early years of my marriage to Edward, for which I was particularly grateful.

Consequently, his demise threw me into a great sense of grief as I observed forty days of mourning, dressing in black as well as abjuring the wearing of any jewellery. I was shaken and saddened, feeling somewhat weakened by the loss of my strong ally. My grief was compounded by the knowledge that so many of Edward's subjects afflicted by famine were in a state of great suffering during a long, wet winter.

Yet, for all that, my personal life had never been better as Edward came to my bed more frequently and the bond between us continued to strengthen. He seemed to both want and need the physical comfort that I could offer him. I rejoiced in the joy he clearly felt when we made love. Furthermore, it was a great joy to both of us that our infant son was thriving.

Of course, we railed against the financial restraints that Lancaster and his fellow Ordainers were placing upon us. Our mutual sense of grievance against them deepened when in February they forced Isabella de Beaumont and her brother Henry to leave court yet again. I was furious and made my feelings plain to Edward.

'Lancaster and Warwick have done this to spite us. Not content with the power they already hold, they now seek to deny us the support of those who are closest to us.'

Edward gave me a weary look of resignation. 'That's typical of them, I'm afraid. After all, they've done it before.'

'But Gaveston was still alive then. Now he's gone, God rest his soul, they've no cause to act in this fashion.'

'I tell you; they never had any just cause!'

'No, of course not, forgive me, I did not mean...'

'I know, I know. They simply relish rubbing salt into my wounds because they can. I pray that one day I will have my revenge on them!'

'...Well, in the meantime I shall maintain correspondence with Isabella. That at least is something they cannot prevent.'

Bread was also now so scarce and expensive that the famine grew worse, whilst the weather brought no relief with the wettest and coldest spring I could ever recall. My heart bled for the suffering of the people, so in what was a miserable June with almost every day bringing rain, Edward and I made a point of once again going on a pilgrimage to Canterbury to make offerings to St Thomas. Sadly, this along with our fervent prayers, had no effect on what continued to be an awful summer of cold, wet weather, causing immense distress across the length and breadth of the country.

Then in August, the Earl of Warwick died. Neither Edward nor I shed any tears at his passing as he had contrived with Lancaster to be our enemy. Nonetheless, his death now left Lancaster in a position of unrivalled supremacy amongst the Lords Ordainers, making him more insufferable than ever.

'He will not even attend meetings of the Council, but rather forces me to send him messages,' Edward complained. 'I tell you he behaves as if he is the King, and I am merely his subject. There seems to be no limits to his presumption!'

'No, I agree. Do you remember that day when we were at Berwick and he made you come to him by crossing the bridge over the Tweed?'

'Aye, how can I forget. It was humiliating. I just pray that one day he'll overreach himself.'

When the harvest then failed for a second successive year, the suffering in large parts of the country grew even worse with too many poor souls starving to death. I handed out what alms that I could to the poor, but I was only too aware that there was little or nothing that could be done for the overwhelming majority of those who were afflicted by this terrible famine.

Christmas festivities that year were a subdued affair with the mood at court made all the worse by bad news from Ireland where Edward had once again sent Mortimer to rule on his behalf. Buoyed up by their victory the previous year, the Scots had mounted an invasion of that country and now, so the messenger informed us, inflicted a terrible defeat on Mortimer's forces. The new year had not long begun, when he returned to court, as handsome and robust as ever, making it clear that without more men Ireland was likely to be lost to the crown completely.

As if our woes were not bad enough, there came news of a rebellion in Wales, which Edward asked Mortimer to put down. Thankfully he was able to do so with ease, although the news from Ireland continued to be as bad as he had predicted with that country now largely under Scottish rule. Meanwhile, I discovered that I was expecting another child, something which I was happy to rejoice in as a further demonstration of the growing affection that Edward had for me.

At the same time, it was plain to me that the time had come for me to allow my dear nurse, Theo, to retire from her duties as she was growing old and suffering increasingly from the pains in her bones that so often come with age. She had been my dearest companion all my life and I knew I would miss her constant presence but decided it was for the best. It was easy to persuade Edward to grant her a pension along with some land in Gascony, where she would be able to live comfortably. He knew how much I had valued her and indeed, loved her.

Then in June more sad news arrived from the French court. My brother Louis who had ascended the French throne at the age of twenty-five upon my father's death, had also died, apparently of pneumonia, leaving his Queen pregnant. Given the age difference between us, we had never been close, but all the same I was still shocked, and yet again reminded of my Godfather's curse, making me increasingly fearful for the future of my family. I also still felt a strong sense of grief, wishing that I had been closer to him.

In July, grateful that we were at last enjoying some warm, dry weather, I withdrew to Eltham Palace in preparation for giving birth and praise be to God was safely delivered of a second healthy boy on the fifteenth of August. He was christened John. Thankfully, my labour was shorter than when I had given birth to my first born, but I was somewhat disappointed that Edward had chosen to take himself off to York. His justification for this was the need to prepare for another campaign against the Scots, a decision of which I was outwardly supportive.

'I hope you don't mind us being so far apart when you give birth?' he had asked me. 'It's just that if we are to succeed against the Scots, I must ensure that I have sufficient support in the north.'

'No, no, you must go, of course. I am perfectly well, after all.'

In truth, though, when the pains of my labour began, I would have much preferred him to be only a courtyard's distance from me rather than all of two hundred miles.

Shortly before his departure, Edward had suggested that as a gesture of reconciliation, Lancaster should be invited to be my newborn's Godfather. I doubted that he would ever set a good example to any child of mine but did not demur. Indeed, John had barely entered this world when I had a letter dispatched to my uncle inviting him to attend the christening in that capacity.

He chose to totally ignore this, so the event proceeded in his absence. I wasn't sorry but nevertheless such a snub underlined the extent of the hostility that now existed between Edward and my uncle. Earlier in the year Parliament had chosen to appoint Lancaster as chief councillor to the King. Yet, ever since, he had largely absented himself from any of its meetings, preferring to attend to his own affairs rather than those of the State.

Now, upon learning of Lancaster's refusal to acknowledge the invitation, I had sent him to become John's Godfather, Edward was not just angry but also concerned that my uncle might be planning to try to seize the throne. For our safety, he therefore summoned me to join him in York with all due speed, bringing with me both our sons, even though it was less than a month since I had given birth.

Fortunately, I felt sufficiently recovered to be able to set off within about a week of receiving this summons. In contrast to the previous September the weather was fine, enabling a decent harvest to be brought in to alleviate the suffering of the people. When we reached York after several days travelling, it was a pleasure to be able to present Edward with his newborn son, who, to his evident delight, smiled at him.

'It's a great relief to have you all with me, safe and well,' Edward told me. 'After the way Lancaster's been behaving, I'm more fearful than ever that he means to start a war, so I've had to abandon my plans to attack the Scots. I fear it would have been too expensive, anyway.'

I had no doubt that my uncle posed a serious threat to Edward's rule, but, for the time being, whilst we remained in York, a fragile peace was maintained. I was pleased, too, when Edward invited me to attend meetings of the council. It was a demonstrable sign of his respect for me as our union deepened. At the age of twenty-one, in the ninth year of our marriage, I believed I had truly come of age, confident that Edward now held me in high esteem. I was an asset to him after all as well as the mother of his sons and heirs.

As it happened, I was soon able to turn the influence I now enjoyed to my advantage when the rich Bishopric of Durham became vacant. Despite her exclusion from court, I had maintained a close correspondence with Isabella de Beaumont, who urged me to support the candidacy of her brother, Louis de Beaumont. I told her that Edward favoured someone else but promised to do what I could. When I then learnt that the monks of Durham had chosen Edward's preferred candidate, I hastened to speak with him.

'Edward, is it true that your man, Henry de Stanford, is to be made Bishop of Durham?'

'Yes, the monks have chosen him and as you know I have supported his candidacy.'

'Then I would beg you to reconsider.' Spontaneously, I fell to my knees in what I accept was a melodramatic gesture. 'I am certain that Louis de Beaumont will be a 'stone wall' against the Scots at a time when that is what you most need.'

'Yet I am advised that he's not a very learned individual.'

'Perhaps not, but he has strength of character and understands the need for firm action to keep the Scots at bay.'

'Very well, be assured that I will give your plea every consideration.'

To my delight later the same day Edward assured me that he had changed his mind and would now seek to overturn the monk's decision. I immediately sent a letter to Isabella telling her the good news.

A few days later, more sad news arrived from France. The

child of my late brother, Louis, had lived barely a week with the result that my brother Philip was now King. It appalled me that in little more than two years I had lost my father, my brother Louis, and now a baby nephew, so my Godfather's curse was seldom out of my thoughts for long.

That Christmas we spent at the royal palace of Clipstone on the edge of Sherwood Forest. It was a happy occasion during which I looked forward to the future with some measure of confidence. For all the supposed weaknesses of my sex, I now rightly saw myself as the most powerful woman in the country. Furthermore, along with my youth and beauty, I had wealth as well as lands in my own right, and was conscious, too, that I was increasingly admired and respected by those around me.

I remember well that Mortimer attended court, accompanied by his pretty wife, Joan, having been made Edward's principal lieutenant in Ireland. During the festivities, we saw a great deal of each other, often participating in courtly dances together, particularly the carola.

This brought us into physical contact when we found ourselves side by side and were required to hold hands as we processed from right to left. Whenever this occurred, I couldn't help but experience a certain frisson of emotion. I found him to be so compelling it was difficult not to be distracted by him.

Occasionally, too, our eyes would meet, and with a hint of a smile he would hold my gaze, albeit briefly. It was then that I could sense that he was as attracted to me as I was to him. I took a great deal of pleasure in his company, perhaps too much for safety's sake.

Moreover, when the court assembled in my presence it was his face I was drawn to along with his forceful voice whenever he spoke. It seemed to vibrate through my body, touching my very core.

For all that I convinced myself that I was now content with my life, I knew full well by now that Edward would never be my soulmate, however much we had come to feel genuine affection for one another. Mortimer was different, he was exactly the sort of man I would have happily married for love had I ever been free to do so. As it was, I resolved to merely take pleasure in his presence in the expectation that we could always enjoy a respectful, arms-length, relationship.

I knew in my heart that this would be difficult to achieve given that my attraction to him was growing daily. I hoped that we would both be strong enough to resist any temptation to act upon these dangerous, though rather delicious and exciting feelings. How, I reasoned, could such a strong emotional and physical inclination be so wrong?

# CHAPTER 16

# DIPLOMACY

With the coming of the new year, continuing our nomadic existence, we travelled south to the fine royal hunting lodge at Clarendon, near Salisbury. My sons were still with us, but our intention was to be in Westminster by April for a sitting of Parliament. Once there, I intended that they should both reside at Eltham Palace. Much as I would have loved to always keep them with us, I had decided that it was in their best interests to remain in familiar surroundings in the care of trustworthy individuals and Edward agreed.

He then called a meeting of the Council before telling me he had received reports that were deeply disturbing.

'As you know the Scots are continuing to carry out raids in the north, yet I now have reliable reports that they're leaving Lancaster's estates untouched. That can only mean that he's in league with them.'

'To what purpose, do you think?'

'Why, their support when he seeks to seize the throne from me.'

'But they'd want something substantial in return.'

'Oh yes, I expect they would. Berwick for a start, but probably much more, particularly in Ireland where it seems Mortimer is holding his ground against them.'

'So do you intend to raise this accusation against my uncle at the forthcoming meeting of the Council?'

'Most certainly, though, of course, Lancaster may not even deign to attend it.'

Somewhat to my surprise, he did in fact appear, and predictably denied any collusion with the Scots when Edward made his accusation.

'How dare you suggest such a thing,' he retorted angrily. 'The Scots are leaving my lands untouched, but that's only because they know they're well defended and there are easier targets for them to strike at.' He then banged his fist on the table. 'I'll not stay here to be insulted!'

With that he simply got to his feet, turned his back on everyone present, and stalked out of the chamber, leaving an awkward silence in his wake, before Edward, a look of cold fury on his face, spoke up.

'That man is insufferable. Now, I suggest we continue with the business in hand…'

In May we were then beset by events that further soured Edward's already terrible relationship with Lancaster. As I recall, I first heard what had happened from my ladies-in-waiting, and it was very soon on everyone's lips at court. That Lancaster's wife, the wealthy Alice de Lacy, should elope with a squire to the Earl of Surrey, by the name of Lebulo Lestraunge, was certainly most shocking. Nonetheless, given Lancaster's unprepossessing personality, I had some sympathy for her. More so because their marriage of over twenty years was childless, whilst it was common knowledge that they lived separate lives and that Lancaster kept mistresses.

When I first spoke with Edward about this news he even laughed, clearly taking pleasure in Lancaster's discomfiture. However, he was less amused when my uncle started to complain that we had encouraged Alice to elope.

'What an outrageous suggestion!' he exclaimed angrily.

Even so, whether as a convenient excuse or not, Lancaster let it be known that he would no longer come to court because he feared treachery.

'Good riddance to him then,' was Edward's response. 'I shall be delighted if I never have to set eyes on him again!'

After the sitting of Parliament, I was able to enjoy a period of relaxation at Eltham Palace with my children. Edward also visited regularly from Westminster so there were days when we were able to enjoy life as a family in the pleasant spring sunshine. On such occasions, Edward was also happy to put affairs of state to one side to give his full attention to our two boys. He was relaxed as well as playful in their presence so that I thought him a good father and we were as happy as we had ever been in each other's company.

Meanwhile, Lancaster was now embarking on what amounted to a private war with the Earl of Surrey, sending his soldiers to ravage his lands in the North. Edward appealed to him to desist, but, of course, this fell on deaf ears as Lancaster still felt powerful enough to do as he pleased.

'The day is coming, though, when I shall have my revenge on him,' Edward declared to me, portentously. 'I now have more barons who are loyal to me rather than Lancaster, than at any time since that wretched defeat by the Scots.'

He was referring to men like Hugh Despenser and Roger d'Amory, which troubled me. I feared that he might fall under the spell of another Gaveston and again consequently reap the whirlwind.

In July we resumed our annual peregrination around the country, not returning to Westminster until December, by which time I discovered that I was once again pregnant. I was truly delighted and prayed that, having previously given birth to two healthy boys, I might be blessed with a healthy girl. I even went as far as imagining what our daughter would look like and the times that I would spend with her. These musings were so precious to me as I had not been able to spend time with my own dear mother.

Meanwhile, the well-intentioned Earl of Pembroke made strenuous efforts to bring about an accord between Edward and Lancaster and bring an end to his private war with the Earl of Surrey. Unfortunately, in return for peace, Lancaster made demands that I thought were totally unacceptable. I decided to make my feelings plain to Edward.

'Much as I do not want to see this war to simmer on endlessly, a settlement cannot be achieved at any price. Give him what he wants and many who are loyal to you will be worse off financially, including myself.'

'Dear Isabella, I agree. You are not the first to put that argument to me. I will be making it clear to Pembroke that Lancaster will have to modify his position considerably before there can be any question of an agreement between us.'

This was something that Lancaster at first refused to do, by which time my confinement was fast approaching. I had decided to retire to the attractive royal manor of Woodstock in Oxfordshire where I was safely delivered of a baby girl, just as I had hoped, on the eighteenth of June. My labour was, thankfully, not too long, or painful, so feeling in good spirits I made a quick recovery.

I was pleased, too, that Edward was soon with me, expressing his delight at the birth of a daughter who was christened

Eleanor in memory of his mother. Like her two older brothers, she was also well-formed and healthy, giving me every reason to give thanks to almighty God for the blessings he'd seen fit to bestow upon me.

We were on the road again by the end of the month, in truth, too soon after giving birth, but I was naturally very strong . Taking Eleanor with us in the care of the wet nurse I had selected, we travelled to Northampton for another sitting of Parliament where the ongoing negotiations with Lancaster took centre stage. To his credit, Pembroke pressed on with his efforts to achieve an accord, and after a further meeting with Lancaster reported to me in person that he had been able to make some progress.

'I'm pleased to say that I've now persuaded the noble Earl to compromise somewhat on the demands he's been making. Furthermore, I believe that if you, as his niece, were to make a personal appeal to him in the interests of peace and good governance, he might be willing to go even further.'

'For all that he's my uncle, there's no love lost between us.'

'That I understand, but he still respects you as Queen; he's told me so.'

'Very well, I'll write to him . That is, once I have spoken with my Lord, the King. I'm not prepared to act without his full approval.'

'That I understand, but could you not go further than that by suggesting a meeting? I believe an appeal in person is likely to be more effective.'

I agreed to put this suggestion to Edward, uncertain as to what his response would be, but in the event, he was perfectly amenable to this happening.

'I will never cease to hate Lancaster for what he did to Piers, you know that. Nevertheless, I need more time to strengthen my position, so go to him with my blessing. Remember, though, that he's cunning and untrustworthy.'

I assured Edward that I would do no more than make an appeal to my uncle's better nature, and the same day dispatched a letter to him, which led to him promptly inviting me to visit him at his castle at Pontefract. I now felt sufficiently recovered from giving birth to ride side saddle, but even so the journey there from Northampton still took three and a half days, travelling via the royal manor of Clipstone.

I felt a certain nervousness at the prospect of a meeting with my uncle. He had never shown me any measure of affection despite our kinship, and I had always found him to be both distant and taciturn. To bolster my confidence, I decided to travel with a significant entourage of squires and ladies-in-waiting, as well as servants, sending word to my uncle to expect this.

When we arrived at the castle on a hot, summer's day, I was impressed by its size, as it had high walls and towers as well as an imposingly large keep. To give him his due my uncle greeted me with perfect courtesy as befitted a Queen and daughter of a King, before inviting me to join him at the high table of the castle's great hall for a meal. This was provided for the benefit not just of myself, but also all of my entourage as well.

'Beds have also been prepared for your use and that of your ladies-in-waiting in the castle's keep. The rest of your party can be accommodated in its towers. Once we have eaten, I will also be pleased to discuss with you the matter that has brought you here.'

As the first of four courses were served to us, I thought

that the word feast more accurately described what was being provided for our delectation. Each course consisted of several dishes, cooked to perfection and finely presented. It was certainly a meal fit for any King or Queen.

'I thank you for providing such a delicious repast, uncle,' I said graciously.

'I like to eat well as befits my rank. It's also a rare honour to be able to entertain a Queen.'

'It would be less so if a peaceful settlement could be achieved between you and my lord, the King.'

'Perhaps so. I assure you that I am as anxious as any man in this Kingdom to see such a settlement achieved so long as the terms are just, but let us talk of that further when our meal is done.'

I nodded my head in agreement and offered my uncle a smile, though he did not return this. I would indeed have been pleasantly surprised had he done so as I seldom remember him wearing anything other than a stern, aloof expression on his face, much like my father.

Wine was also served with each course, but I was careful to drink as little of it as possible, taking only occasional sips and declining offers to replenish my glass. I was determined to remain sober, though the temptation to drink more grew by the time we reached our final course as the wine was of the best quality. Certainly, I was aware that many around us were drinking to excess whilst the babble of conversation in the hall steadily increased in volume. My uncle, though, appeared to my eye to drink little more than I did, presumably for the same reason.

It must have taken the best part of an hour to finish our

meal, whereupon he suggested that the two of us withdraw to his private solar in the castle's keep.

'We can then speak frankly to each other, I trust?' was my response.

Our eyes had hardly met since my arrival even though we had been seated next to each other, This time, however, his eyes seemed to bore into mine as if he was in search of my very soul. 'Why, of course.'

The solar we soon entered was as richly furnished as any I had ever set eyes upon; its walls hung with several large, beautifully colourful tapestries, depicting scenes from the book of Genesis. With their intricate patterns, there were also several expensive Turkish rugs adorning the floor, whilst the chair he gestured me towards was padded with sable.

I took my seat and he then sat down as well, his chair a respectful distance from mine. I decided to come straight to the point,

'Will you give up the demands you have been making now, in return for peace?'

'I am willing to modify them, somewhat.'

'So, I understand, but I've come here to ask you to give them up entirely. You must appreciate how much they would harm my interests as well as those who are loyal to me and the King. I thought your quarrel was with Surrey rather than with me.

'And so, it is.'

'Then, for the sake of our kinship, I would appeal to you to do as I request. You surely have wealth and power a plenty without seeking yet more.'

'But what I have asked for is no more than a restitution of what I am entitled to.

'My Lord the King only withheld them because of your war with Surrey.'

'That may be so, yet in return for my giving up that struggle, I consider it only reasonable to seek their return. It was none of my doing that the King chose to bestow these on others including your good self. But I hear your appeal and to achieve a settlement I'm prepared to go further than I have before and ask only for the grants I've been demanding, over a period of four years rather than eight. The harm to your personal interests would then be minimal, I believe.'

I had sought this meeting in the knowledge that it might well be impossible to persuade my uncle to give up his demands completely. There was also no denying that what he was now offering was also a significant improvement on anything he'd previously suggested, so part of me thought I should not press for more. Yet I still did so.

'Dear uncle, that is gracious of you. If you will but agree to let what you are still demanding be arbitrated upon by Parliament, I will happily withdraw my objections to a settlement and encourage others to do likewise.'

'...Very well, that is reasonable enough. You may tell Pembroke that if he sends his envoys to me again, it should be possible to finalise a settlement based on what we have just agreed.'

'I thank you.'

'You must understand that I have only ever sought to do what is best for the Kingdom. If Gaveston had remained in exile, he would still be alive today and had my wife not eloped, any conflict with Surrey would have been unnecessary. Now, I suggest we drink to the success of your visit.'

He offered me a rare smile and standing up summoned one of his servants to bring us wine. It had been easier than I had anticipated to win him round, which suggested to me that he had already made up his mind to modify his demands before I even arrived. His war with Surrey along with his refusal to attend council meetings had left him isolated and unable to hold sway over Edward as he had been accustomed to doing in the past. Prolonged conflict was also, no doubt, draining his resources, so it was probably that, more than anything else, which had encouraged him to adopt a more flexible approach.

Only a few weeks later the so-called Treaty of Leake was drawn up, which included a clause whereby my uncle gave up his control of the royal council in return for Edward agreeing to continue to abide by the Ordinances and dismiss the likes of Roger d'Amory. Given how much he reminded me of Gaveston, I wasn't sorry to see the back of such a man, though, of course, Edward was far less enamoured.

'This is but a first step towards regaining my full powers as King,' he confided in me on the very eve of his meeting with my uncle to give him the kiss of peace along with a pardon for waging war against Surrey. 'What he did to Gaveston was still unforgivable and one day I will have my revenge.'

For my part, I was happy with the contribution I had been able to make towards achieving peace. In a world ruled by men, I now enjoyed as much wealth, influence and even power as I thought it possible for any woman to enjoy. What was more, at the age of twenty-three I knew that I was as beautiful as I might ever be. I understood that there were probably few, if any, other women anywhere in the country who could match my looks, Of course, I also understood that I had the means and wherewithal to ensure that I always looked my best, whilst most women did not enjoy such good fortune. I was conscious, too, that my bearing and grace caused even the greatest men in the land to stand in awe of me.

# CHAPTER 17

# DANGER

I had more reason to feel optimistic about the future than at any time since the disastrous defeat inflicted by the Scots four years previously. Lancaster's powers had now been limited, I was as content as I could expect to be with my marriage to Edward, and ever grateful to almighty God to be the mother of three healthy children. Furthermore, within weeks of the Treaty of Leake, the news from Ireland could not have been better. Roger Mortimer, for whom I had long had such a high regard, had triumphed over the Scots. By the end of the year, they had withdrawn from the island for good, at which point Mortimer had returned to court to great acclaim for his endeavours.

I had high hopes that he might become Edward's right-hand man, but instead Edward preferred to appoint Hugh Despenser to the post of Chamberlain. This soon began to trouble me as I saw in Edward's demeanour towards him the same attraction that he had had for Gaveston. There were also aspects of Despenser's character that mirrored those of Gaveston. Both men were intelligent as well as handsome, and dressed extravagantly, whilst also possessing the same streak of arrogance, leading them to speak dismissively of others behind their backs.

By June the following year Mortimer had returned to Ireland to take up his position as Edward's Justiciar on that island. Despenser's star at court continued to rise as his position gave him control over who was allowed access to the King. I suspected that he was more than capable of using his powers to feather his own nest, but for the time being I decided to keep such a thought to myself.

I concentrated on my relationship with Edward, being an attentive and dutiful consort, whilst remaining alert where Despenser was concerned. I tried to put myself between the upstart and the King as often as I could, without seeming to do so at all.

For his part, Edward pressed on with plans to recapture Berwick from the Scots, so in the spring we travelled to York for a meeting of Parliament where it was agreed that an army would be mustered to achieve that objective. It was apparent that such a campaign was likely to preoccupy him for the remainder of the summer and possibly longer. I also found that I was missing my children more, particularly Edward, who was now nearly seven years old.

I was grateful to be spared so much of the hard work involved in looking after infants, but enjoyed the company of children once they grew old enough to be inquisitive, and certainly did not want to be constantly separated from any of them.

'Edward, may I have the children brought to me here in York whilst you're away on your campaign against the Scots?' I asked.

He gave me a gentle smile. 'Why, of course. If that is what you want, you really don't require my permission.'

It was mid-July before the campaign finally got underway, by which time the children had been with us for about a month, enabling us to enjoy one of those joyous periods as a family that I still recall with pleasure. We withdrew from the bustle and sometimes noxious odours of the city to the Archbishop of York's Palace at Bishopsthorpe, which he had graciously put at our disposal, some three miles away to the south.

It was at times like this that Edward demonstrated that he could be an attentive, kindly father to our children, enjoyed playing with them in a boisterous fashion, and was essentially a man of peace rather than war. It was this along with the common touch he possessed with even the basest of individuals that endeared him to many of his subjects, but could also so exasperate his warlike peers.

We managed to re-ignite our physical relationship as well, I worked on this by wooing and gently pursuing my husband. There had never been any great passion between us, more of a gentle, respectful affection, but I was determined to continue in that vein. Particularly now that I perceived an irritating threat on the horizon of our personal life, in the shape of Despenser.

Once Edward had departed, on what I saw as yet another expedition, I enjoyed the remainder of the summer in this most tranquil of settings with my children. We were a hundred miles from Berwick and I never imagined that we were in any kind of danger. But then when September had barely arrived, one fine morning I looked out of the solar window and spied a body of horsemen approaching.

'We're not expecting any visitors today, are we?' I asked Eleanor de Clare, wife of Hugh Despenser, who had recently been made one of my ladies-in-waiting. Another of my ploys was to keep the Despensers under my surveillance as far as possible.

'No, your Majesty, not to my knowledge.'

I then pointed towards the approaching riders. 'I recognise the Archbishop of York. What brings him here, I wonder, without any prior notice?'

Ten minutes later when he entered my presence he had some shocking news.

'I beg to inform you that a Scottish army is approaching fast. I fear that its express purpose is to kidnap you... You and your children need to seek safety inside the walls of York without delay.'

Within the hour we were ready to depart and less than an hour after that entered the city. I was terrified, not just for my own safety, but more so for my children. The Scots venturing so far south, and even more so what their purpose was, filled me with dread. I wracked my brains to try and discover how they knew where to find me.

'Have they a spy in our midst?' I asked. 'Or, more likely, is someone playing the traitor?'

But no one could answer these questions and to this day I've no idea who the guilty party was. Certainly, the arrival of this army so close to where I was staying was no mere chance, although, thank God, I managed to escape. However, the ramifications of what had happened were still awful as many brave men died in a terrible defeat inflicted by the invaders. When Edward learnt what had happened, he abandoned the siege of Berwick. It was then that the recriminations began.

Lancaster's enemies accused him of being the traitor, whilst those who had come to dislike Despenser pointed the finger at him. Worst of all, by the time Edward had been left with no alternative but to agree a truce with the Scots, his standing amongst the nobility was at its lowest ebb since the defeat at Bannockburn. He was downcast and bitter.

'I am being blamed for our defeat by the Scots, but it was hardly my fault that someone chose to betray your whereabouts and I was left with no choice but to abandon the siege of Berwick,' he complained to me.

I was duly sympathetic. Yet, I had been safe enough once I reached York, and I knew it was said that Edward had simply used the news of my lucky escape as an excuse to abandon the siege. The fact of the matter, I feared, was that he was not the soldier his father had been and consequently was no match for the King of Scots.

The ramification of this setback was that Edward became increasingly introspective, dismissing court entertainers and even creating a private retreat within the precincts of Westminster Abbey. Worse, Despenser inevitably became more powerful, along with his acolytes, who were appointed to influential positions within the government of the realm.

This change in his outlook also caused Edward to be more distant from me despite my best endeavours. I tried to improve his spirits, I tried to involve him in minor diversions and frivolities to take his mind off his woes, but he showed little interest. This began to place a renewed strain on our union with which I had until then been increasingly content.

The fact of the matter was that we had very different personalities. Yet we were still good friends, and, whatever his limitations, so long as I felt he was doing his best to do his duty as King, I was happy to be as supportive as possible. When he began to neglect this, however, by shutting himself off from the world, I became frustrated and even angry with him.

'You cannot afford to neglect your responsibilities as King,' I chided him on one of the increasingly rare occasions he came to my bed, so we were alone together behind the curtains which surrounded it. 'This will only encourage the likes of my uncle,

Lancaster, into making more trouble.'

'I'm not neglecting them, I assure you. I rise earlier than I used to in order to attend to affairs of state and try harder, too, to listen carefully to the advice I receive.'

'That's all very well, but then you disappear to this retreat you've created for yourself. It's the behaviour of a hermit rather than a King.'

'I need time to myself for contemplation. It helps to settle my mind. You know I do not find that being King gets any easier. In fact, it just irks me. You know when our son, Edward, is of age, I'd like to be able to abdicate the throne in his favour.'

I wasn't surprised by this revelation, I knew that my husband found the burden of kingship to be a heavy one, but now he had openly admitted it to me.

'But that is still many years in the future. He's only seven years old, don't forget.' I reminded him.

Our conversation then turned to the prospect of our making a visit to France to pay homage for Gascony now that spring was almost upon us. It was something that I was increasingly looking forward to as I still missed the land of my birth, and most especially its warmer weather. We were emerging from what had become another harsh winter, with bitter north winds and heavy snowfalls that had settled for weeks on end.

We had already made one attempt to make the journey, even travelling as far as Canterbury, before having to return to Westminster because my brother, Philip, had neglected to issue the necessary safe conduct. Now that it had finally arrived I hoped we could travel again soon, but Edward was far less enthusiastic and to my growing annoyance, it was mid-June before we sailed.

My expectation that this visit would bring us closer together again both physically and emotionally, was somewhat undermined by Edward choosing to include both Hugh Despenser and Roger d'Amory in our entourage as he spent so much more time in their company than mine. It raised the spectre of Gaveston in my mind, and to such an extent that there were occasions when I fancied that it was him standing next to Edward rather than Despenser. Of course, I tried to dismiss any such notion as a nonsense, but it kept recurring to me.

After Edward had paid homage to Philip for Gascony, at the high altar in Amiens Cathedral, we sat down for fruitful talks in which Philip promised military assistance in the event of an armed struggle with my uncle, Lancaster. We then remained in France for about a month. There were a few wet days, but the weather was mostly warmer and sunnier than I had grown used to in England, which pleased me greatly.

It had also been a pleasure to be reunited with my brother, Philip, though I still felt a keen sense of loss at the passing of my siblings, Robert, and Louis, as well as that of my parents. So much so in fact that I made a point of visiting their tombs where I lit candles in their memory.

By the time we returned to England I was becoming increasingly concerned by what I felt to be Hugh Despenser's malign influence on Edward. The time I had spent in his company whilst we were abroad, also convinced me more than ever that he did not like me, and I must say that the feeling was mutual. It was not just that he reminded me of Gaveston, either. Once we had become better acquainted, he had at least deigned to always be polite and even offered me the occasional smile. Despenser, on the other hand, was thoroughly cold, never offered me any eye contact, let alone a smile, and did his upmost to ignore me, which I considered disrespectful to the point of rudeness.

In August Despenser's father, who was a Godfather of my son, Prince Edward, suddenly and without any explanation, stopped paying me rent for his use of the Manor of Lechlade, which I had let to him. I had always got on perfectly well with him and suspected that it had been his son who had encouraged him to behave in such a fashion. I immediately sought some explanation for the withholding of this money but received no reply. My dissatisfaction lingered, unassuaged, whilst I knew it was hopeless to appeal to Edward for help in this matter.

I was also aware of Despenser seeking to profit from Edward's favouritism. This reached a head in the autumn when he encouraged Edward to confiscate lands on the Gower peninsular, in South Wales, from one of the Marcher lords, John Mowbray, who had recently acquired them, with a view to bestowing them on him, instead.

Admittedly, Mowbray had neglected to obtain the necessary royal license required to purchase the land, but I have no reason to think this more than an oversight, which could have been easily corrected, albeit retrospectively. Rather, when Mowbray declined to surrender the land, Edward sent soldiers to seize it from him, though not before I had tried to persuade him not to do so, which led to a confrontation with Despenser in Council.

'My blessed Lord,' I said to Edward,' surely sending soldiers to seize the land is too heavy handed. It risks angering Mowbray's fellow Marcher Lords to the advantage of your enemies, especially once they learn what you then intend to do with the land.'

'But I am perfectly within my rights as King to seize the land. Mowbray knew full well that his purchase required my license and preferred to ignore this.'

'Forgive me, Edward, are you certain this was no more than an innocent mistake?'

An uncomfortable expression formed on his face whereupon Despenser interjected, directing his gaze on Edward rather than me. 'Of course, it was more than an oversight. Mowbray acted as he did quite deliberately and deserves to pay the consequences.'

I felt the cold wind of trouble blowing all around me.

'But even if that's true, is it wise to then bestow these lands on Baron Despenser. It will be said that you have merely found an excuse to seize land that does not belong to you.'

'Nonsense,' Despenser retorted, again looking only at Edward. 'The likes of Mowbray need to understand that they are not above the law. Once the land has been forfeited you will then be well within your rights to bestow it on whoever you choose.'

'Yet, my blessed Lord, what the Baron here fails to mention is that he already possesses a significant amount of land in South Wales as well as Lundy Island. Grant him much of the Gower as well and I must say that you will only create antagonism towards both yourself, and the Baron, which could even lead to armed conflict.'

Despenser looked angry. 'That's a completely exaggerated fear. My Lord the King, you must act decisively to assert your royal authority, otherwise the requirement for royal licences will become totally disregarded.'

Edward smiled at him. 'Quite so, Hugh, quite so.'

It was evident to me that I was losing the argument, but I made one final appeal. 'Seize the land, then, but at the same time make it very clear that you only intend to keep it in your possession until Mowbray offers sufficient compensation for his denial of your authority.'

Despenser snorted. 'Her grace, the Queen, fails to understand the seriousness of Mowbray's offence. Only a total seizure of his land will deter others from acting in a similar manner. My Lord King, you must make an example of him.'

Edward nodded. 'Yes, of course, Hugh. You're quite right.'

From that moment onwards I knew that he was under Despenser's spell, so history could be about to repeat itself. Within months my fears proved to be well founded as the Marcher Lords, including Roger Mortimer, who had recently been recalled from Ireland, were so appalled by Edward's conduct, especially when he stubbornly refused to countenance any compromise, that they withdrew from court.

I was angry with Edward and angrier still with Hugh Despenser for his avaricious manipulation of Edward's largesse. Worst of all, it was now clear to me that he was as much in thrall to Despenser as he had previously been to Gaveston, which deeply upset me. When he had been under that man's spell, I had been just a slip of a girl, but now I was a beautiful young woman, who had given Edward nothing but my loyal devotion for the best part of twelve years as well as three healthy children. As such, I was not just going to stand back and let this happen again. I also had trusted friends with whom I could share my fears.

'I'll not stand in the shadows as I did when Gaveston was alive,' I exclaimed to Isabella de Beaumont in a letter. 'Edward insults me by preferring both the advice and the companionship of a man as avaricious as Hugh Despenser, who has not the least regard for my position as Queen.'

I added in my letter that I was now pregnant again, which should have been a cause for great joy. Instead, my emotions were on fire as I feared that all my efforts had been in vain. Edward had fallen under the spell of a man I detested!

# CHAPTER 18

# OUTRAGE

Hearing that the Marcher Lords, including Roger Mortimer, had met with my uncle, Lancaster, and had resolved with his support to demand that the Despensers be sent into exile, I decided to insist on a frank conversation with Edward in private. I was determined to be forthright and speak my mind.

'We must speak alone about Hugh Despenser,' I said to Edward as we ate together. He raised his eyebrows and gave me an anxious glance. 'It's important. Do not deny me this request.'

'Oh, very well, once we've finished eating, I'll dismiss the servants.'

Half an hour later I had him to myself and came immediately to the point. 'I want to know if Despenser has replaced me now in your affections?'

'No, of course not… I swear it.'

'Then why do you spend so long in his company and give way to his every demand, even though it's only leading to confrontation with the Marcher Lords as well as my uncle?'

'I don't spend too long in his company…'

'Does he come to your bed?'

'No! Certainly not. How dare you suggest such a thing.'

'But you care for him, don't you.'

'He's become a good friend, nothing more.'

'But he's leading you by the nose. Don't you see that it's just taking you down the same road as you went with Gaveston? That ended terribly and, mark my words, this will as well.'

'Not if you stand by me. Together we can defeat those who oppose my royal will.'

'But you're even making enemies of once loyal supporters, Roger Mortimer for one.'

'That's regrettable but I'm determined to assert my authority. Will you help me?'

'How can I do that?'

'By making your castles at Marlborough and Devizes available to those who support my cause.'

'I have always been loyal to you, so alright, I will do as you ask. Please, though, promise me that I will continue to come first in your affections?'

'That I gladly do.'

'I ask, too, that you think carefully about my advice that what you're embarking upon will not end well.'

'I respect your judgement, but my mind is made up. Remember that the Marcher Lords have decided to enter an alliance with my now, sworn enemy, Lancaster.'

I took a deep breath and calmed myself; perhaps a compromise could be reached, nay, should be reached. So, I steadied myself and resolved to still support Edward, though with some not inconsiderable qualms. I knew that I had to think like a tactician, a politician even. I had my children to think of, not least the one I was now expecting imminently.

The conversation between us had given me a certain measure of reassurance and I subsequently kept to my undertaking to hand over my two castles. Yet, as if to confirm my worst fears, the Marcher Lords, led by Mortimer, launched an attack on Despenser lands in Glamorgan and Gloucestershire, seizing castles and leaving crops burning in the fields. By the time my confinement due close in June, they had also sworn to disinherit both Hugh Despenser and his father, bringing the country so close to outright civil war that, for my personal safety, I took up residence in the Tower of London.

This may have seemed like a drastic measure, but I needed to be assured that I was safe, especially as I was at such a vulnerable time.

It was here that my second daughter, Joan, was born on the fifth of July. Yet again, praise be to God, my labour was neither too long nor too difficult. Unfortunately, the royal apartments were in such an appalling state of disrepair that, when it rained, water dripped through the ceiling onto my bedclothes. This made me so angry that I didn't hesitate to inform Edward, whereupon he summarily dismissed the Constable of the Tower from his position.

By the end of the month Roger Mortimer had brought an army to within a few miles of London and he was soon joined by my uncle, Lancaster. They then demanded that Edward dismiss the Despensers but he told me bluntly that he would not do so. It was all too reminiscent of the struggle he had had with his Earls over Gaveston's fate. So much so in fact that I laughed ruefully at his response, thinking it better than weeping, though in truth I was more than ready to shed bitter tears. I remained strong.

'What choice have you?' I asked him. 'I did warn you it would come to this.'

Edward just flew into a temper. 'Damn their eyes and damn

yours!' He then flounced off, surely knowing full well that he was in an impossible situation and would have to accede to their demand sooner or later. I was naturally upset by his outburst, though he did have the grace to apologise for it later the same day. He was somewhat cowed and tender on his return, acknowledging that I had so recently given him another beautiful child, which he professed to love.

Meanwhile, the Earl of Pembroke, a man I was coming to admire for both his sound judgement and negotiating skills, sought to act as an intermediary again, but to no avail as Edward still stubbornly refused to listen to reason. This brought Pembroke to my door, asking me if I might persuade Edward to change his mind.

'My dear Earl, I can assure you I have already tried but without any success. My Lord the King simply became angry with me so you can appreciate my reluctance to raise the matter again. History is repeating itself, I fear, so I warned him that if he fails to give way, this can only end badly. However, hearing such a remonstrance from my lips simply upset his pride. What he hates most of all, you see, is having to give way to my uncle, Lancaster, and that yet again his royal will counts for nothing.'

'Then your Majesty, might I suggest a different approach. Declare your wholehearted support for the King's cause, but emphasise, too, that the time is not yet right for a confrontation with an army he cannot hope to defeat, in which event Hugh Despenser could well be executed just as Gaveston was.'

'Very well, I will try, but do not be surprised if he will not listen.'

Later the same day I interrupted a meeting that Edward was having with some of his courtiers and in a deliberately dramatic gesture went down on my knees before him.

'My Lord King, I humbly beseech you to hear my most urgent plea…'

'What is this? Do get up…'

'No, I will not! Hear me out, I beg you.'

'Yes…, yes, alright…,' he said, in a fractured and irritated manner.

'My Lord Pembroke has told me that you are still refusing to dismiss the Despensers. Of course, I understand why this is so and do not think that I am prostrating myself before you out of sympathy for those who are challenging your royal will. I simply appeal to you to understand that if you do not dismiss them, you will be putting Hugh Despenser's life in grave danger. If for no other reason than his personal safety I therefore beseech you to dismiss him along with his father. Think, too, of the blood that will be spilt amongst your loyal subjects if there is civil war. This will inflict untold misery upon them. For their sake as well, I beg you, my Lord King, give way.'

I had my hands placed together in humble supplication as I spoke, and looking steadily into Edward's eyes, was willing him to accede to my plea. He had rarely seen me in such a humble position, begging at his feet like this. I felt that it was what I needed to do, to shock him into listening and realising how serious my request was.

'I will think on what you've said and let you have my decision tomorrow. Now please, Isabella, do get up off your knees.' And with that he held out his hands to me.

I was satisfied at least that I had done all I possibly could to win him round but was by no means certain that it would make any difference. I was therefore delighted to learn from his own lips the following day that he had indeed changed his mind.

A few days later the Marcher Lords assembled in Westminster Hall to be told by Edward that he was prepared, after all, to dismiss the Despensers from his service and send them both into exile. At the same time, he was also forced to pardon my uncle, as well as all the Marcher Lords who'd taken up arms. Of course, he only did this through gritted teeth, storing up yet more hatred of my uncle, and he told me afterwards, in no uncertain terms, that he still intended to have his revenge.

'I will bring him down one day, as God is my witness.'

Deprived of his favourite's presence, Edward was moody and irritable in mine, which wasn't all that often, as he increasingly preferred his own company. Yet again, I was reminded of how he'd behaved in Gaveston's absence. I knew without having to ask, that he was probably scheming to bring the Despensers home again. I was losing patience with him.

Towards the end of August Edward unexpectedly suggested to me that we might care to go on a pilgrimage together to Canterbury. He knew how much I revered St Thomas, and I had previously mentioned to him a wish to revisit his shrine, so I gratefully agreed. I also hoped that his kind offer was a demonstration of his desire to keep me first in his affections. What I did not, however, appreciate was that he had an ulterior motive.

During our journey, Edward admitted to me that he was in contact with Hugh Despenser. 'Once we've visited Thomas's shrine my intention is that we should travel further east to Thanet, where I've arranged to meet with Hugh. He has his own ship and can put into port there.'

I drew in my breath. 'Is this necessary? He's supposed to be in exile.'

'And will continue to be so, more's the pity, but I surely still have the right to meet with him from time to time.'

Yet again I was reminded of his relationship with Gaveston and knew in my bones that Edward was now playing just the same game as he had with him.

When we then approached Canterbury, news was brought to us by a messenger whom Edward had sent ahead into the city to announce our arrival, that it was full of the armed retainers of Lord Badlesmere, who despite being steward to the royal household, had allied himself with the Marcher Lords, as well as my uncle, Lancaster.

'Apparently, there's much drunkenness in the city and some violence, too. The Archbishop is not in residence, and the Cathedral monks have advised that if you enter the city you risk a hostile reception.'

This was frustrating news, which I was inclined to disregard, but Edward decided to avoid any unpleasant confrontation, pointing out that we had insufficient armed retainers with us. We therefore simply bypassed the city and continued on our way towards Thanet.

We then crossed to the island by ferry and met with Despenser at the small cinque port of Sarre, not that I did more than nod my head to him before he and Edward, having embraced warmly, walked away.

They were gone for upwards of an hour and when they returned Despenser immediately boarded the ship that had brought him to the island. For his part, Edward was in a very good humour and told me that they had decided upon a strategy, which would hopefully bring down his enemies and enable Despenser to return to court.

'We mean to begin with that turncoat, Badlesmere, who now lords it over Canterbury with his armed retainers

'But how exactly?' I asked.

'As you well know, his castle at Leeds, here in Kent, was originally bequeathed to you...'

'Yes, you chose to give it to Badlesmere in exchange for land in Shropshire.'

'Quite. At the time I thought it a fair exchange. Anyway, it's still a former royal residence and if as Queen you should request the right to stay there for a night or two, during your travels, Badlesmere should not refuse you. Indeed, if he were to do so, it would be an insult to the crown that would justify me in acting against him.'

'But do you seriously imagine then that he would refuse to offer me hospitality?'

'I think it possible. The castle is not all that far from Canterbury and you could request your right to stay there on the way to St Thomas's shrine. I take it you'd like to try and visit it again?'

'Why yes, but why can't we do so together?'

'I have matters requiring my urgent attention and must return to London as soon as possible...'

'...And I now wish to spend time with our children, especially Joan.'

'She has her wet nurse...'

I tutted. 'I am still her mother!'

Edward gave me a contrite look. 'Do so, but pray, only for a week or so. Then it would help our cause if you set out for Canterbury again, by way of Badlesmere's Castle.'

'But I still don't see what purpose that will have served if in fact I am offered every hospitality.'

'At the very least it will have been a test of where his ultimate loyalty lies.'

'Very well, I'll do as you ask, though Canterbury could still be overrun by Badlesmere's men.'

'Take as many armed men with you as are necessary to offer you protection.'

Scheming such as this had never been in Edward's nature, so it was clear to me whose idea this was. Nonetheless, being anxious to visit St Thomas's shrine once more, I was content to go along with what was proposed, imagining that the worst that could happen was that Badlesmere would refuse to open his gates to me.

Having spent a few days pleasantly, in the company of my children, I travelled through some beautiful Kent country-side that I had never previously seen until we came within sight of Leeds castle. The weather was dry fortunately, and autumn having set in, the leaves on the trees had turned to some lustrous shades of red and gold. I then decided to send a messenger forward to announce my arrival and request entry. Twenty minutes later he returned, looking out of sorts.

'Lady Badlesmere spoke to me from the battlements. She said her husband was away and that he had left her strict instructions to deny entry to any strangers...'

'What, even if that stranger is the Queen of England?'

'That is how she chooses to interpret his instructions. She suggests that you find accommodation elsewhere.'

'Insolent woman!' I declared. 'I've a mind to speak to her in person.'

I rode forward, until I was within yards of the castle's Barbican. This guarded a short bridge over the castle's moat, which at its full extent was the size of a lake, making its setting exceedingly pleasant to the eye.

'Call out, announcing that the Queen of England demands to speak to Lady Badlesmere,' I said to the same messenger who had previously spoken to her. He bowed his head to me and duly did as I had asked. A few minutes later I saw the face of a woman looking down at me.

'I am Lady Badlesmere and regret, your Majesty, that I cannot allow you entry in the light of my Lord's express instructions.'

'But in God's name, I am your Queen. He surely did not intend that his instructions should apply to me. May I also remind you that this was once a royal castle that was pledged to me.'

'With respect, your Majesty, the castle was gifted to my Lord; he has every right to deny anyone entry. I fear that I must follow his instructions without exception.'

I found her manner so irritating that it made me angry. 'Damn your eyes, I and my party need a night's rest and it's growing too late to find anywhere else. Your attitude is insolent to the point of being treasonous. If you'll not open your gates, I'll direct my men to force entry.'

At this moment, she simply disappeared. Then I made what was to prove to be a fatal mistake, ordering my men to cut down and then fashion a tree into a battering ram so that they could break down the gate with it. This they proceeded to do but, as they approached the gate, archers appeared on the battlements and fired at them with devastating effect. Six men soon lay dead or dying and I was forced to call a retreat.

'Foolish woman,' I muttered under my breath, knowing that she'd unwittingly played right into Edward's hands. That said, I was both shocked and angered that she had ordered her archers to do such a thing before my very eyes. I had never been in any personal danger, but nonetheless to see six healthy young men needlessly killed in front of me was deeply unpleasant and it is an image that has continued to disturb my dreams even into old age.

After being forced to spend an uncomfortable night in a nearby priory, I sent a letter to Edward the following day explaining what had happened. Of course, I emphasised the affront to my royal dignity, and knowing full well that this was what Edward wanted to happen, demanded that action be taken to punish Lady Badlesmere for her outrageous behaviour.

Then I travelled as far as Rochester castle where I took up temporary residence in its splendid keep. I learnt, subsequently, that Edward had complained to Lord Badlesmere about his wife's behaviour, only to receive an utterly defiant reply stating that he completely approved of what his wife had done.

Such a provocative response utterly amazed me, I can only assume that it demonstrated in how much contempt Edward was held by far too many of his barons. I expect, too, that based on Edward's past behaviour, Badlesmere imagined that there would be no retribution for his defiance, but on this occasion, he could not have been more wrong.

Whatever his faults, Despenser seemed to have put 'fire into Edward's belly' as he assembled an army to put Leeds castle under siege. This eventually numbered several thousand men, so not surprisingly the castle soon surrendered, whereupon Edward, who was present, wreaked a savage retribution, the likes of which he had never demonstrated before in his entire reign.

The constable of the castle along with thirteen of his men were summarily hanged before the castle gates and Lady

Badlesmere sent as a prisoner to the Tower of London. At last Edward had acted with the kind of decisiveness that I would have expected of my father. I was reunited with him at Tonbridge castle and delighted when he bestowed Leeds castle upon me.

My pleasure at this turn of events was, however, soon tempered when Edward moved to annul the Despensers' exile. This was hardly unexpected, but I still felt that it was Hugh Despenser who had given Edward his stomach for a fight and that once restored to a position of power he would be as malign an influence on him as Gaveston had ever been.

# CHAPTER 19

# A TERRIBLE JOURNEY

Encouraged, I expect, by Hugh Despenser, Edward now displayed more unaccustomed energy in moving against the Marcher Lords, including Roger Mortimer. This upset me as I was personally in sympathy with their desire to protect their interests, which were after all threatened by Despenser's high-handed ambitions.

Edward, though, was simply angry with them for forcing his favourite into exile as well as allying themselves with his greatest enemy, namely my uncle Lancaster. Appreciating that it would be pointless to try and persuade him to take a different course, I decided that it was best to keep my own counsel.

While I stayed at the Palace of Langley in Hertfordshire, Edward marshalled an army, which was too powerful for the Marcher Lords to have any hope of defeating. They therefore retreated in the face of his advance until, following many desertions, Mortimer surrendered to Edward, who promptly imprisoned him along with his wife and sons. By mid-January Despenser and his father had returned to England and by February the last Marcher castle had surrendered.

This was a triumph for Edward but at the same time I was cast down by more sad news from France. My brother, Philip, was struck down by dysentery, and having sired only daughters was succeeded to the throne by my last remaining brother,

Charles. Of course, Philip's premature demise, again brought home to me my Godfather's terrible curse, making me fearful that my family was damned in the eyes of God.

When Edward returned to me at Langley, it was immediately obvious to me that his recent success had boosted his self-confidence hugely.

'Now I'm determined to bring down Lancaster, as well,' he declared to me as we ate together. 'I know I can muster a large enough army, whilst apart from Hereford he's bereft of allies. At last, I shall have my revenge on him for what he did to Piers.'

For all that Lancaster was my uncle I had never liked him and ever since Gaveston's death had lived with the knowledge that a confrontation between him and Edward was almost inevitable one day. Certainly, I had no desire to discourage Edward, especially after the support Lancaster had given Badlesmere and my wretched experience before the walls of Leeds Castle, which still gave me nightmares.

By the end of February Edward was ready to put his plan into effect, and, within a short while, had captured one of Lancaster's castles, as well as having evidence that he had been colluding with the King of Scots. It was just what he needed to have Lancaster declared a rebel. My uncle then tried to flee but his forces were brought to battle at Boroughbridge in Yorkshire, Hereford was mortally wounded, and after many of his men deserted him, my uncle was left with no choice but to surrender.

In a twist of fate, Edward then very deliberately dealt with him in the same way as he, Lancaster, had dealt with Gaveston. At his trial he was not allowed to defend himself and having inevitably been found guilty of treason was beheaded. It was a humiliating end for such a proud man.

The letter I received from Edward informing me of the execution, also added that he'd had several of my uncle's supporters executed as well. The tone was triumphant, even gloating, which shocked me. I had never thought of Edward as being a cruel man and had expected him to respect my uncle's royal blood by casting him into prison rather than having him executed. I did not revel in the bloodletting that was my uncle's end. Rather, I advocated mercy, which was surely preferable.

Edward invited me to join him at Pontefract, and once I arrived there, I learnt from his own lips the extent to which he had revenged himself on those who had, as he put it, long humiliated him. It was clear to me just how much pent-up anger and frustration had caused him to behave in such a merciless fashion, even imprisoning my uncle's estranged wife, Alice de Lacy, as well as her mother. Seeing, Hugh Despenser, at Edward's side, also made me suspect that he'd encouraged such conduct. Yet again, I was reminded of Gaveston, making me fear for the future.

I brought with me to Pontefract a petition I'd received from a certain Lady Jane Knovill, pleading with me to intercede with Edward to spare the life of her husband, Lord Knovill. I felt enough blood had already been spilt so decided that I would do so. Seizing the moment, I chose to address Edward on the subject at a meeting of the Council at which Hugh Despenser was present.

I felt his cold eyes on me as I spoke and could sense that he was displeased by my appeal. When I had barely finished speaking, he spoke out against it.

'Sire, I believe it would be a sign of weakness if you were to allow this. We're agreed, are we not, that all traitors deserve nothing less than death?'

'But surely, enough men have been executed already,' I retorted. 'I beg you, my noble Lord, to show Lord Knovill mercy.'

I smiled plaintively at Edward as I spoke, willing him to accede to my request. At first, he looked uncertain, clearly torn over what to do the best.

'Oh, very well, on this occasion I'll let him live.'

Despenser snorted. 'But noble King, you're surely not going to allow him to walk free? Spare his life, if you must, but at least make him pay a heavy price for his freedom.'

'What do you suggest would be suitable?'

'I'd say twenty thousand pounds in silver.'

'But that's a huge amount. I doubt he'll ever be able to raise such a sum.'

'Then keep him in prison until he does.'

At this point I intervened. 'In which case he'd likely die there. Might I suggest that he be released upon payment of five thousand pounds, with the remainder being payable by annual instalments of the same amount.'

Edward smiled at me. 'Yes, I think that an excellent idea.'

I could tell that Despenser was still less than pleased with my intervention, but I really didn't care. His relationship with Edward was irritating me more than ever, making me wish that he had never returned from exile. I was delighted to have gained a victory over him on this occasion. My persuading of Edward to save a man's life, and even to make him pay the price for his freedom over a more manageable period, was no mean feat considering how much influence Despenser appeared to wield.

In May Edward and I travelled to York where a meeting of Parliament repealed the Ordinances that had for so long shackled his ability to rule as he pleased. After almost fifteen years on the throne, he had every reason to see this as his finest hour, but I struggled to share his happiness.

For one, I was increasingly anxious that the execution of my uncle created a dangerous precedent, given that no one with royal blood had been treated in this fashion in two hundred and fifty years since the battle of Hastings. Furthermore, I was, of course, deeply perturbed by Hugh Despenser's malign influence, which I strongly suspected had encouraged Edward to deal so harshly with not just my uncle but many others besides.

My dislike of Hugh Despenser intensified when in the summer, without warning, he stopped paying me the rent that was due to me for a farm in the vicinity of Bristol, which was in his possession. By then I was also growing frustrated that my castles at Marlborough and Devizes showed no sign of being returned to me.

Meanwhile, Roger Mortimer and his father were brought to trial at Westminster Hall, accused of treason. Given the high regard I had always had for him this naturally perturbed me, and then, the day before the trial was due to take place I received a plea from his wife to beg Edward to be merciful in the event of his being sentenced to death. Without hesitation I sent a reply promising her that I would gladly do so. Then I ordered one of my squires to attend the trial with a view to bringing me immediate news of the sentence.

Sure enough, he came to me in the early afternoon with an expression on his face that told its own story. The Mortimers had indeed been sentenced to death without delay so I sought out Edward, who to my annoyance was in the company of Hugh Despenser. As a child Queen this might well have deterred me, but those days were now long gone.

'Edward, I must speak with you on an important matter...'

'As you wish. What might that be?'

'It concerns the sentence of death passed on the Mortimers. I have received a plea from Roger Mortimer's wife that you show them mercy by commuting their sentence... May I speak to you alone about this?'

I could see that Despenser was already scowling at me while Edward hesitated. 'Please?' I added earnestly.

'Very well. Hugh, could you leave us for a short while?'

'Of course, Sire, but granting this plea would be just another sign of weakness. They deserve only death.'

Once he had withdrawn, I looked Edward in the eye. 'You don't believe what he just told you? Many men including my uncle have already been executed. You surely do not need yet more to demonstrate that you are not a weak King. The Mortimers also surrendered themselves to you without any struggle and Roger Mortimer has shown you loyal enough service in the past to merit clemency.'

'Yet they've still been found to be traitors, does not that deserve death?'

'...That must be for you to judge, but you certainly have the power to spare their lives, and I can only repeat that it would simply not be any sign of weakness if you were to do so.'

The expression on Edward's face softened. Indeed, he even smiled at me a little with his eyes. 'As it happens, I already had in mind commuting their sentences to life imprisonment, so let me assure you that that is what I shall do, forthwith.'

I returned his smile, gratefully. 'Thank you, Edward, I believe you've made a wise decision.'

Spontaneously, I then placed a kiss on his right cheek, which brought an even more affectionate smile to his face. 'When I begin my latest campaign against the Scots, I want you to come north with me as far as Northumberland. You could stay at Tynemouth.'

I did not have happy memories of this place so was less than enthusiastic about this suggestion. 'Would it not be better if I were to remain in York?' I would be safer there if the campaign should fail.'

'But there's no reason at all why it should end in anything other than success. I've had my revenge on your uncle and now I mean to have it on the Scots as well.'

'You can't be too sure of that. The Scots will not make it easy for you.'

'I don't expect them to, but the army I'm assembling is a formidable one. This time I shall win, I know it.'

I was concerned that Edward was being over-confident but was content to travel north with him as far as Tynemouth whereupon he led his army into Scotland, accompanied by Hugh Despenser. By then it was August, which I thought was late in the summer to begin such a campaign. Yet, the weather was still fine, and in early September I received a letter from Edward informing me that his army was encountering no resistance.

This only made me feel uneasy, worrying that the Scots might be luring his army into some sort of trap, after which I received no further news for several weeks, making me increasingly anxious. Finally, in early October, I received a letter from him telling me what I had most feared. The Scots had laid waste to their own land and refused to give battle. Consequently, his army had run out of supplies and then been wracked by dysentery, resulting in many deaths. Of course, he'd been left with no choice but to retreat as far south as York.

'How can this be?' I exclaimed to my ladies-in-waiting, feeling utterly shocked that he should have travelled so far south without making the least attempt to secure my safety. 'Has my Lord, the King, deserted me?'

I knew in my heart, that I had not been a priority to Edward. Certainly, there were others he thought of before the safety of his Queen. I was, yet again, let down and disappointed, as well as left to fend for myself, no doubt.

I was met by embarrassed glances, but upon reading on was somewhat reassured by his promise that he had sent a body of troops to my rescue. Nonetheless, I was naturally concerned that the Scots might reach me first so sent some of my squires on a reconnaissance to try and establish just how close they might be. The news that one of them soon returned with, convinced me that if I was to escape capture, I had no choice but to ask my squires to requisition a suitable ship with all possible speed.

The first time I set eyes on the cog, a single-masted vessel, that I and my ladies were invited to board, I was concerned that it might not even be seaworthy, given how old it looked.

'Is this the best you've been able to find us?' I asked, somewhat dubiously.

'I'm afraid it is, your majesty,' my most trusted squire, John de Lacy, responded. 'But I'm assured by its master that it's in perfectly sound condition.'

'But it's on the small size, wouldn't you say?'

'Perhaps it is, your Majesty. I think its cabin should still accommodate you and your ladies-in-waiting, though.'

'Which will no doubt be dark and uncomfortable, whatever the weather.'

'But if it's fine you could remain on deck.'

I smiled at him. 'Better that if any of us are seasick.'

As it turned out, the elements in mid-October proved to be anything but kind to us. On the morning of our departure, it was raining steadily and windy, too, whilst the waves racing towards the shore were certainly most perturbing.

'Don't you think we should delay our departure?' Hugh Despenser's wife, Eleanor de Clare, my chief lady-in-waiting, asked me.

'I wish we could, but I fear the Scots are too close. If we don't leave now, we may never do so.'

So, we set-off, setting course for Scarborough, some ninety miles to the south. We were never out of sight of land, which was just as well as the weather soon became rougher, causing such a swell that several of my ladies-in-waiting became seasick.

For my part, I still felt well, having always previously enjoyed being at sea, but it soon became clear to me that we were heading into a storm, which might endanger all our lives, especially if our ship was driven onto the rocks. Naturally, I was fearful, yet I considered it my responsibility to remain as outwardly calm as possible, and to her credit so did Eleanor de Clare.

We were both only too aware that she enjoyed her position entirely due to her husband's influence over the King, but I did not resent her. On the contrary, we got on perfectly well, as she was a handsome, intelligent woman, possessed of much dignity. I also felt we had much in common, for like myself, she had been married off whilst still young, and had borne Despenser seven children.

As the storm grew louder, our ship began to creak and roll even more violently, making some of my ladies-in-waiting even more distressed, to the point that they began to sob loudly, as well as wringing their hands in dread.

'We must pray to almighty God to grant us salvation from this tempest,' I called out. 'We can but trust that he will hear our prayers and that this ordeal will soon end.'

Unfortunately, the storm worsened, causing me to fear that our ship might break up, sending us all to a watery grave. I decided that I must speak to the ship's master, but he assured me that we were holding to our course and making good progress.

'Are you confident we won't run aground?' I asked him.

'Yes, yr Majesty, just so long as the wind doesn't change. If anything, we're being taken a little further out to sea.'

This last remark offered me little comfort. 'Your ship's old, is it not; is it capable of surviving this storm?'

'It's still sound, yr Majesty. I've sailed 'er through worse storms than this one.'

I took encouragement from what he said and hoped my ladies-in-waiting would do the same. Yet, our confinement was still most unpleasant, and though it was now dark I saw little prospect of being able to sleep. Nonetheless, at some point I must have managed to do so as the next thing I remembered was being vaguely aware of a scream.

'What's happening?' I called out. 'Has someone been hurt?'

At that very moment I heard the door of our cabin open,

bringing with it a blast of cold air. 'Forgive me, your Majesty, something terrible's happened.' It was my trusted squire, John de Lacy. 'One of your ladies has been swept overboard and drowned. It was a huge wave that took her.'

'No! No, this is too awful. What was she doing outside?' Who was she?'

When Eleanor told me that it was Margaret Valence who had died, I was quite distraught for she had been a delightfully engaging person, whose company I had always enjoyed. I also recalled how bitterly she had complained about our confinement, especially as it grew darker.

'Was no one aware of her going outside?' I then asked.

'Your Majesty, I knew the door had been opened,' came a reply from out of the darkness. 'But it was very quickly closed again.'

I imagined how desperate she must have become and thought it utterly tragic that this should have led to her death when she was still not yet twenty-five and the mother of two small children.

I was angry, too, that we had ever been forced into this situation because Edward had failed in his duty to give us adequate protection until it was far too late.

By the time we finally reached the safety of Scarborough's port, the storm had all but blown itself out although the sea was still choppy. Though I had not been physically sick, I felt utterly exhausted for want of enough sleep or a properly cooked meal. Most of my ladies-in-waiting, with the notable exception of Eleanor were in a distraught state, making me feel even more angry. What's more, to compound the horrors of our journey, we had not long touched dry land when one of our number, who was pregnant went into premature labour.

When her babe was stillborn and she then bled to death, I wanted to scream out in anguish at the cruelty of this world. Only the strong sense of self-discipline that I had learnt at my father's knee constrained me, but inwardly I was seething. What's more, that emotion remained within me like a coiled viper all the way to York where I was finally reunited with Edward.

## CHAPTER 20

## FROM BAD TO WORSE

When we first met again, Edward behaved in a solicitous way towards me as he always did. 'Welcome, welcome, I'm so pleased you're safe,' he said with a warm smile of greeting.

Then he placed his arms around me, I let him place a kiss on my cheek, but I could not bring myself to return his smile. I wanted to say no thanks to you but constrained my anger, not wishing to admonish Edward in the presence of others. Once we were alone together, I was, however, quite determined to make my feelings clear. The sight of Edward in close company with Hugh Despenser had also done nothing to improve my mood. Their relationship reminded me more and more of the one Edward had enjoyed with Gaveston.

'My journey from Tynemouth by sea was dreadful. Two of my ladies-in-waiting are dead.'

He looked suitably shocked at this news. 'Oh dear, how did this happen?'

'I ask that we talk in private about this.'

His response was to look in Despenser's direction, which irritated me. 'Not now, I'm afraid, but this evening I will come to you, I promise. In the meantime, take your ease. I can see how tired you must be.'

'Oh, very well.' I felt thwarted, not so much by Edward, more by the influence Despenser clearly had over him.

Edward kept to his word, but we had barely greeted each other before he began to bemoan the loss of so many valuable possessions that he'd been forced to abandon while fleeing from the Scots. 'And worst of all, Richmond's forces have been routed and he's now a prisoner of the Scots. There'll be a heavy ransom to pay before they'll release him.'

It was all too reminiscent of the disastrous campaign against the Scots eight years previously, but I was not inclined to express any sympathy. Instead, my pent-up emotions burst forth like the waters of a swollen river.

'How could you abandon me and my ladies-in-waiting? We were placed in such terrible danger!'

'I didn't abandon you. On the contrary I sent men to your aid.'

'But by then it was far too late. And surely you understood that Tynemouth Abbey is no fortress. If we had not fled by sea when we did, the Scots would have taken all of us prisoner and think what ransom you'd have had to find.'

'It was all very unfortunate...'

'Unfortunate! Is that all you can say? Your duty to me as your faithful Queen was to come personally to my aid when you first retreated out of Scotland. Had you done so, two of my ladies-in-waiting would still be alive today!'

'I'm sorry. Their fate's most regrettable.'

'But why, why did you wait until you'd retreated as far as York before thinking of my situation?'

'We were in a difficult position. So many men were ill, we had insufficient food, whilst I did not want to expose either you or your ladies to such suffering.'

'You could still have communicated with me sooner and

given me the choice. I think in your haste to escape the Scots, you simply abandoned me.'

'No, that's unfair. I spoke to Hugh about your situation when we first turned back. We agreed that for the time being you were safest where you were at Tynemouth.'

'Ah, so this was all his idea, was it?'

'No, no, I simply sought his advice.'

'And then bowed to his better judgement, I expect!' I exclaimed, sarcastically. 'It would suit his purposes very well, I'm sure, if I was to die.'

'Such a suggestion is unbecoming of you…'

'Is it? I don't think so. He knows I don't like him and never will. Why, why, do you allow a man of such grasping ambition to gain such a hold over you? He's just another Gaveston, isn't he, who you care for far more than you do me!'

'You're talking nonsense.'

'No, I'm not. I've seen the way you look at him, just as you once looked upon Gaveston. You're thick as two thieves, which is why my safety and that of my ladies was just an afterthought. I tell you; I'll not stand for it. As your child Queen, I had no choice but to suffer humiliation, but now let me make it plain that it's Despenser or me. If you truly care for me dismiss him from your services.'

'Absolutely not! You've no right to tell me what I can or cannot do.'

'I've still the right to expect you to place me first in your affections and if you'll not do so then I tell you now that I'll devote myself to going on pilgrimage and otherwise to the interests of our children.'

'Very well, I've no quarrel with that, if it's what you want.'

'So, you put him first then?'

'He's my trusted adviser, nothing more, '

'I don't believe you.'

'Oh, God. Please, don't try my patience any longer.'

'Then don't try mine.'

'Enough! Enough! I'm going!' And with that he brought his fist down on the table in front of us with such force that, as had happened before when he couldn't contain his temper, a goblet of wine spilled its contents in my direction, splashing my dress. Then, without another word, he stood up and walked towards the door. I was naturally distressed, feeling quite tearful. Indeed, in the fourteen years of our marriage I couldn't recall such a terrible argument between us.

Yet, after what had happened so recently, I was still very angry, and felt fully justified in being so. Furthermore, I was absolutely determined not to endure any repeat of what I had previously suffered because of Edward's infatuation with Gaveston. What I could not yet know was that this moment marked the beginning of the end of our marriage.

We remained in York until the turn of the year but relations between us were exceedingly frosty and Edward spent no time whatsoever in my company except on those occasions when we were expected to be seen together in public. Even then, he barely said a word to me personally and barely even offered me a smile. Despenser, too, barely acknowledged my existence until on one occasion, shortly before Christmas, when every man present at an Advent feast had drunk more wine than was good for them, I caught him staring at me.

The look in his eyes was one of undiluted hatred, which for all that this was shocking did not really surprise me. As an act of defiance, I decided to stare back until a lascivious leer spread across his face and he then turned his head towards the man sitting next to him. If I'd harboured any doubt before this that he was my deadliest enemy, this occasion put paid to it. I was convinced that Edward must have also spoken to him about our quarrel and that once he'd done so Despenser had chosen to capitalise on the rift between us to reinforce the hold he already had on him.

That very evening, I was disconcerted when Edward came to my chambers for the first time since our quarrel. I even contemplated seeking to deny him entry and could easily have made some excuse to do so. Instead, I made the mistake of hoping that he was seeking a reconciliation, but the moment he entered I was horrified to see that he was arm in arm with Despenser. Both men were also clearly the worse for drink, as they were giggling, inanely. I shrunk back in a state of total shock.

'…What's he doing here?' I asked Edward, tremulously, having discovered my voice. He looked at me somewhat shame-faced and it was Despenser who answered, slurring his words.

'Your Lord, the King, demands his conjugal rights. I'm here to act as his witness, should you seek to deny them.'

'How dare you!' I screamed, advancing towards him. 'Get out!'

Instead, he stood his ground. 'Only if my liege Lord, the King, wishes it.'

'Edward, tell him to leave before I begin to scream!'

'…Yes, Hugh, I think you'd better.'

With that Despenser bowed to Edward and left the room, though not before giving me a disdainful look of utter contempt. I waited a few moments for his footsteps to die away before turning my wrath on Edward.

'How could you behave in this manner towards me? It is utterly humiliating! I must ask you to also leave me. I can tell you're the worse for too much wine.'

'...I...I...Yes, alright. Forgive me...'

'I imagine what's just happened was all Despenser's idea?'

'Yes, I suppose it was.'

'My God, Edward, he plays you like a puppet on a string, don't you see that?'

His only answer was to shake his head before leaving me in peace. I felt completely furious and made up my mind to leave York on my own, if necessary, once the Christmas festivities had come to an end. The following day I received a curtly written message from Edward, which made no reference at all to what had just occurred, but rather simply asked if it was still my intention to go on pilgrimage and, if so, for how long.

'He wants rid of me!' I exclaimed to my old friend, Isabella de Beaumont, who was with me at the time. 'It's all because of Despenser, of course. That dreadful man.'

I had confided in her what had happened, and she was duly sympathetic. Better than anyone, she understood what I had endured during the early days of my marriage thanks to Edward's infatuation with Gaveston, and because of that how intolerable it was for me to have to suffer in much the same way again at the hands of Despenser.

'What will your answer be?' she asked me after I had shown her Edward's letter.

'Oh, I don't know. I'm so angry with Edward that I'm tempted to say that I'd like to travel as far as the Holy Land, and perhaps never return, but for the sake of my children I won't do that.'

Instead, after a little reflection, I informed him that I was preparing to go on pilgrimage for up to nine months, whereupon he promptly announced this to the entire court, which felt as if I was being sent into exile. Of course, I was the one who had first threatened to go on pilgrimage, but I believed I had been provoked into doing so. Certainly, I saw no justification in his announcing my plans to all and sundry.

I was left feeling intensely uncomfortable throughout the Christmas festivities, being angrier with Edward than ever, whilst the very sight of Despenser offended me. Outwardly calm, I was intent on maintaining my dignity, but every time I saw Edward fawning over Despenser I wanted to scream out that I was being betrayed. For his part, Edward barely said a word to me and avoided any eye contact.

It came as relief when we finally set out for London in January, at which point I told Edward that once we arrived there my firm intention was to stay with our children at Eltham Palace.

'They aren't exclusively yours; you know. I want to spend time with them, too.'

'You're welcome to come with me, then.'

'No, no, that's not possible, but Prince Edward can be brought to the Palace at Westminster. He's old enough now to begin to see something of the world.'

'I agree, but as that's your wish can he not reside with me in the Tower for a few weeks?'

'Yes, alright, so long as he comes frequently to the Palace.'

'Of course, as much as you like. I can then take him back to Eltham...'

'...Do you still intend to go on pilgrimage?'

'Why yes, once I've spent some time with all our children. In two days, I can be in Canterbury. You know St Thomas is one of the saints I most revere. I might even take Edward with me. That is, if you approve?'

'Why yes, that's a good idea.'

For the first time since our dreadful argument, we had managed a civil conversation, for which I gave thanks. Even so, there was still an awful rift between us, underlined by my determination to reside at the Tower rather than the Palace of Westminster.

I had not set eyes on my eldest son for several months and when we were reunited, I immediately recognised a change in him. He was taller, less child-like in appearance and beginning to show signs of being as handsome as his father. I could only pray that he had not inherited the same weaknesses of character. In any event, it was a pleasure to spend time in his company, at the end of which I was satisfied that he was growing into a fine young man.

When I came to reside in the Tower, I was also conscious of the fact that Roger Mortimer was being held prisoner there. The more antagonistic I had become towards Hugh Despenser, the more my sympathy for the Marcher Lords and Mortimer in particular, had grown. Ever since my days as a child Queen, I had thought him the handsomest of men and had happy memories of the occasions when we had danced together. Now, I had only been in residence at the Tower a short while when I happened to catch a glimpse of him taking exercise close to the castle's walls.

I felt a pang of pity for him. He was poorly dressed, heavily bearded and, of course, under guard, but I still recognised him immediately. He then looked in my direction and we seemed to hold each other's gaze for just a few seconds before he moved on. His plight also recalled the fate of his imprisoned wife, which struck me as being an even worse injustice, given that she had committed no crime and certainly posed no possible threat to Edward's rule. Only a few days later, the deputy governor of the Tower approached me with a letter in his hand.

'Your Majesty, I have been asked to give you this.'

I took it from him and upon breaking its seal realised that it was from none other than Mortimer himself. The letter begged me to intercede on behalf of his wife, whom, so the letter claimed, was being held prisoner in poor conditions without the benefit of even adequate food or clothing because even the sum allocated towards her expenses had not been paid. Remembering my thoughts when we had seen each other, I promptly decided to accede to his request, though I was conscious of the fact that the amount of influence I had over Edward had waned considerably since our terrible quarrel.

It then occurred to me that if Despenser's wife, Eleanor, who was, after all, still my principal lady-in-waiting, was willing to add her name to a petition to Edward to ensure Mortimer's wife received what was due to her, it might enjoy more chance of success. We had also grown more intimate since my estrangement from Edward, sharing with each other our frustration and even anger at our husbands' behaviour.

I had told her of my awful quarrel with Edward and admitted to her that I was very uncomfortable about his relationship with her husband. I had half-expected her to come to his defence, but instead she had confessed that despite the many children she had borne him their marriage had never been a happy one.

'He has his way with me when the mood takes him, but there has never been any real love between us. He can be cruel and overbearing, I'm afraid.'

Now, when I asked her if she would support my plea, she readily agreed to do so, but added a suggestion that I was happy to agree with.

'Rather than trouble the King, why not simply petition the royal treasurer. After all, this is a matter within his control. He must have the power to ensure that the payment is made.'

Within a week or so of sending our petition we received a favourable response from the treasurer. This assured us that the failure to make the necessary payments had been an oversight that would now be corrected without further delay. I had already taken the step of informing Mortimer of the action we had taken on his wife's behalf, and now I was pleased to let him know that our efforts had been successful. A day later I received his profound thanks.

I was tempted to let him know that I only wished I could have done more for both his wife and him, but the thought that Despenser might well have his spies in the Tower observing everything I did, inclined me to caution. In any event, with March approaching, heralded by less wintry weather, I was ready to accompany my son back to Eltham, and from there to journey on towards Canterbury.

# Chapter 21

# My world in ruins

It was an absolute joy to be reunited with all my children at Eltham and by the time I had visited St Thomas's shrine in Canterbury in the company of my eldest son and then returned to Eltham once more, spring had arrived, bringing with it mild and mainly dry weather. I was thus able to pass a good deal of the time enjoying my children's company out of doors until, with May approaching, I learnt that Edward was about to pay us all a visit.

I feared that he might be insensitive enough to bring Despenser with him but to my great relief he spared me that tribulation. Arriving on a beautiful spring day in early May, he also went out of his way to behave in a solicitous manner towards me before asking if I might be willing to agree to a reconciliation.

'I miss your presence at court,' he added.

'Do you really?'

'Why yes, of course.'

'Yet, you informed the world that I would be absent from court for nine months, and that was barely five months ago. Are you tiring of your favourite?'

'No, but he can hardly perform the role that you do as Queen. There are occasions when I need you by my side.'

My heart sank. 'So, that's all I am to you; a useful figurehead for special occasions?'

'Of course not. You're being unfair.'

'Am I? I wish to God you were tiring of Despenser. He will still be the ruin of you, believe me.'

'No, he will not. Even as we speak he's on his way north to begin negotiations with the Scots, which should bring about a lasting truce. Assuming that can be achieved then my intention is to hold a celebratory feast in York with you at my side…if you'll come?'

'To celebrate that, why yes, I'll do so… But not otherwise.'

'Look, Parliament will also be sitting at York at the end of the month by which time we should know the outcome of the negotiations. If you wait here for news, it may well be too late for you to attend. I beg you, come north with me in anticipation of the negotiations succeeding. I'm not seeking to impose any onerous conditions on the Scots so I see no reason why Hugh should fail to secure a truce.'

'Very well, I'll come with you, but I'd like to be back here by the end of the next month so that I can enjoy the remainder of the summer with our children.'

'I'm perfectly happy for you to do so. I may also join you here again so we can be a family once more.'

That night, for the first time in months, we even shared a bed. He made no real effort to make love to me, though, and I was quick to wish him a goodnight before turning my back. I thought he might be upset but he said nothing, no doubt appreciating that I was still upset with him, and I was soon asleep.

Over the course of the next few days and weeks, as we travelled north to York together, the former equilibrium of our marriage was restored, at least superficially. Nonetheless, as far as I was concerned the prospect of being joined there by Despenser was ever a dark cloud heading in our direction.

As Edward had anticipated, a truce was indeed announced at the sitting of Parliament, but that, of course, helped place Despenser even higher in his affections. Furthermore, a particularly unpleasant incident cast an awful shadow over what was intended to be a happy occasion.

Isabella de Beaumont's brother-in-law, the Bishop of Durham, had been repeatedly criticised by Edward for failing to fulfil his promise, upon attaining office, of making every effort to stand firm against the Scots. Whatever the justification for this criticism, Isabella's husband, Henry, thought that his brother was being singled out, unfairly, and made the mistake of making his feelings plain in Parliament on an occasion when I was present.

As a consequence, he was ordered to leave the chamber and although he did so, at the same time shouted out the words 'nothing would give me greater pleasure.' This outburst was taken to amount to a contempt of Parliament, for which he was so charged, a step I considered unnecessarily harsh. Worse than this he was then required to swear an oath of loyalty to Despenser and upon refusing to do so was thrown into prison. I was incensed.

'How can this possibly be justified?' I asked Edward, angrily, in the presence of several courtiers including Despenser, which I knew was brave to the point of being reckless. 'I thought you were King but now it seems your favourite here has taken on that role.'

Edward stared at me. 'This is none of your concern.'

'Of course, it's my concern. Henry's an old friend who's

always been one of your most loyal supporters. If this goes on, you'll soon have none left.'

'Desist! I'm not prepared to listen to any more of this.'

'Very well, but I tell you this is a grave injustice to a good, decent man.'

After this confrontation, I sadly concluded that any reconciliation between us was unlikely to occur, so long as Despenser continued in power. At the earliest opportunity I was on my way south again, but not in Edward's company, having decided that I would make a pilgrimage to the shrine of the blessed Mary at Walsingham, in the county of Norfolk.

Consequently, it was early August before I returned to Eltham, having received some momentous news as I passed through London. Roger Mortimer had managed to escape from his imprisonment and his whereabouts were unknown.

In the light of everything that subsequently occurred, I know that there are those who've suggested that I must have been involved in this escape, or in any event been given some prior knowledge that it was to be attempted. Let me say in all honesty that this was simply not the case. I was certainly amazed that anyone could achieve such a daring feet and at the same time felt a mixture of pleasure and anxiety. The former, because I believed it wrong for Mortimer to have ever been imprisoned in the first place, and the latter because I knew that if he was recaptured, he might well be executed.

Over the years I had also maintained a regular correspondence with my last surviving brother, King Charles, in which I had kept him appraised of events in England and on occasions expressed my opinion on what I thought of certain people. He therefore knew how much I had come to despise Despenser as well as the fact that I disapproved of the imprisonment of fine men like Mortimer, who had dared to oppose the hold he had over Edward.

Now, I decided to inform him of Mortimer's daring escape and added, purely as a matter of conjecture rather than any actual knowledge, that I thought it possible he might be heading for France.

...In that event, dear brother, should he solicit your aid, I would hope that you will not be slow to offer it, as I believe he's an honourable man who's been wronged by the actions of Despenser. As I've previously made plain to you, that man has brought me nothing but unhappiness and is an upstart tyrant...

As it transpired, when I received a reply from my brother a few weeks later, it told me that my conjecture had proved to be prescient and that he had been pleased to receive Mortimer with all due honour at his court when he arrived in Paris. I was greatly relieved to learn that he was safe, laughing gleefully at the thought of how much his successful escape would have infuriated Despenser.

In the meantime, I continued to enjoy the company of my children at Eltham, though all the while being conscious of the fact that Edward was likely to pay us a visit sooner or later. As summer turned to autumn without him appearing, I dared to hope he had forgotten us all but eventually in mid-October he finally arrived.

At first, he was tolerably courteous in a rather distant fashion, seldom making any eye contact with me and keeping his own counsel. At the same time, though, I gave him due credit for being relaxed and warm hearted in the presence of our children, which naturally endeared him to them. Then one evening, under the influence of too much wine, he began to heap abuse on Mortimer as well as certain persons he suspected of abetting his escape. I sat stony-faced.

'You're pleased he escaped; I expect?' he asked me in an accusing tone of voice.

I held his eye. 'I think he was ill-treated by your favourite, certainly, so yes, I am quite pleased.'

'I could regard such a view as treasonous.'

'Oh, really? You asked me a direct question and I gave you an honest answer.' I was determined to stand my ground.

'Hm…Well, I still expect you to do your duty as my Queen and not hide yourself away here at Eltham.'

'That I accept… I'm quite prepared to return to court whenever you wish.'

'Good. There's no need to do so immediately, but I'll want you by my side during the Christmas period and probably into the new year as well.'

So by December, we were on our way north again, spending a few days in Lichfield, before celebrating Christmas at Kenilworth Castle in Warwickshire, which had once belonged to my uncle, Lancaster.

Of course, Despenser joined us there, which made me exceedingly uncomfortable, I was becoming tired of this and increasingly irritated. I understood it was my duty to be by Edward's side, but I felt a renewed sense of humiliation by the attention he gave to his favourite, who barely even acknowledged my existence, which I thought rude and disrespectful. To compound this, with the turn of the year, we were invited to stay at his castle at Hanley, where, for the few days we remained there. I felt utterly ignored.

Nothing gave me greater pleasure than when we departed on a journey to the southwest without Despenser, before then returning to London. I was left to reflect on the fact that at the age of twenty-eight, I had now been married for almost sixteen tempestuous years, which had brought me little happiness beyond the birth of my beloved children. I longed for real intimacy, a loving, caring, true partnership; my marriage was just a sham.

What was also beginning to trouble me were increasing tensions with France over the future of Gascony. Some six months previously, as was his right, my brother, Charles, had summoned Edward to pay homage for it. This, I'm sure, had made Despenser nervous about the possibility of a rebellion in the King's absence, so diplomatic efforts had secured a year's postponement. Unfortunately, a dispute had then arisen over a fortified town that the French had built, which encroached on Gascon territory, causing the Gascons to attack the place.

By the time I returned to Eltham in February, Charles had made it plain to me in a letter that the situation had become so serious that he was prepared to contemplate an invasion of the province unless he received redress for what he considered to be unwarranted behaviour on the part of the Gascons. He also added, with some justification, I'm sure, that he was sceptical of Edward ever paying him the homage for Gascony to which he was entitled.

To my dismay, within a month or so the money which was my due as Queen was suddenly reduced without explanation. I was nonplussed by this so decided to seek a personal explanation from Edward by visiting him at Westminster. When I arrived there, the reception I received proved to be so upsetting that I began to fear that our marriage was now on a downwards spiral. I was fearful about my future, as well as suspicious of whatever poison Despenser had been pouring into my husband's ears.

Edward went out of his way to avoid me, so I was finally forced to confront Despenser; a meeting that left me feeling deeply displeased as he was thoroughly unpleasant. When I put to him my complaint as politely as I could he gave me a look of total contempt.

'Be grateful you've not been arraigned for high treason,' he declared, coldly.

'What on earth do you mean?'

'We know you favour that traitor, Mortimer, and that you correspond regularly with the French King...'

'But he's my brother. I'm perfectly entitled to write to him whenever I choose. Are you telling me my letters to him are being opened by one of your spies?'

He sniffed. 'I didn't say that, but I fully expect their content is disloyal to his Majesty the King.'

'Imagine what you like, but I tell you I've never been disloyal to my Lord, the King.'

'You cannot deny that you favour Mortimer, though?'

'I merely believe that he and his wife have been harshly treated. I have said as much to Edward. Making an enemy of a man of his stature was very unwise.'

'But he took up arms against the King.'

'No, he took up arms against you and with good cause, it seems to me. But you've still not answered my question. Why have payments that are due to me been reduced?'

'Because you favour Mortimer, and also because of your connection to the French crown, which is now prepared to attack Gascony.'

'So, has this reduction been made with Edward's full knowledge?'

'Of course.'

'I don't believe you. Edward cannot possibly doubt my loyalty. I think this is all your doing.'

'Certainly not, I am merely his Majesty's loyal servant.'

'Then I insist on seeing my Lord, the King.'

'I've told you, he's not available.'

'Then kindly inform him of my considerable displeasure at the way in which he is treating me as his loyal Queen. It's a vile calumny to suggest that I have ever been anything less than that.'

'Very well, I shall convey your words to him, but I doubt it will change anything.'

# CHAPTER 22

# HUMILIATION

Despenser's tone was dismissive as well as utterly disrespectful of my royal blood and status as Queen. I maintained my dignity but inwardly I was seething. By the time I returned to Eltham my overwhelming emotion was one of bitterness at the way I was now being treated. All I could do, I decided, was to devote myself even more to the welfare of my children.

A few weeks later I received a letter from Edward, which was nothing more than a perfunctory demand that I write to my brother to plead with him not to carry out his threat to invade Gascony. The letter also required me to remind him that the whole purpose of our marriage had been to prevent any war between England and France. I knew I could not refuse Edward, but I still felt that I was being put in the invidious position of having to effectively say that without peace my marriage served no purpose. Perhaps I felt so uncomfortable because I knew there was more than a grain of truth in that thought.

In any event, at first my letter appeared to have achieved its desired effect, for in his reply Charles assured me that so long as Edward was still prepared to pay homage by July, he would not invade.

While I continued to live quietly at Eltham, I then learnt that the Earl of Pembroke, a man of honour and integrity, had been sent to Paris to mediate with Charles, but news soon reached me that unfortunately he'd been taken fatally ill within a short while of arriving there.

I feared that, with his demise, Despenser's power over Edward would become even greater, and saw his hand at work when a very foolish attempt was made to postpone, yet again, the requirement for Edward to give homage for Gascony. Not surprisingly, Charles lost his patience and ordered an invasion. A truce was eventually agreed, but the ill-advised foray had led to most of the province being held by the French crown.

Sadly, the consequences for me of this conflict could not have been worse. It began with a demand from Despenser that I swear an oath of loyalty to him.

'The nerve of the man! How dare he require me to do any such thing,' I declared angrily. 'Have I not, as Queen, already sworn an oath of loyalty to the King. I owe this upstart absolutely nothing. He deserves only my contempt!'

I then sent him a very curt reply, merely stating that I had no intention of complying with his demand as he had no authority over me as Queen. I knew that this would result in greater friction and probably further dire consequences, but I could not withhold my disdain. In response, I wasn't deprived of my liberty, but all my property was sequestered by the Crown. Even worse, the allowance I received from the King was reduced from eleven thousand marks to a mere thousand marks a year.

I was utterly appalled, so once again sought an audience with Edward, only to be rebutted by Despenser in another draining confrontation.

'You have brought this on yourself by failing to swear your loyalty to me. Agree to do so now and the King might be willing to treat you more generously.'

'I will never do that.' I couldn't believe his sheer effrontery.

'Then you will remain under suspicion of being untrustworthy.'

'On what possible grounds?'

'That your first loyalty is to your brother and to France.'

I stamped my foot, unable to hold back my anger. 'That's false and you know it. You have poisoned the King's mind with your foul aspersions, I know you have. You wicked man!'

'Take care. You've been very foolish to make an enemy of me. The King trusts my good judgement and be assured he'll continue to do so.'

With that I turned my back on him and walked away, barely able to contain my fury at the way I was being treated. I feared that I was on dangerous ground, but I was not prepared to cede anything further to that villain. As soon as I returned to Eltham, I sent a letter to Edward pleading with him to restore what was rightfully mine.

...My Lord, King, I have ever been loyal to you and any suggestion to the contrary is totally false.

It is thus totally unjust to deprive me of my property as well as much of my income. Nor is there any truth in the suggestion that because France has invaded Gascony I can no longer be trusted.

Please, if nothing else, grant me an audience so that I might look you in the eye and reaffirm the oath I made you at our coronation. I remain your ever loyal consort.

Sadly, this letter was ignored. Indeed, I even wondered if Edward ever read it. Shortly thereafter my circumstances deteriorated still further when Parliament ordered that all subjects of the King of France in my service be banished. This was another hammer blow as several of my French servants had been with me ever since I'd arrived in England.

Worst of all, within a few more days my three younger children were removed from my custody. Had he not already been given his own household no doubt my eldest son would have been taken from me as well.

The spurious grounds for this cruel act were that I might encourage them to treason against their father.

I was totally devastated, thinking my world in ruins. Yet still Despenser strove to grind me down, when Eleanor, his wife, told me that she was now required to be my constant attendant and as part of that role to examine all my letters.

'I'm sorry, your Majesty, but I have no choice but to obey my husband,' Eleanor said to me.

'So, you are now my gaoler?' I asked, bitterly.

Eleanor looked embarrassed. '...This is none of my doing.'

'Your husband's actions against me are intolerable. It leaves me with no choice but to ask my brother to intervene on my behalf. Please, I beg you, allow me to do this?'

Eleanor shook her head, regretfully. 'No, your Majesty, that's not possible.'

Her response exasperated me beyond measure, so I decided I would have to send a letter to my brother anyway without Eleanor's knowledge. Some of my loyal French servants were still preparing to return home, making it easy enough for me to surreptitiously ask one of them to carry a letter on their person as far as my brother's court. There was then the task of writing the letter in the first place without Eleanor's knowledge, but fortunately she was not constantly by my side for every hour of the day, so I was able to accomplish this without much difficulty.

Unfortunately, though my letter was received by Charles, the letter he wrote in turn to Edward complaining about his behaviour towards me, was completely ignored. What's more, Edward cut my allowance still further, whilst apprehending the French members of my household who had not already returned to France, and then confining them to various religious houses around the country. Initially I felt a huge sense of loss and despair, but I drew on my reserves of inner strength to rally again.

I decided to make one more plea to him to behave in a more reasonable manner. In a letter I begged him to restore to me what I believed to be rightfully mine as Queen under the terms of our marriage settlement as well as to allow me to provide a surety for the future good conduct of my imprisoned servants. Even as I wrote I was dubious that it would persuade him to change his mind and rightly so, for the only response I received was notification that he was seeking an annulment of our marriage from the Pope.

'This is the final humiliation,' I exclaimed. 'He has no grounds whatsoever for taking such a vindictive step against me. In the name of all that's holy, haven't I given him four healthy children including two sons! Does he seriously wish to make them illegitimate?'

# PART 3

# A WOMAN SCORNED

# CHAPTER 23

# ESCAPE!

Edward's only possible ground for seeking an annulment against me was that we were distant cousins, my paternal great-grandmother, Beatrice of Savoy, also having been his great-aunt. However, as I understood it, all necessary dispensations had been granted by the church prior to our marriage. It therefore came as no surprise to me that the Pope declined to grant an annulment. Nonetheless, the very fact that Edward had been prepared to countenance such an extreme step was enough to satisfy me that our marriage of almost seventeen years was now all but finished.

To be cast out like this after the loyal support I had given Edward over all these years made me not just sad but angry, too. I was after all still beautiful and not yet thirty, so I refused to accept that my life was all but over. Yet, that could very easily have been the case, had the Pope not put a suggestion to Edward, which he found too tempting to refuse. To me it was simply a godsend.

It was in early January that I first learnt, through a letter from my brother, that what was being proposed was that I should be allowed to travel to France with the objective of seeking to negotiate a lasting peace, which would resolve the dispute over Gascony. My heart leapt at the prospect of being able to escape my virtual imprisonment, so I decided to write a letter to Edward telling him that I would be pleased to act in this capacity if asked to do so.

After that, all I could do was wait on events, until later the same month I learnt from Eleanor that both the royal council and Parliament would be considering the Pope's proposal. At this juncture I realised that I needed to garner as much support as I could for my mission. I therefore made approaches by letter to those I thought would be sympathetic towards my cause.

Then I received another letter from Charles telling me that he was going to let it be known that if my oldest son travelled with me as Duke of Aquitaine, he could pay homage on Edward's behalf for Gascony, following which all French soldiers would withdraw from the province.

This excellent news persuaded Edward that I should be allowed to travel to France, so preparations for this to take place were underway by mid-February on the basis that once I'd been able to conclude a peace settlement my son would then follow me. I was also given no choice as to who should be included in my retinue, but decided that it would be most unwise to complain as this might cause Edward to change his mind.

In early March, he arrived at Eltham with Despenser at his side to accompany me as far as Dover. I was determined to set aside my differences with both men in order not to jeopardise my departure so went out of my way to be perfectly pleasant to both. Of course, behind my mask of conviviality I still loathed Despenser, but I was less ill-disposed towards Edward for all that he had treated me abysmally in recent years. He was after all still the father of my children and for many years I had been content with our relationship. As I saw it, he had allowed himself to be duped by Despenser, whom, above all, I blamed for the failure of my marriage.

Until the very evening before my departure, I was careful to make absolutely no mention of the several ways in which Edward had offended me and would have kept to that resolution to the very last had Edward not gone out of his way to speak to me alone in my chambers in Dover Castle. He began with a justification of his actions.

'I know that you think I have treated you harshly of late, but I have done so upon good advice to protect the realm during a time of war. Once peace has been successfully attained, I assure you that I will be willing to restore what I have taken away.'

'My Lord King, I hope you can accept that I have only ever striven to be your loyal consort?'

'I understand that that is your contention and I have no wish to argue with you about that at all. I merely wish to stress that assuming your mission is successful, I would like you to resume your full role as Queen.'

'So, will our three younger children be returned to me?'

'Yes, I see no reason why not.'

'And my estates and income, will they be restored?'

'Certainly.'

'And I trust I will no longer be spied upon, and my letters read?'

'No, that too can end.'

'But you'll keep Despenser as your favourite and also your lover, I assume?'

Edward stiffened. 'He will remain my trusted adviser, nothing more.'

There was no point in his making a direct denial, I knew

what I knew. His evasion and unwillingness to engage with my assertion regarding the nature of his relationship with Despenser spoke for itself.

'Then if all those things you are promising come to pass, I hope I'll be able to find it in my heart to forgive you so that our relationship can be restored to its former amity.'

Edward offered me a gentle smile. 'I hope so, too. And now I wish you a good night's rest.'

Long after he'd left me, I pondered our conversation, wondering at the likelihood of his ever fulfilling his promises. I was entitled to have grave doubts that he would ever do so if he remained under Despenser's pernicious influence. Nonetheless, I hoped that he had meant what he said and that this could lead to a reconciliation between us. It was also in this spirit that I bade him farewell the following day before setting sail for France. It was the ninth day of March in the year of our Lord, thirteen hundred and twenty-five, so we had now been man and wife for a full seventeen years.

—⁓—

It was a joy to me to return to the land of my birth. It was also a delight to once more be treated with the dignity and respect, which was my due, as well as to feel that for a time at least I had escaped from the malevolent control of Despenser. Within a few days of landing, I also had the pleasure of being reunited with my brother, King Charles, who in his looks and bearing reminded me so much of our late father.

We embraced each other warmly, following which I was quick to thank him for the support he'd endeavoured to give me during the tribulations I'd endured at the hands of Edward and Despenser. Then I went further.

'You know how much I've been ill-treated and humiliated. Since my children were so shamefully taken away from me, life has barely been worth living.'

'Dear sister, be assured that I'll always continue to offer you whatever support I can.'

'Thank you, brother, that's a great comfort to me.' With that, overcome by emotion, I went down on my knees before him, whereupon he helped me back onto my feet and I began to recover my composure.

Whatever my sense of relief at once more being on French soil, I remained conscious that I had come there to fulfil a specific purpose and remained determined to focus on that. At first, though, it proved harder to achieve than I had imagined because of my brother's desire to retain control of some of the territory which his soldiers had occupied. It took the help of the papal legates who had come to support my mission before I was able to achieve a breakthrough, enabling a draft treaty to be agreed upon by the end of the month.

I was then able to make a state entry into Paris on horseback as befitted my status as Queen of England, accompanied by my entourage along with many French nobles. The early spring weather was kind to us and I felt a real sense of achievement. Meanwhile, the actual peace treaty still needed to be drawn up and signed, a process that took several weeks, during which time I was able to enjoy my brother's company, as well as restore my spirits after the way I had been treated in England.

Understandably, I was also in no great hurry to leave, although I had not forgotten Edward's promises to me. The trouble was that he had also made it clear that nothing would induce him to give up his favourite. This made me fear that once I returned to England these promises could all too easily be reneged upon. Furthermore, it had been a particular delight to me to be reunited with some of my loyal servants who had been forced to leave England and I certainly did not want to have to give them up a second time.

Edward had also readily agreed to my remaining in France until all the necessary formalities had been concluded and he had provided me with sufficient funds. However, these formalities were concluded by the end of May whereupon I received more than one letter from him requesting that I return home.

Still, I hesitated to do so, and consequently, by the middle of June, all my income was abruptly cut off. To remain in France, I was therefore forced to turn to my brother who fortunately did not disappoint me, although in an endeavour to reduce my expenses I took up residence in much reduced circumstances in a royal castle outside Paris.

I then learnt from Edward that he intended to travel in person to France to pay homage for Gascony, giving me a perfect excuse to wait on his arrival, which was expected to be in August. I had my doubts that he would in fact ever appear as I understood full well how nervous Despenser would be about the mischief his enemies could get up to in Edward's absence. I was not therefore surprised that in the event he changed his mind, albeit the night before he was due to embark to France from Dover.

Instead, he once more proposed that my oldest son should pay homage on his behalf, yet again providing me with an excuse to remain in France, with payment of my expenses being resumed. I was also content to ask my brother to re-affirm his consent to such a process, which he willingly did in early September.

Some ten days later I was at Boulogne to greet my son as he set foot on French soil for the first time, having two days previously been created Duke of Aquitaine by his father. He was accompanied, too, by my old friend, Henry de Beaumont, and it was a huge delight to be reunited with them both.

I then took great pleasure in accompanying my son to Paris, where he was introduced to my brother for the first time. It was an entirely happy occasion and two days later at Vincennes, in a brief ceremony, my son duly paid him homage for Gascony.

Now I was faced with a dilemma; should I return to England or not? On the one hand, my task completed and remembering, too, the promises Edward had made me, I really had no justification for lingering more than a few more days in France. On the other, I simply didn't trust Edward any longer, and having tasted freedom and respect for the last six months, the last thing I wanted was to once more place myself at the mercy of Despenser, a man I had come to despise.

As it happened, my brother Charles gave me some excuse for putting off any decision, at least for a short while, when he announced that he was not in fact prepared to give up some disputed territory in Gascony. When I reported this to Edward, I received an understandably angry response along with a request that I attempt to persuade my brother to change his mind. I'm not ashamed to admit that my loyalties were with my brother, based upon my personal feelings as well as family loyalties.

At the same time, I decided to seek advice from those I felt I could trust on what I should do for the best, turning first to my beloved cousin, Robert of Artois as well as Henry de Beaumont and Sir John Maltravers, an exile from England, who was tall, heavily bearded, and had once been a close ally of my uncle, Lancaster. All three of them were of much the same opinion.

'Your Majesty,' Sir John said to me, 'before you return to England insist to your Lord, the King, that he dismisses Despenser from court.

'But he will never agree to that.'

'Perhaps not, but in that event, he cannot expect you to return to England. Do not forget, either, that you are not without power in this situation.'

'What do you mean by that?' I hadn't thought of my own strengths.

'Why, you have your son and heir to the throne, in your custody. If Edward will not dismiss Despenser then keep your son by your side here in France.'

I smiled at him. 'Dear Sir John, that is wise counsel, I must say.'

It was advice that was also endorsed by Henry de Beaumont as well as no less than the Earl of Richmond, who had been serving in France as Edward's principal envoy for about a year. During my conversations with such men, I came to appreciate that we had one great thing in common and that was a shared loathing of Despenser.

It wasn't long before I received a letter from Edward, commanding me to return home with our son, to which I felt obliged to respond. I did not yet feel myself ready for outright confrontation so merely stated that the two of us were being treated very well at the French court, and that I hoped I might still be of some service to the cause of peace, given the ongoing dispute over part of Gascony. Not surprisingly, this didn't satisfy Edward who instructed his envoy, Bishop Stratford, to raise the issue with my brother.

To his credit, Charles was not prepared to have any discussions behind my back and summoned me to be present at the royal palace in Paris when he spoke to the bishop. I decided that I had no choice but to make it clear just how unhappy I still was at the way Edward and his favourite had treated me whilst I was in England.

'My Lord, the King, acting under the influence of Hugh Despenser, has behaved appallingly towards me in the past, dispossessing me of my lands, depriving me of income as well as the services of servants who had been loyal to me for many years, and above all even taking my children away from me. The justification for all this was also never more than a flimsy excuse. Just before I left England it's true that my Lord, the King offered me certain assurances that all would be put right, but I have to say to you, bishop, that I do not believe him.'

'But the King is a man of his word.'

I shook my head. 'Sadly, he's demonstrated all too often that he's not. There is only one thing that would induce me to return to England...'

'What is that?'

'Hugh Despenser must be banished for ever. His power over the King is entirely malign as he does everything in furtherance of his own interests rather than what is in the best interests of the Kingdom.'

'Your Majesty, with all respect, it is not for you to dictate the terms upon which you will return to England. Your conjugal duty is to obey what the King commands.'

At this remark I began to grow angry. 'Do not speak to me of duty, bishop. For seventeen years, despite many humiliations, I strove to be nothing but a loyal wife to the King and yet I was still treated shamefully. I will not place myself under the power of Despenser ever again. After all, he is not my husband, and let us face up to the sad fact, that he is influencing Edward's every move. Either he is banished, or I must remain here in France.'

I could have added that I would also keep my son by my side as well, but for the time being at least was prepared to resist making such a threat. I did not, after all, want to anger Edward too much out of concern that he would once again cease to pay my expenses, though within a matter of weeks that happened anyway.

At that juncture I made the dramatic decision to wear the black robes of widowhood and sent Edward a letter making it clear that Despenser had come between us and that until he was banished would continue to do so. I also added that I would keep our son by my side. Predictably, this angered Edward, whereupon I went further by warning him that there would be direr consequences if he failed to act against Despenser. I felt deep distress, it had never been my intention to go against Edward, but he had left me with no choice.

My warning to him was not an altogether idle threat as I knew from my conversations with men like Sir John Maltravers that their ambition was to return to England with an army capable of overthrowing Despenser's rule over Edward. Furthermore, my brother remained fully supportive of my position and continued to make it clear to Edward that I was welcome to stay in France for as long as I wished. I felt bolstered by his strong support.

Whether he would go so far as to commit resources to an invasion was an open question that I had not yet discussed with him. However, I was reasonably confident that he would be willing to do so, and this was certainly the implication behind the threat contained within my letter.

The response I received came not from Edward but from the bishops. It proclaimed that Despenser had declared himself innocent of ever having acted against me, before going on to appeal to me to return to Edward's side. It also expressed the fear that a French invasion would lead to great suffering.

Of course, I did not want to bring suffering on anyone other than Despenser and knew his declaration to be a lie. I was not prepared to be moved by this appeal. I was, though, beginning to run short of money, so once again my brother had to come to my aid.

Then, in early December, I received another letter from Edward himself, commanding me to come home, which when I read it simply made me more determined to do nothing of the kind.

'How can he possibly assert the utter falsehood that his favourite has always acted in an honourable way towards me!' I declared to my ladies-in-waiting. 'Nor is it fair to suggest that I am the cause of increased tensions between England and France. He is so intent on pleasing that man, to the detriment of myself, his children, and even his beloved kingdom. I fear that the King is a lost man.'

I said this with anger as well as a deep well of sadness in my heart for all the efforts I had made to be his loyal wife and a good queen, which had now crumbled away.

Shortly afterwards I learnt from my brother that he, too,

had received a personal letter from Edward appealing to him to compel me to return to England, taking our son with me. The messenger who brought me this news also told me that my brother wished to discuss its contents with me. We met the following day and Charles promptly showed me what Edward had written.

'But this just contains the same old lies about Despenser behaving in an honourable way towards me. I admit that in the weeks before I left England, I went out of my way to behave in a courteous fashion towards Despenser. Yet, I tell you, this was pure subterfuge on my part, born out of a fear that if I didn't curry favour with him, he would do all his power to prevent me from leaving his grasp.'

'That I can well understand, dear sister, and have no fear; I've no intention of compelling you to return to England. Nor shall I take any steps to send your son there.'

## CHAPTER 24

## A FATEFUL MEETING

It was a cold, miserable day, at the Cathedral of St Denis where we gathered for the funeral of my uncle Charles, Duke of Valois, a kindlier man than my father, of whom I had always been fond. Amongst my fellow mourners was his daughter, my cousin, Jeanne, Countess of Hainault in the Low Countries, which bordered Northern France. I hadn't set eyes on her since childhood, and was struck by how much like her late father she looked.

Amid her retainers, I also instantly recognised none other than Roger Mortimer, looking as handsome as ever. I was aware that following his escape he had chosen to live in Hainault, but it had not occurred to me that he would choose to attend the funeral. I thought that he must now be in his late thirties, his hair greying somewhat at the temples, but otherwise he still appeared quite youthful. His presence naturally excited my curiosity and once the funeral rituals were complete we were invited to the Louvre royal palace in Paris where refreshments were provided. This afforded me an opportunity to speak to both my cousin and Mortimer.

Jeanne in fact was quick to seek me out, curtseying to me as befitted my rank before we embraced each other. Mortimer, meanwhile, was just behind her and bowed his head to me.

'Your Majesty, I'm so pleased to meet you again,' he said,

fixing his eyes upon me; his abundant strength of character a huge contrast to that of my dissembling husband.

I returned his gaze in kind. 'And I'm most delighted to meet you, Sir Roger. You did well, I believe, to escape your captivity in such a daring fashion.'

'With the help of my friends, yes, and now I owe a great deal to the countess and her husband, Count William, for the hospitality they've shown me.'

'Sir Roger would like to raise an army to invade England,' Jeanne added.

'So that I might overthrow that tyrant, Hugh Despenser,' Mortimer emphasised, whereupon I proffered him a warm smile.

'You should know that I'm entirely sympathetic to your cause. He has caused me much misery.' I replied emphatically.

'I was hoping you might say that. You see, I want to suggest that we work together to bring him down.'

I hesitated. 'As you see I am wearing a widow's clothes and I am dependent on my brother's charity, so I have nothing material to offer you.'

'No, but you are still our rightful Queen. It's my belief that men will rally to your cause, knowing how badly you've been treated.'

'It's true, I'm not without my supporters here in Paris. I include the Earls of Richmond and Kent amongst these.'

Mortimer nodded. 'And could you not persuade your brother to provide soldiers to aid our cause?'

'I've considered doing so but don't you agree that an invasion by any army perceived to be largely French could rebound against us. It would surely be claimed, with some justification, that this is just a foreign army intent on overthrowing the Kingdom. Even members of the nobility who are sympathetic to our cause, may still rally behind my Lord, the King, as well as Despenser.'

'Your brother could still provide some financial backing.'

'That's possible, I agree. And you see my son over there...' Having attended the funeral, he was standing across the hall from us engaged in conversation with another young man of a similar age. 'As heir to the throne of England, he's my most valuable asset as I have every intention of keeping him by my side so long as Despenser remains in power.'

'That is very wise of you, I must say.'

At this juncture, Jeanne re-entered the conversation. 'I can also vouch for the fact that my husband, Count William, would not be averse to an invasion of England being launched from Hainault. From what he's said to me he might even be willing to provide soldiers in support.'

'He's also told me that,' Mortimer added. 'Yet, without your active support, your Majesty, I'm still a long way from being able to assemble a force capable of crossing the channel and then overthrowing Despenser.'

'We need to talk more of this. Do you intend to remain in Paris for long?'

'To promote my cause, I will remain for as long as I need to.'

'Then I'm willing to speak to my supporters to establish their views on what you're seeking to achieve. I can do this in a matter of a few days and then we can meet again.'

For a short while, we talked on about some less consequential matters until he again bowed to me before walking away. Throughout our conversation, I was conscious that he hadn't taken his eyes off me and nor, frankly, had I been able to take my eyes off him. Ever since I had first met him as a child bride, I had been physically attracted to him. Now, I realised that this attraction was stronger than ever. There was an instant frisson between us when we were in each other's company. I was certain he felt it too.

As I pondered this, what struck me most of all was that for the first time in my life I had a measure of freedom to love whom I chose, and on my terms. Of course, there would be huge risks involved, which I could never under-estimate, but in the most unusual circumstances in which I found myself, taking a lover was certainly possible so long as we were careful and discreet.

I was also now open to ignoring my own marriage vows before God, because I believed vehemently that Edward had not only betrayed me through his love for his two favourites but also allowed Despenser to treat me shamefully. Further, I had no wish to cause pain to Mortimer's wife by allowing him into my bed, but hoped she could remain in ignorance of his adultery.

Above all, I just knew in my heart that there was a strong likelihood that Mortimer would become my lover. My over-whelming feelings also overrode any sense of guilt and were essentially those of joy, excitement, renewal, in anticipation of a pleasure I had not felt throughout my marriage. I had lived for duty thus far, and had put this above my own happiness, now there was a chance to live differently. I rejoiced in that idea.

After some thought, I decided that it would be beneath my dignity to throw myself at Mortimer's feet like a wanton woman. If he should choose to pay court to me, however, I was prepared to be persuaded, upon the proviso that we behaved with the upmost discretion.

As I had promised Mortimer, I now had a series of meetings with the likes of Richmond and Maltravers to garner their support to an invasion of England for the purpose of over-throwing Despenser.

'And who would lead this invasion?' Maltravers asked me.

'Sir Roger Mortimer is best qualified to do so, I believe. What's more, he has the support of Count William of Hainault, whom I have reason to believe might well provide both ships and men.'

'And do you think the prospect of such an invasion would persuade the King to give up his favourite?'

'It might, but if not, I believe most of the nobility detest Despenser as much as they ever detested Gaveston. Consequently, the King would be unable raise any army against our forces. We would thus be victorious in our endeavour without even having to strike a single blow in anger.'

'And after that would you trust the King to do our bidding?'

'No, I would not.' I said, resolutely.

'Then Despenser would need to be put to death just as Gaveston was.'

'Yes, indeed he would.'

'Well then, for my part I would support an invasion so long as it's undertaken in your name, as our rightful Queen, with the express purpose of unseating Despenser.'

My conversations with Richmond and Kent followed a similar course save that it was apparent to me that Kent was far less enthusiastic about any army being led by Mortimer. He looked glum at the very mention of his name and like Richmond made it clear that he would only lend his support to an invasion undertaken in my name.

I then took the fateful step of sending a message to Mortimer inviting him to dine with me. I was careful to add that it was for the express purpose of discussing our plans for overthrowing the hateful tyrant, Hugh Despenser.'

He arrived alone and I was once again struck by his handsome appearance, which gave me immense pleasure. I had already decided that once we had been served with our food and wine, I would dismiss all my servants from our presence. I had no need to explain this, and of course discussion of affairs of state was not my only, or indeed, my main motive.

In order to look my very best I took care to bathe using expensive oils and perfumes from the south, while I dressed , not in my widow's black, but rather my finest, richly embroidered, silk dress, which was purple, a colour that not only befitted my rank, but I knew suited me very well. I applied more perfume made from lavender to both my neck and arms. After that I selected a simple cross made of pure gold to wear around my neck before turning my attention to my hair, which I did not want to cover as was the normal expectation. For modesty's sake, I chose to contain it within a crespinette, under which it was still perfectly visible. Showing my luxuriant tresses would be, I knew full well, a signal of encouragement to him. I wondered if as a Queen I was behaving too brazenly, but I quickly dismissed that thought.

From the moment Mortimer entered my presence it was obvious to me that he had also taken care with his appearance, and I could feel the overwhelming sexual tension between us, I did my best to ignore it; at least while we enjoyed our meal. I'm sure, though, that he was aware of the smile that played upon my lips throughout our meal and which I couldn't suppress.

'I have good news for you,' I told him. 'I've had conversations with Richmond, Kent and Maltravers, and all have told me that they would support an invasion so long as it was carried out in my name as Queen with the express purpose of removing Despenser from power. They also accept that it would be necessary to put him to death rather than accept any false promises from the King.'

He smiled at me appreciatively. 'That's well done, your Majesty.'

'They'd also accept your de facto leadership of the invasion force though Kent only grudgingly so.'

'That doesn't surprise me. There's never been any love lost between us.'

'And there's an aspect to the situation we find ourselves in that we've not even begun to consider...'

'Oh yes, what might that be?'

'If we invade England together, it's unthinkable to me that anything can go back to the way things were before Despenser came to power. I tell you; Edward was heartbroken when Gaveston was put to death and vowed vengeance upon those he held responsible; principally my late uncle, Lancaster, of course. Once Despenser suffers the same fate he'll be even more distraught and hold both of us accountable. I'll never be able to sit beside him again as Queen and your life will always be in danger so long as he retains any power.'

'I concur with everything you say. To be blunt, it will be necessary, I believe, to make him abdicate in favour of your son, Edward.'

'But what if he refuses to do that?'

'Then regrettably it will be necessary to depose him.'

'Hm, that's the conclusion that I've also reached. I wouldn't want him put to death, though. He's the father of my children and for some years we were tolerably happy together. He's too easily led and can be vengeful, but I don't believe he's an evil person. Despite everything, and for all that I believe our marriage to be beyond repair, I still retain some affection for him.'

'That I can quite understand, but it would still be necessary to hold him in custody. He could then, when the time is right, be sent into exile.'

I now felt that we understood each other better, though there was an implication to what we had just agreed that I did not yet feel ready to discuss. If Edward was to be deposed, then my son was still too young to rule so would need a regent. It was a role that I believed I could fulfil but this is, of course, a man's world, so I could imagine Mortimer coveting it. I might not be averse to him being the power behind the throne, but I could imagine it making him enemies, whilst I would certainly not be pleased if he sought to retain such power for longer than was proper. I also appreciated that the position of regent was likely to be precarious. After all, it meant ceding power eventually to the younger and rightful heir, which might not be easy once the regent had developed a taste for power.

In any event, for the time being at least, such considerations remained purely theoretical. Much remained to be done before any invasion fleet could even be assembled and without it Despenser would simply remain in power.

My mind turned once more to a far more personal matter, namely the intense attraction I felt for Mortimer. Would he or wouldn't he begin to behave flirtatiously toward me, I wondered? Furthermore, if he did, would I respond in kind, or feel compelled to regard that as an almost unforgivable sin, which at all costs must be kept at bay? The war within me was between a strong sense of duty and propriety and an even stronger physical and intellectual desire. I really wasn't sure of how I would respond but sensing a heightened physical tension between us, I began to take more and more sips of wine, which gradually helped me to relax.

'Leave us,' I heard myself say to my servants whereupon they instantly withdrew, bowing to me as they backed away. I then took another long sip of wine, looked straight into Mortimer's eyes, and smiled at him. I believe my desire was writ large. Holding my gaze, he returned this before bringing his right hand to his mouth and clearing his throat. I had always thought him to be the most confident of men but for the first time I could tell he was slightly nervous.

'Your Majesty, what I am about to say may make you extremely angry…'

'Then perhaps it might be best if you don't say it.' I was still smiling at him, and the tone of my voice was gently teasing.

'No, I must say it. I could not live with myself if I remained silent.'

'So…?'

'…For as long as we have known each other, I have thought you the most beautiful of women; spirited, capable, and now deeply wronged. Since… since we met again here in Paris, I've also realised that I feel more than just admiration for you; I feel love… I feel desire.'

'Fie, Sir Roger, this is bold of you, I must say, given that we're both married.'

'I merely speak the truth. I wonder do you have the same feelings for me?'

'...You're most handsome; I've always thought that. And a finer man than my husband could ever be, of that I'm certain. I'll confess, too, that these last few years have left me unloved and lonely.'

'It's been the same for me, I can tell you. I've not set eyes on my wife in three years... But you've not really answered my question...'

'I know I feel a certain passion for you which could easily grow into love. This could in turn be very dangerous if we were to indulge these feelings. We would need to be very discreet and even then, servants aren't blind. I could swear them to silence, I suppose, yet the chances are someone's tongue will still start wagging. And then there are my ladies-in-waiting who were foisted on me by Edward. They looked thoroughly shocked when I told them that I intended to dine alone with you. They understand only too well that adultery is sinful and seen as more so if you are a woman.'

'I can't deny this, but we're all sinners before God. The circumstances we find ourselves in are also surely exceptional. Fair minded people will make allowances, I'm sure.'

The political and strategic nature of our conversation began to turn as he touched, first my arm and then gently caressed my cheek.

'You know I cannot afford to find myself with child. Unless it is fathered by the King, tolerance might be stretched beyond all limits. Even as Queen, I might find myself ostracised. The common people might also cease to hold me in high regard, damaging our cause against Despenser.'

Roger shrugged. 'It might still be possible to keep it a secret.'

'I very much doubt that, though I suppose we could try.'

'Well, only you can decide if you're willing to take the risk. His voice fell to a whisper, and I could feel his breath against my skin. You know I will never force myself on you.' A smile played upon his lips.

I smiled back at him. 'I know that but if you wish you may kiss me.'

He took me into his arms, gently at first but then with full force. I responded with equal vigour.

—ᴍ—

I led him to my bed chamber, and we began to undress each other, slowly exploring each other. I looked at his beautifully formed body with joy and hunger. I had never experienced this level of excitement with Edward. Every part of my own body was filled with desire and passion. He had ignited something new in me and I didn't want it to end. His touch was magical, I was fully alive with him.

Before the night was done, we had discovered ecstasy in each other's arms; it was as though we were both intoxicated. Never, had I experienced such carnal lust before and I told Roger, as he now was to me, that I loved him deeply. In the morning, when I awoke, I also felt a satisfying sense of fulfilment rather than guilt. I wanted to savour the memory of such a night of pleasure, the like of which I hadn't known was possible. In truth this did not feel wrong. I believed that I had discovered how love was meant to be, having been kept in the dark for so long.

Sometime later, I sought absolution for my sinful behaviour from my confessor, but having done so knew I would gladly sin again. I had been given a new sense of freedom, which I was determined to enjoy while I could.

# CHAPTER 25

# PLAYING GUINEVERE AND LANCELOT

Of course, my servants were the first to know that I had taken Roger to my bed, so I told them in no uncertain terms that I expected them to remain loyal to me by saying nothing about what they had seen and made each of them swear to this. Even so, I still had my ladies-in-waiting to contend with and unfortunately one of them saw Mortimer leaving our residence. After that, I soon found myself confronted by my chief lady-in-waiting, Alice, the Dowager Countess of Warwick.

Some twenty years my senior, we got on tolerably well, but there was little warmth in her personality, and I thought her very dull company. Now, she took it upon herself to warn me against continuing to enjoy any intimate relationship with Roger.

'Your Majesty, with the greatest of respect, I believe your behaviour to be utterly, utterly...' At this point she stopped, struggling for the right word or words.

'Yes, utterly what?' I asked her.

'...Utterly scandalous and sinful.'

'No more so than my husband who indulges in sodomy with other men,' I retorted, feeling in no mood to be lectured to. 'He and his favourite have treated me appallingly.'

'I accept that you've been placed in a difficult position.'

'I'd say I've been put in an impossible position; deprived of my estates, deprived of my children, deprived of all self-respect after years of being a loyal wife to the King. Well, now I seek no more than a small measure of personal happiness. Of course, I know it's sinful, but I put my trust in the Lord's forgiveness as he'll certainly know how much more I've been sinned against. Beyond the walls of this household, I also intend to continue to behave with the upmost discretion so I trust I can rely upon you not to ferment any scandal?'

'Indeed, you can, your Majesty.'

I accepted this assurance, though only with a full measure of caution as I thought her more than capable of sending a letter to Despenser reporting on what she'd discovered. 'Let her do her worst,' I thought, having also decided, defiantly, that I had lived too long in the King's shadow.

As a token of this, I promptly took the initiative of suggesting to Roger that I seek to arrange an early meeting between the two of us and my brother, to which Countess Jeanne could also be invited before her imminent return to Hainault. He greeted this suggestion with enthusiasm and fortunately my brother was happy to consent to it taking place.

Two days later we all gathered at the royal hunting lodge at Vincennes on what was to prove a fateful occasion, setting in motion a momentous series of events. Naturally, it was my brother who spoke first.

'We are here today to discuss what is to be done to overthrow the tyrannous rule of Hugh Despenser in England so that my dear sister may once again enjoy all that is rightfully hers. I know, too, Sir Roger, that you have been grievously wronged by Despenser's conduct, leading to your exile in Hainault. Also, you are not the only man to have suffered at his hands. The question, I believe, is whether anything less than an invasion of England will bring about Despenser's downfall? What say you to that, dear sister?'

'...I say that King Edward makes promises to me and may well continue to do so concerning everything that is rightfully mine, but what he'll never do is voluntarily dismiss Despenser from his court and send him into permanent exile. Furthermore, so long as Despenser remains at court, he will, I have no doubt, do everything in his power to deprive me of my estates and even the right to be with my children. There'll be no end to his tyranny and the injustice that has led to. The conclusion, I draw from all of this is that only an invasion will achieve our aims.'

'...And I agree with everything her Majesty has said,' Roger added.

'But will an invasion succeed?' my brother, asked, looking Roger in the eye.

'Your Majesty, I have the upmost confidence that any invasion launched in the name of your sister as Queen of England will enjoy overwhelming support. She is greatly loved by the people, whilst Despenser's tyranny is despised.'

'So, you're suggesting you might be able to achieve your objective without force of arms?'

'Indeed, I am. Of course, I cannot be certain of that, but I will add this, Despenser is no soldier and nor is King Edward. Even if we had to give battle against them, we would win.'

'So, are you asking me to support this proposed invasion with French soldiers?'

'Certainly not. Your sister and I are fully agreed that this would be totally counter-productive. King Edward and

Despenser would assert that England is threatened by nothing less than a French invasion. This would be likely to shore up their support to such an extent that our enterprise could even end in failure.'

'But you'll need soldiers from somewhere, won't you, unless you're certain that men will simply flock to my sister's cause once you've landed?'

'As I believe the Countess here, will confirm, her good husband is willing to support our cause by providing some soldiers.'

'And what of ships?'

'Again, we look to the Count to provide these, but we do ask for some financial support from your Majesty's coffers.'

My brother chuckled. 'Ah, I thought you might. I've already given that some consideration and am pleased to tell you that I'm willing to provide such support. So, when do you think you might be ready to mount your invasion?'

'I would hope, by this coming February,' Roger replied.

'My, that's no time at all.'

'The sooner we put an end to Despenser's rule the better.'

'I agree, but the sea can be a dangerous place in winter. I suggest you should wait until the spring.'

By the time the meeting closed there had been talk of a formal alliance between Hainault and France, making me more confident than ever that the hoped for invasion would take place. In the following weeks a fleet of ships began to be assembled, though what preoccupied me more than anything else was my love affair with Roger. The need to be discreet still kept us apart far more than I would have wished for. I found myself longing for the next occasion when we would be together.

Gradually, in the knowledge that our relationship was by now widely known about anyway, we became less cautious. I was also increasingly determined that we should be able to spend longer in each other's company.

'I have an idea as to how we can be totally alone together,' I told him.

'Oh, yes?' He was already smiling at me in anticipation of what I was about to say next.

'There's a small hunting lodge in the royal forest, not all that far from here, which I've known since childhood. I realise it's wintertime but to the best of my knowledge it's always kept well furnished with comfortable beds. There should also be plenty of wood for its fire as well as wine in its cellar. If we wanted to spend a night there, we'd just need to have a little food with us.'

He beamed at me. 'That's a wonderful idea.'

It was not, though, somewhere we could expect to visit in total secrecy. To begin with, it was kept locked when not in use, and whilst I was entitled to have it unlocked for my personal use, this obviously entailed my having to ask for it to be opened. Similarly, I couldn't avoid asking for preparations to be made for our visit, including the lighting of a fire as well as the provision of food.

I was confident, though, that I could rely on the loyalty of my most trusted servants and so it proved. Nevertheless, the existence of a 'love nest' was too much for those amongst my retainers who had been imposed upon me, amongst them the Countess of Warwick, who soon returned to England.

'Good riddance to them,' I told Roger as we enjoyed the privacy afforded us by the hunting lodge. We were seated together, drinking wine, in front of a well-banked fire, which was giving off a pleasant amount of heat,

He gave me an anxious look. 'As soon as they return to England, they'll tell the King about our relationship.'

'So, they will. I just know life will be easier without their prying eyes and ears.'

We had in front of us a beautifully illustrated manuscript of Chretien de Troyes story, Lancelot, the Knight of the Cart, which I had brought with us as we had discovered a mutual love for the stories of King Arthur and his knights. Amongst these none had more appeal to me at this time than this story by de Troyes, given that it describes the adulterous love affair between Queen Guinevere and Lancelot. Of course, it wasn't lost on either of us that their story had significant parallels with our own.

'Shall you be my Lancelot and I your Guinevere?' I suggested to Roger, teasingly.

He bowed his head. 'I would be proud to accept his role and rescue you forever from Despenser, just as Lancelot rescued Guinevere from the evil Maleagant.'

'And so enjoyed his lady's favours ever after.'

'Should you be gracious enough to bestow them upon me, I can think of no greater honour.'

Yet for all this talk of noble deeds and courtly love, there were times when I awoke in the middle of the night in a cold sweat, thinking myself mad to have, some might say, rashly begun an adulterous affair with a married man. It wasn't too long, either, before another letter arrived from Edward. It made no reference to Roger but admonished me for not returning to England, bringing our son with me.

I decided to defend my position by making it clearer than

ever how much I believed myself to have been wronged by Despenser. I ended my letter by suggesting that only he stood between us, when this was no longer really the case. Seized by feelings of guilt, I simply couldn't bring myself to admit in writing that I had now fallen totally in love with Roger.

In any event, I expected that events would soon move on apace with the planned invasion. But then, no doubt encouraged by Edward, the Pope now intervened by appointing two papal nuncios to mediate between us. At the same time, fearful of renewed warfare between France and England, he also persuaded both my brother and the Count of Hainault to put any invasion plans on hold pending the outcome of this mediation.

By the middle of March, I was coming under immense pressure from the papal nuncios to seek a reconciliation with Edward. They went out of their way to emphasise that I risked hellfire if I continued to repudiate him. I had always striven to be a devout Christian who was willing to confess all my sins, but since the previous December, I had increasingly refrained from doing so. Now, the dilemma I faced, provoked my first argument with Roger.

I told him that the nuncios had persuaded me to say that I would agree to return to Edward so long as Despenser withdrew from court and my status as Queen was once again fully respected. This would mean that my estates would be restored to me and I would once again have custody of my three younger children. In response he glared at me.

'So, our declarations of love for one another mean nothing to you!'

'No, no, of course that is not what I mean, but what am I

to say to the nuncios when they threaten me with hellfire if I fail to abide by my marriage vows?'

'Tell them that Edward and his favourite are sodomites who've robbed you of all dignity.'

'That's precisely what I have told them, but they insist that this doesn't absolve me from my vows. Don't you see that I am being placed in an impossible situation?'

'Just don't listen to them. We've freely vowed undying love to one another as a man and woman, whereas you were no more than a child when you married Edward. Go back to him now and I'll… I'll kill you.'

I was stunned. 'Roger…, for God's sake, I know you don't really mean that. Edward will never agree to exile Despenser so the nuncios' efforts are bound to end in failure, as I swear to you, I would never return to Edward unconditionally.'

'You should never contemplate returning to him under any circumstances, if you truly love me.'

'Alright, alright, I'll never go back to him, but I can't tell the nuncios that; not when they're threatening me with hellfire and damnation. Surely, you can understand that?'

He grunted. 'I suppose so.'

'And please don't ever threaten me again if you wish to retain my love?'

He held up a hand. 'I'm sorry, the thought of you ever returning to Edward makes my blood boil with anger.'

'Well, I'm not going to, whatever I might feel obliged to say to the contrary in order to placate the papal nuncios.'

# CHAPTER 26

# PLANS

Of course, I was right to think that Edward would never exile Despenser, but now he did his best to undermine my position by writing directly to both my son and brother, denouncing my relationship with Roger. At the same time, he begged my son to return to him, while asking my brother to facilitate this.

Fortunately, my brother was deaf to Edward's overtures and there was no question, either, of my allowing my son to return to England. Nonetheless, it was evident to me how unhappy Edward's letter had made him, so I tried to be reassuring. It was all too easy for me to regard him as no more than a child, yet at thirteen he was already older than I had been when I married his father. Further, he was quite old enough to know his own mind and to express forthright opinions.

'My son, you know how grievously I have been treated at the hands of Hugh Despenser. I have therefore told your father that he must send him into exile before there can be any question of our returning to his side, yet he refuses to do so. There is thus an impasse between us.'

'And, I take it, you intend to resolve this by invading England?'

'Yes, with the purpose of overthrowing Hugh Despenser's tyranny, to which your father is sadly blind.'

'Whilst, in the meantime, must I be made to live in the company of Mortimer, whom I thoroughly dislike? My father regards him as nothing better than a traitor.'

'Sir Roger is no traitor. Like many others he has suffered at Despenser's hands. He wishes only to see that evil man brought down. Otherwise, be assured that he has your best interests at heart.'

'I doubt that. I think he covets my father's throne. That's why he's so close to you.'

'No, no, that's not true.'

'I think it is!'

I was shocked by his expression of such a strongly negative opinion. My son was growing up faster than I had realised and he was becoming very much his own man. He had formed his own perceptions of my relationship with Roger, and they were clearly unfavourable. This conversation both frightened and upset me, I felt that I was losing my child.

And with that he turned his back on me and walked away, refusing to halt even when I called out to him. I found his dislike of Roger troubling, as I had decided that they should spend time together in the expectation that Roger would be a mentor to him and that they would become friends. Instead, no doubt missing his father, who I knew he loved, he merely resented Roger's presence. Whatever I might aver to the contrary, it was also plain to me that he believed Roger to be an unworthy interloper, who was to blame, at least in part, for destroying my marriage to his father.

Nevertheless, though it might be wishful thinking, I hoped that with time he would come to respect Roger for his strength of character, which sadly his father so often lacked.

Edward then took the punitive step of confiscating all of Pembroke's lands, though if he thought this would act as a deterrent to our plans, he was much mistaken. On the contrary, it served to make Pembroke even more determined to bring down Despenser.

Meanwhile, with the coming of spring, I continued to standby my conditions for returning to Edward's side, which I had set out in my letter to him that had aroused Roger's anger. There was no response from Edward, however, so as a last resort, the papal nuncios decided to send a request to Edward that they be granted a personal meeting with him. At first, too, it appeared that this was being ignored, so my attention turned to the forthcoming crowning of my brother's third wife, Jeanne of Evreux, our cousin.

With all due ceremony, this took place in the magnificent Saint Chapelle in Paris, at which I was delighted to be present with my son as guests of honour. With my beauty still untarnished by the marks of time, I took care to wear my finest jewels along with an exquisite blue-silk dress that had been made especially for the occasion. Roger, too, was in attendance, whilst the coronation was followed by a sumptuous feast. Inevitably, I couldn't help but contrast this with the disastrously poor one, which had been prepared for my own coronation.

For me, this was a happy occasion that I now look back upon nostalgically. Yet, I know it was far less so for either my son or Mortimer. The former was at that awkward stage in life, no longer a child but not yet a man, so looked uncomfortably self-conscious. The latter, despite my assurances, had continued to be decidedly grumpy, particularly as only the day before, Edward had finally agreed to a meeting with the papal nuncios.

'Nothing will come of it, I promise you,' I had said to him.

'But what if Edward surprises you by agreeing to exile Despenser?'

'He won't. I know him too well.'

'You'd better be right,' he'd snapped at me.

I wished that he trusted in my prediction of what would happen. Looking back, I can see that he was afraid of losing me as his lover. We had become as one; our union one of soul mates.

In the event, my prediction was well founded. The papal nuncios returned to France having achieved nothing. By the middle of June plans for an invasion of England were yet again well advanced, whereupon Edward tried again to persuade our son to forsake me and return home.

The letter, which described my relationship with Mortimer as being notorious and attacked him as a traitor and mortal enemy, caused my son renewed heartache, so that he was practically in tears when he showed it to me. Remembering his most recent outburst against Mortimer, I did my best to be gentle and understanding, appreciating that the letter had placed him in such a difficult position.

'I realise this isn't easy for you, but I swear to you that Sir Roger is no traitor. The villain of the piece is and always has been Hugh Despenser. Our sole purpose is to bring him down and free your father from his evil influence.'

'So, would you have me ignore this letter?'

'Yes, I think it best that you do so. Before long, our invasion fleet will be ready to set sail for England.'

'I still do not like Mortimer. You're too trusting of him.'

'You've made that plain before now, but I believe his

intentions are entirely honourable.'

'Very well, but we must return to England soon.'

'We will, my son, we will, and when that happens, I'm more confident than ever that we will enjoy overwhelming support. I can tell you that I, too, have received a letter. It comes from several Barons who assure me that out of loathing for Despenser they will rally to our cause.'

Unfortunately, I had not reckoned on the Pope now turning against me. Within a short while I received a request from my brother for a meeting. As soon as I entered his presence, I could tell that all was not well. He looked decidedly glum.

'See here this letter I've now received from the Holy Father. He chastises me for harbouring adulterers and threatens me with excommunication if I continue to do so.' He then waved the letter in my face. 'Well, what do you say to this?' he demanded.

I took a deep breath. 'Brother, I cannot deny that the King's behaviour towards me has forced me into the arms of a better man. I know that I have sinned, and I pray to God every day for forgiveness. With your support I will, though, soon be able to return to England. A few more weeks is all I believe we require to be ready.'

Charles shook his head. 'No, I can't support you any longer. As if being threatened by the Holy Father isn't bad enough, Edward has now declared war, which means further conflict over Gascony. I simply can't afford a war on two fronts. I can only advise you to immediately cease your relationship with Mortimer and abandon these notions of invading England. If you don't do so I'll have no choice but to command that you to leave my Kingdom.'

'Brother, I beg you to reconsider.'

'No, my mind's made up. I'll give you a week to think about your position. No longer.'

Later, when I told Roger what had happened, he suggested my brother was simply frightened of the Pope.

'What's more, unless you want to return to Edward's side, how can you possibly agree to what your brother's demanding? I suggest you call his bluff. With luck, he'll change his mind.'

Instead, at the end of the week he sent me a message confirming his threat and adding that if I didn't leave immediately, I would be made to do so.

At first, I was utterly downcast, but Roger did his best to reassure me.

'All is not yet lost, I tell you. Our plan has always been to invade England from Hainault and that can still happen. In the meantime, we've spoken before of your raising funds for the invasion in your dower lands in Ponthieu, so I suggest you proceed to do so.'

'And would you come with me?'

He shook his head. 'If the invasion is to go ahead, I need to be in Hainault as soon as possible. I will also be welcome there, of course.'

'As I should be, surely?'

'I agree, but nonetheless I think it would be wise for you to visit your dower lands first.'

'Alright, but what most concerns me is that without my brother's support, we will never be able to invade.'

'After the pledges of support you've received in England, I believe we can still succeed without his help.'

I was less confident, but I knew that I had to trust Roger,

believing him to be a man of great ability and determination. Within a day or two we were ready to depart, but not before I had received a visit from a cousin, Robert of Artois, who told me he came on behalf of my brother.

'In strictest confidence the King has sent me to assure you that he still wishes you well. He has acted in the way that he has to appease the Holy Father and for no other reason. In the circumstances, he cannot be seen to be helping you, but believes that you can count on the aid that Count William of Hainault is able to offer you, which should be sufficient for your purposes.'

'Tell my brother that I am grateful for this reassurance, and that it's my intention to travel forthwith to my dower lands in Ponthieu. Whilst there, I intend to raise funds to aid my cause. Then I will travel on to Hainault.'

The visit from my cousin helped to lift my spirits as my party, which included both my son and the Earl of Kent, set off on our journey to my dower lands, while Roger headed for Hainault. We had grown so close that I found it painful to be apart from him, so hastened to confine my visit to a matter of just a few days. Then I followed him north, arriving in Hainault by early August

# CHAPTER 27

# THE DIE IS CAST

Count William and Countess Jeanne showed us great hospitality during my stay with them at Valenciennes, even covering my expenses out of their own pockets. Best of all, they were also willing to lease one hundred and forty ships to our cause, upon my pledging to reimburse them for any losses out of the revenues from my dower lands in Ponthieu. It was not long since I had been utterly downcast by my brother's rejection of me, but now I dared to hope that our invasion plans were, after all, about to come to fruition.

I was also aware that the Count and Countess had four healthy daughters and my eyes lit up when I was introduced to them, for they were all pretty girls, especially the second oldest, Philippa, who was much the same age as my son. To secure the alliance, I had made with the Count and Countess, it made perfect sense to me to ask for the hand of one of their daughters in marriage to my son.

With every passing day in the company of these girls, it was also apparent to me that Philippa and my son were attracted to one another, so I quickly decided that she was the daughter to whom I would like him to be betrothed. To take such a step without consulting Edward was, of course, something that I knew would greatly displease him, but I was past caring about that. I wanted my son to marry for love, I wanted him to be so much happier than I had been.

When the time came for us to leave Valenciennes to take up residence in Mons, my son embraced all the Count and Countess's daughters and when Philippa's turn came, she suddenly burst into tears.

'What on earth is the matter?' Countess Jeanne asked her.

'I'm sorry. My fair cousin of England is about to leave me, I have grown so used to him!'

We all smiled, or indeed in some cases laughed at this outburst, whilst I was more convinced than ever that my judgement was well-founded. On our way to Mons I therefore asked my son if he would be happy to be betrothed in marriage to one of the Count and Countess's daughters.'

'That would depend on which one it was?'

'You may choose,' I responded with a teasing grin.

'Really?'

'Why, of course.'

'Then, please God, let it be Philippa.'

'An excellent choice. She's clearly in love with you and I believe would bring you every happiness.'

'I thought Kings weren't meant to marry for love?'

'Perhaps not. Certainly, your father didn't. But then I'm not aware of any divine rule that forbids it.'

At the end of the month, I signed a treaty with Count William providing for the betrothal of my son to Philippa. Vitally, the dowry that came with this was the provision of soldiers, ships, and money to support an invasion. Meanwhile, in early September, I also concluded an agreement with my subjects in Ponthieu under which they would provide me with financial assistance. Roger and I were also busily engaged in garnering support amongst the local nobility, with many prominent knights joining our cause, including Sir John of Hainault, who took command of seven hundred men.

Even more crucially, Roger had been anxious for some time that once our invasion took place, the Scots might seize the opportunity of doing the same. We had therefore made overtures to the Scottish ambassador at my brother's court, which now led to a secret agreement being concluded, whereby in return for the Scots taking no such action, we would upon seizing power recognise Scotland as an independent nation.

There was now no reason to delay the invasion any longer so on the twenty-first of September I bade farewell to the Count William and Countess Jeanne, while at the same time offering them my profuse thanks for their support. Our party then rode to the port of Dordrecht, where the following day, helped by favourable winds, our armada of ships set sail for the coast of England.

It was an impressive sight with so many banners unfurled, helping to give me confidence that our invasion would be successful. Roger, for one, certainly had no doubts.

'Be assured that once we land on English soil the nobility will flock to our cause,' he told me.

'I pray to God that they will, for I know we come in the name of justice.'

We did not speak of what exactly we would do once we had succeeded in ousting Despenser, but to me it was now abundantly obvious that Edward would have to be forced to abdicate in favour of our oldest son. Being mindful of his accusation that Roger was intent on seeking power for himself, I could envisage dangerous waters ahead, but for the time being it was easy enough to ignore these in favour of devoting all my energies to the immediate task in hand.

We soon sailed into a storm that initially, I feared might undo all our ambitions. Fortunately, after altering course, we were able to sail on, and after two long nights at sea, during which I slept poorly, the English coast came into view.

Continuing to wear my black widow's dress as a powerful symbol of my distress, I was soon brought ashore in a small boat. I had not set foot in the realm of which I was Queen for more than eighteen months and did so with a certain trepidation, knowing what was at stake. However, I held my head high before making a solemn declaration.

'Let it please God, I return to this land to undo the injustices that have been done to me and to so many others under the tyranny of Hugh Despenser and those who support him. May God bestow his blessings upon our cause for we know it to be righteous.'

This was met by cheers as well as cries of 'God bless your Majesty' from those gathered around me, which included my old friend Henry de Beaumont along with the Earls of Kent and Richmond.

We had landed on the coast of Essex near Walton, where we found shelter for the night. I knew how important it was to secure the maximum amount of support with the minimum of delay so didn't hesitate to send a letter to the Mayor of London and also letters to the mayors of other important cities. In these I repeated the declaration I had made upon coming ashore, whilst adding, too, that I came to avenge the murder of my uncle Lancaster. Since his execution he had come to be seen as a martyr by many men whose support I now counted upon, not least his younger brother, the Earl of Leicester. I understood full well that it was essential to capitalise on this.

Before we ventured inland, I watched the fleet of ships that had brought us to England sail away. It was a sight that brought home to me the enormity of what we had undertaken and that there could be no turning back. Once again, I resolved to hold my head high and be resolute, whatever lay ahead of us.

We marched first to Bury St Edmunds, finding it necessary to live off the land. I was mindful that this could easily have provoked animosity amongst the common people, so was insistent that they were paid a fair price for all the goods that we took from them.

'We must keep the people on our side,' I said to Roger. 'It is both politic and just that we do so.'

'I don't disagree, though it will surely be expensive.'

'I tell you; every coin will be well spent if it helps us achieve our objective.'

As we moved on in the direction of Cambridge, I was delighted by the good wishes that were offered to us. Better still, once we arrived there, several Bishops joined us, led by the Bishop of Hereford who donated a substantial sum to our cause and encouraged his fellow bishops to be similarly generous.

This encouraged us to advance next upon Oxford, where we thought we might meet some resistance. Instead, when we arrived there in early October, the Burgesses of the city came out to greet us. It was apparent that they saw us as saviours rather than invaders and I was pleased to accept the gift of a silver cup which they presented to me.

Since our arrival in England, I had been determined to keep

my love for Roger as discreet as possible, so we tried not to be seen together too often in public and were assiduous in never sleeping under the same roof, never mind the same bed. This frustrated me at times and Roger even more so.

'Let me visit you under cover of darkness?' he whispered to me when we had a brief opportunity to be out of anyone else's hearing. 'I miss you not being in my arms.'

'I feel the same, I promise you, but we must be patient. We cannot afford to risk provoking any scandal when all is going so well.'

'Alright, I can see the sense of that.'

Our principal aim was to advance on London, by far the most important city in the Kingdom, so long as we could be reasonably confident that we would be welcomed there. When news then reached us that the Earl of Leicester had seized the city of Leicester, along with treasure belonging to Hugh Despenser, and was marching south with a large force of men to rendezvous with us, we decided that we should not delay any longer.

We moved south to Dunstable, only thirty miles from London, from where I sent a second letter to its mayor, this time calling on all its good citizens to rally to our cause in overthrowing Despenser's tyranny. Once joined by Leicester's army, we then advanced on Wallingford, which although further from London possessed a mighty fortress overlooking the Thames, and was thus of great strategic importance. It was surrendered to our forces without any resistance.

The following day I was quick to issue a proclamation condemning Despenser and his supporters. It was given in not just my name, but also that of my son and the Earl of Kent. In this we were careful to emphasise that we were seeking to act in the interests of both the Holy Church and the Kingdom, and that Despenser's tyranny made him the enemy of both as well as the King.

Only a day later news arrived from London that its citizens had risen in our support, seizing the Tower of London, and murdering one of Edward's supporters, the Bishop of Exeter. We had also learnt that Edward and Despenser had retreated westwards, so rather than head for London it was decided that we should pursue them.

'Victory is within our grasp,' Roger declared. 'We mustn't let Despenser escape us.'

The citizens of every town we passed through then greeted us as saviours, and when we reached Gloucester we were joined by forces from the north as well as Marcher barons and some men from Wales. A party also joined us from London bearing a gruesome trophy.

'Your Majesty, the men wish to present you with the head of the late Bishop of Exeter,' I was told.

I took a deep breath. This was the last thing I wanted. Yet, I decided that it would not be politic to appear ungrateful. 'Very well, let them come forward.'

One of three men was carrying a basket with a cloth draped over it. He bowed to me. 'If it please, your Majesty.' He then removed the cloth, exposing the head. I barely glanced at it.

'I thank the Mayor for this bloody act. It's an excellent piece of justice.'

In truth, I felt almost physically sick, but was pleased to be able to disguise this as well as I had.

I was also anxious about the well-being of my younger son,

John, who had been in the Tower of London when it was seized. Accordingly, I dispatched a letter asking that he be sent to me.

—⁊⁊—

Next, we advanced on the city of Bristol, which was held against us by Hugh Despenser's father, though not for long. After a few days its citizens threw open the gates. To my absolute delight, I was then told that my two young daughters, Eleanor, and Joan, had been found. They had been in the elder Despenser's guardianship.

'Bring them to me, quickly,' I cried.

Shortly thereafter, I had tears running down my cheeks as we were finally reunited, and I was able to take them both into my arms. We had been apart far too long and they had both changed in appearance, though they were still my daughters, just more grown up. I was deeply moved that they were filled with joy to be with me once more. For sure, this was one of the happiest days of my life.

The following morning news reached us that Edward had fled the Kingdom. We had invaded in the certain knowledge that many barons would rally to our cause. Yet I had never expected to achieve total victory with such speed, or without the spilling of any blood save that of the Bishop of Exeter.

'We must proclaim your son Keeper of the Realm in the King's absence,' Roger suggested.

'Yes, of course. I shall call a council meeting. By what authority should we say that we're entitled to act?'

'Let it be by the consent of the community of the realm.'

At the same time the council also agreed to put Despenser's father on trial in just the same fashion as my uncle Lancaster following his defeat four years previously. Accordingly, he was not allowed to offer any defence and was sentenced as a traitor to be hung, drawn and quartered.

'Must he be dealt with so cruelly?' I asked. 'He's an old man, after all.'

However, the Earl of Leicester, whom the council had agreed should succeed to his older brother's title as Earl of Lancaster, was not prepared to show any mercy. 'Your Majesty, I must remind you of your undertaking to destroy all the King's favourites.'

The execution was carried out as ordered, the very same day. It was a foretaste of the fate that awaited Hugh Despenser. It then became clear that Edward's attempt to flee the realm had failed due to a storm having driven his ship back to land and that he and his favourite were presently in Wales. Meanwhile, upon hearing that a state of near anarchy prevailed in London, I sent John of Hainault there, along with a small body of knights, with instructions to take control of the Tower and to act as my son, John's, protector.

At the end of the month, remaining determined to bring Despenser to justice, we advanced on Hereford where we were joyfully received by its citizens. I then took up residence there with my son and within a few days received overtures from Edward for a negotiated peace.

'There can be no negotiations with traitors,' Roger insisted. 'It's clear that the King has no support and he and Despenser must be captured.'

'I agree. I'll send an armed force into Wales with that express purpose.'

Less than two weeks later, Hugh Despenser along with his close associate, Robert Baldock, were delivered to me as my prisoners, whilst Edward was held under arrest at Monmouth castle. In the meantime, Edward's one remaining supporter of any substance, the Earl of Arundel, had also been arrested. He was a particular enemy of Roger's, and it was upon his orders that the Earl was summarily executed. This troubled me and I told Roger so. I was beginning to worry about Roger's zeal in acting against his enemies, usually without consulting me.

'I know you hated the man for seizing some of your estates and I disliked him, too, but you still exceeded your authority by having him executed without trial. We cannot be seen to replace one tyranny with another.'

'He deserved his fate.'

'That's not the point, which you surely realise.'

'Very well, you have my word it won't happen again.'

'I hope not, for both our sakes.'

It was my wish to put Despenser on trial in London, but he refused either food or water to cheat justice, becoming so weak that it was feared he would not survive the journey. We were left with no choice but to try him in Hereford. At the same time, having proclaimed my oldest son, keeper of the realm, I appreciated that it was essential to persuade Edward to surrender the Great Seal of England, so assigned to the Bishop of Hereford the task of achieving this by dispatching him to Monmouth.

A few days later Despenser was brought to trial in my presence, a pale shadow of his former self, being weak with hunger. Still, I could feel no pity for him, and, of course, there could be no question of allowing him to defend himself. His indictment was merely read out, citing his many crimes against me and many others, including my uncle, Lancaster, as well as Roger.

Naturally, he was then convicted of all of these before being sentenced to be hung, drawn and quartered.

I did not welcome having to watch him being put to death in the market square but felt that it was my duty to be present. This was the necessary climax of all that I had set out to accomplish when I had decided upon an invasion. At first, he also showed great courage, but then let out a dreadful howl of pain and anguish, the memory of which will remain with me to my dying day.

After his death, by way of celebration, we ate a great feast for which I had no appetite, as I reflected on the cruel, if necessary, spectacle, we had just witnessed. After I had drunk two goblets of wine, I also felt the onset of a headache, giving me an excuse to retire to my bed where thanks to the image of Despenser's agony praying on my mind, I did not sleep well.

Two days later the Bishop of Hereford returned from Monmouth with the Great Seal in his possession. This completed, in the space of only two months, the success of everything we had set out to achieve. When I recalled how I had first arrived in England as a mere twelve-year-old girl, as well as the many humiliations I had endured since, I reflected that this was a truly astonishing achievement.

# CHAPTER 28

# A NEW KING

Given that my oldest son, Edward, was still a fourteen-year-old youth, I was now the de facto ruler of England. However, let me be frank that as my lover and confidante, Roger enjoyed considerable power. Furthermore, we were left with a serious dilemma, namely what was to be done with Edward's father, still the realm's anointed King?

For the time being, it was merely decided to move him to Kenilworth castle, a more luxurious place of confinement, whilst on one point at least there was no disagreement between me and those whose counsel I had come to rely upon.

'On no account can he be allowed to resume any position of power,' Roger declared to me. 'He has shown himself unfit to rule and that will never change.'

'I entirely agree, but if we merely keep him in confinement, so long as he lives he will continue to be our King.'

'Then we must depose him.'

'Perhaps so, but I suggest this must be a matter for debate both in council and by Parliament. My first priority at this time is to be reunited with my youngest son, John, so we must travel to London without further delay.'

We enjoyed another tumultuous welcome when we reached the city in early December, but nothing gave me greater happiness than embracing John and seeing how well he looked.

Having then issued a proclamation condemning all lawlessness in the city as well as reinforcing the Tower's garrison, I decided to spend Christmas at Wallingford castle. At last, I had all my children with me, which was enough to make me feel a glow of real happiness.

When I held court in the castle's great hall, the nobility and prelates of the realm came to pay me their obeisance, amongst them the Archbishop of Canterbury, who had long been a supporter of Edward. It was my fervent desire to be magnanimous in victory, so when he made his plea to be placed under my protection, I willingly granted this. Then I called a meeting of the Council with the express purpose of considering what should be done with Edward.

This was an important occasion for me. Thanks to my status as Queen I had become used to being a lone, powerful woman amongst many powerful men. Never before, however, had I possessed the ultimate power as de facto ruler so I was determined to assert my authority.

'The most important matter for our consideration today is what is to be done with the King in circumstances where he has demonstrated that he is unfit to rule. I ask for your opinions.'

Lancaster was the first to respond. 'I say his behaviour has been so heinous that he should be executed.'

'No, no, there's no precedent for taking such action against a King,' Kent responded. 'How can he possibly be accused of treason against himself?

'I agree that an anointed King cannot be accused of treason,' John of Hainault added. 'It would be better to merely depose him. He would then have to be kept in a place of secure confinement for the remainder of his days.'

'That accords with my view,' I then said. 'I also suggest that he should be encouraged to abdicate in favour of our oldest son, Edward. Having already given up the Great Seal, I'm confident that he'll agree to take this step as well. But let me make it clear that there can be no question of any reconciliation between myself and the King, his behaviour towards me has been too awful in so many ways. He even came to want me dead. It's unthinkable that I should be expected to share his captivity.'

I knew that this declaration was bound to be disturbing to the prelates who were present, but no one dared to contradict me. I then moved on to one other important matter.

'I'm determined that we should seek a lasting peace with Scotland. I ask for the Council's agreement that commissioners be appointed to begin negotiations to achieve this objective.'

I was pleased that no one spoke out against this proposal and, when I closed the meeting, I was satisfied that it had been as successful as I could possibly have hoped for.

In early January a large crowd of cheering people greeted me as I entered Westminster with Prince Edward by my side. It was also a pleasant surprise to then discover that there was as much as sixty thousand pounds in the royal treasury; a sizeable fortune. Parliament was also due to meet but, of course, it was unprecedented for it to do so in the absence of an anointed King.

'He should be invited to attend,' was the advice I received from more than one prelate, so I decided to send a deputation to Kenilworth. However, this soon reported to me that Edward was completely unwilling to do any such thing. This pleased me as I really felt uncomfortable at the prospect of having to spend any time in Edward's presence ever again. Nevertheless,

I thought it politic to be seen to have done everything possible to persuade him to change his mind, so I sent a second deputation. In the meantime, Parliament dealt with some matters of little importance. After a few more days I learnt that Edward remained intransigent in his refusal to appear.

'He's cursed us all as traitors, but then that was predictable. What matters is that he's been given every chance to appear. Of course, there's no precedent for this, but we simply must proceed without him,' Roger declared to a meeting of the Council to which I had invited several nobles who would not usually have expected to attend.

'Does anyone dissent from that view?' I asked. I looked around and saw no one who wished to do so. 'So be it. Is it also agreed that the King must be deposed?'

Roger immediately spoke up. 'I say that we have no choice. I hear from the Lord Mayor of London that the city is supportive and invites lords, bishops, and commons to attend at the Guildhall to swear an oath to uphold the Queen's cause to the death, rid the realm of the King's favourites, and maintain the liberties of the city.'

It was duly agreed that Edward be deposed, and the same day Roger led a procession to the Guildhall to swear the oath that had been requested. Parliament then reassembled in Westminster Hall. Still wearing my black dress, I was present to hear Roger propose, on behalf of the nobility, the deposition of the King. He spoke well with all his usual authority, ending his address by making it clear that the nobility alone could not depose the King as this also required the consent of the people.

Fortunately, many Londoners, who were vociferous in calling for his deposition to proceed especially after the Bishop of

Hereford preached in support of such a step, had been encouraged to be present.

'The King's behaviour has been childish,' he declared. 'Further, were he to be allowed to continue to rule, the Queen's very life would never be safe in his hands.'

'Away with the King,' the people shouted.

The Bishop of Winchester preached next, also calling for Edward to be deposed whereupon the people cried, 'Let it be done! Let it be done!'

It was left to the Archbishop of Canterbury to declare that the voice of the people is the voice of God, so Edward's reign had to come to an end. 'By the consent of the lords, the clergy and the people, Edward the Second is hereby deposed in favour of his son, Prince Edward.'

His words were met by a roar of approval. It was time to bring my son into the hall to cries of 'Ave Rex!' The lords then knelt to pay him homage, which was all too much for my emotions, which had been increasingly overwhelmed by such a momentous occasion. I broke down in tears.

I shocked myself by being so lachrymose, hastening to restore my normally dignified demeanour as quickly as I could, though, of course, such a public display did not go unnoticed, especially by my son.

'Dearest mother, I'm so sorry that you're so distressed,' he hastened to tell me once we had returned to the palace.

'It was silly of me. I really am quite cross with myself for showing such poor self-control, but what we have been through together has been very emotional.'

'Of course, it has. I must also tell you that I will not accept the crown unless father is prepared to voluntarily renounce the throne in my favour. As his son I cannot otherwise bring myself to dispossess him of what is rightfully his.'

I was stunned by these words. 'Come now, what if he refuses to do so? He's already been obdurate in his refusal to attend Parliament.'

'That will be unfortunate, I accept, but I would rather see him continue as King, at least in name, than take the crown from him without his consent. As his son, I feel I owe him that, if nothing else.'

I sensed that my son still felt a great deal of love and concern for his father, and that he had a strong belief in the sanctity of kingship. Still, I tried to persuade him that it was right for him to accept the role of King now.

'It'll be more than unfortunate; it could ruin everything. Why not just accept that your father has been deposed so you do not require his consent?'

'No, it's a matter of personal honour between me and father. He must give me his consent.'

Roger was furious when I first informed him of my son's position and tried to persuade him to change his mind but to no avail.

'We'll just have to send another delegation to Edward informing him of the people's will and putting it to him that he's no choice but to abdicate in his son's favour,' I suggested.

Two days later such a party, led by the Bishop of Hereford, set out for Kenilworth, leaving me to wait anxiously for news of whether their mission had proved successful. A week later they returned, and I was able to receive the bishop into my presence within minutes of his dismounting from his horse.

'Your Majesty, I am pleased to inform you that the King

has abdicated the throne in favour of your son. The nation's homage to him has therefore been formally renounced and the steward of the royal household has broken his staff of office. What's more, we have the crown and royal regalia with us.'

'You have done very well, Bishop, but tell me, was it difficult to persuade Edward to give up the throne? I have been fearful that he might stubbornly refuse.'

'Your Majesty, I warned him that if he did not do so in your son's favour, the people might choose someone not of royal blood to succeed him. At this he broke down in tears, saying that for the sake of his son he was prepared to do so. He then fainted, but was revived. After that he confessed that he was being punished for his sins and expressed sadness for having incurred the hatred of his people, as well as gladness that they had chosen his son to succeed him. He asked us, too, to show him compassion, and he was assured that he would henceforth be known as Lord Edward, sometime King of England.'

It was a relief to me that there was now nothing to prevent my son from becoming King. At the same time, I felt a certain sadness for Edward's fall from grace. As the father of my children, I had no hatred for him and did not think him evil but rather weak, sometimes spiteful, and, above all else, far too easily led astray by the likes of Piers Gaveston and Hugh Despenser.

The following morning, as I rode through the streets of the city with the heralds announcing Edward's abdication and the new King's peace, the people gathered in great numbers to celebrate. It was almost nineteen years since I had first come to England as its Queen, and I was l amazed at the extraordinary series of events that had led to this day.

# CHAPTER 29

# TRIBULATIONS

On a bright but cold day at the beginning of February my son was crowned, by the Grace of God, King Edward the Third, in Westminster Abbey. It was a splendid occasion in which he behaved impeccably despite his youth, having only passed his fourteenth birthday in the previous November. Once more, I found myself becoming overwhelmed emotionally, but managed to hold back any tears to retain a proper measure of composure.

I was now the Queen mother, intent on ensuring that everything I had lost because of Despenser's malign influence was restored to me. With the treasury in such a healthy state I was also determined to fully compensate myself for having to live on charity for so long. There were debts, too, to be repaid, whilst I was resolved to reward those who had offered their support to my just cause.

At the age of thirty-one, I still looked and felt young. I hoped that my future, along with that of my children was now secure so long as I was careful. I knew that I could not afford to carry on my love affair with Roger in any way that was obvious to public gaze. I was increasingly terrified of becoming pregnant.

In the first heat of lust, I had taken the risk, but now I decided that it was out of the question.

'If it were to happen, it could ruin everything,' I told him bluntly, one evening when we were alone together not long after the coronation.

He grimaced. 'You would just need to withdraw to somewhere out of the public eye for a few months on the grounds of ill health…'

I shook my head vigorously. 'No, no, that wouldn't work. The truth would get out soon enough, even if I bribed a hundred souls to keep their own counsel. And what of the child, assuming it survived? It's identity would need to be concealed indefinitely. Surely, we can still enjoy love making without penetration?' I was still in love with Roger, and grateful to him for all his support. I wanted our relationship to be a complete one, but I was afraid of attracting criticism from many quarters and being seen as no better than the King we had deposed.

He looked at me doubtfully. 'I suppose so. It still won't be quite the same, though.'

'Perhaps not, but I'll not have everything we've striven for placed in jeopardy.'

Aside from this most intimate of matters, our main consideration at this time was the appointment of a regency council and who amongst its members should be my son's official guardian. I was content that this role should be taken by Lancaster, which at first troubled Roger somewhat.

'Will this not then make him the most powerful man in the Kingdom until Edward comes of age?' he asked me.

'In theory, yes, but it's not my intention that he should be so in practice. As Queen Mother, I'm still entitled to keep Edward close to me. What's more, I'll still retain the right, on his behalf, to appoint the Chancellor, Treasurer, and Keeper of the Privy Seal. You could also have a place on the Council if you want it?'

'I have allies aplenty who'll be serving on it; the Bishop of Hereford, for one. They'll be loyal to our interests, I'm sure. Anyway, I dislike protracted meetings. They're thoroughly tedious.'

'In that case, let me make you Justiciar of Wales. It will give you jurisdiction over all the crown lands there. I'll see to it, too, that everything Despenser took from you and your father is restored to you.'

We drank to this before spending our first night for some while in each other's arms. There was a clear understanding between us that we needed to continue to be as discreet as possible, especially while my husband was still alive. Of course, Roger still wanted us to enjoy sexual intercourse, but I remained resolute that any penetration was out of the question, so we pleasured each other instead. Our lust was rekindled by the success we had achieved together.

All the while, I continued to feel a sense of pity for my husband, so decided to ensure that he was able to live as comfortable an existence as possible, making a point of sending him certain luxuries, while at the same time enquiring after his health. In return, I received letters begging to be able to see me and our children, which after some soul-searching I decided to ignore. As far as I was concerned our marriage was utterly dead, so the last thing I wanted to do was give him false hope, even to the extent of allowing him to see our children.

Then, in early March, to my consternation, came news that a plot to free Edward had been uncovered. This would, in due course, lead to indictments against certain individuals. In the meantime, after Lancaster made it clear that he disliked having to be responsible for Edward's security, it was decided, at Roger's suggestion, to move him to Berkeley Castle in Gloucestershire. Lord Berkeley and Sir John Maltravers, both close associates of Roger, were made Edward's joint keepers.

With spring approaching, I was also pleased to be able to go on pilgrimage again to my favourite shrine; that of St Thomas at Canterbury, taking my son, Edward, with me. During my darkest hours under Despenser's tyranny, I had frequently offered prayers to St Thomas, and I saw this pilgrimage as an opportunity to give thanks for the blessings he had seen fit to bestow upon me. I enjoyed spending time in my son's company and was delighted that we got on so well.

'I want to assure you that everything I do in your name is with the best of intentions,' I told him. 'My only wish is that when you come of age you will be able to reign over a Kingdom that is both prosperous and at peace.'

'I appreciate that, mother.'

'With these aims in mind, I must tell you that I remain determined to forge a permanent peace with the Scots in return for their not seeking to take advantage of our invasion last year. I know that isn't welcomed by those who still vow vengeance for our past defeats, but I don't believe victory over the Scots is possible. What's more, fighting any war against them would simply drain our exchequer. When you come of age you may wish to take a different course to mine, but I would counsel you to be wary of doing so. The Scots will never yield without a long and bloody struggle and could well defeat you just as they did your father.'

'Should you achieve your objective, mother, I can assure you

I would be content to observe the terms of any peace treaty.'

'I'm glad to hear that. I hope, too, that you remain happy at the prospect of a marriage to Philippa of Hainault?'

I could see his eyes light up at the very mention of her name. 'Of course, she's a delightful girl. I think about her a lot.'

'Good, good. Your happiness means everything to me. I will shortly be sending an emissary to Count William to formally ask for her hand in marriage.'

As events transpired, within a few weeks of this conversation, in the absence of a peace treaty, the Scots began to muster their forces for an attack on Northumberland. This forced me to accept Roger's advice that we had no choice but to respond in kind.

'We cannot allow the Scots to raid and plunder at will,' he declared firmly.

'I appreciate that.' It was a crushing blow to me, but I knew we could not stand by and allow the Scots to have their way.

'I know you want peace, but I assure you both the nobility and the common people want us to stand up to the Scots. Anything less would weaken your rule.'

By early April Edward was also ensconced at Berkeley castle where I ensured that he continued to be well provided for. Above all else, though I anticipated that he would have to remain in confinement for the remainder of his days, I did not want him to come to any harm.

Of course, I was conscious of the fact that so long as he lived, there would be those, especially within the church, who would expect me to reside with him. I was determined never to do so, but that didn't prevent certain bishops from suggesting it at a meeting of the Council in mid-April.

Relying as I did on the support of the church, I decided that it was politic to say that I was willing to be bound by the council's wishes. However, as soon as the meeting ended for the day without having made any decision, I hurried to inform Roger what had happened.

'If you love me, I beg you to use all your influence to encourage a majority of the Council to vote against my being required to live with Edward.'

'Have no fear on that account, my love. I will speak to the Bishop of Hereford without delay and remind him that the council has already specifically forbidden you to return to Edward on account of his cruelty towards you.'

In the event, the bishop hardly needed to be reminded, speaking forcefully against the proposal that I return to Edward's side. It was then withdrawn, though I remained concerned that the issue would never go away completely. Indeed, the following month a letter arrived from the Pope urging me to achieve a reconciliation. I was disappointed, I had such reverence for the Pope, my conscience was pricked, but not enough to change my heart and mind on the matter.

'Just ignore it,' was Roger's advice, and I duly did so.

The threat of a Scottish invasion also now seemed greater than ever, so I travelled North to York accompanied by my son, Edward. To support our army, I decided as well to invite John of Hainault to return to England, bringing with him as many men as he was able to muster on the basis that they would be well paid for their services. I was delighted when he arrived with five hundred soldiers, but I was then taken aback by what happened next.

Fighting soon broke out between English archers and the

Hainault troops, which resulted in three hundred deaths. After hearing the many detailed accounts of this sorry saga, the archers were accused of having been to blame. Nonetheless, with the benefit of hindsight, although I acted with the best of intentions, I should have realised that fetching so many mercenaries from abroad was likely to cause more trouble than it was worth. This brought home to me more than ever how difficult it is to rule well and that errors of judgement are almost inevitable from time to time. Events, too, can so easily be misread.

Matters then went from bad to worse when attempts to negotiate peace with the Scots again ended in failure and they began raiding once more. This resulted in my consenting to my son going on his first campaign under the watchful eyes of Lancaster, Kent, and Mortimer. Unfortunately, this ended in total failure as the Scots led them a merry dance. Worse, to my absolute horror, at the very beginning of July a messenger arrived from Berkeley castle with dreadful news.

'Your Majesty, I beg to inform you that my Lord Edward, the King's father, is at large.'

At first, I was so stunned that I could barely find the words to speak. 'What!' I finally expostulated. 'In the name of God, how can this be?'

'A band of men managed to break into the castle using trickery and then looted it before carrying off the King.'

'What trickery was this?'

'The castle's been undergoing essential repairs. They entered disguised as simple labourers, with more of them besides, hiding in a cart, who were all armed. Both my Lord Berkeley and Sir John Maltravers were away from the castle at the time.'

'And has anyone any idea where my Lord Edward is now?'

'Not to my knowledge, your Majesty. I bring with me a letter from Lord Berkeley for your kind attention.'

The letter that was then handed to me was full of contrition for what had occurred and offered assurances that everything possible was being done to track down the whereabouts of my Lord Edward.

It was bad enough that he'd been freed. Yet, what caused me the greatest consternation, was the thought that despite his tyrannous rule there still appeared to be a certain number of people who presumably wanted him restored to his throne.

'This is ridiculous,' I complained. 'My son has been consecrated as King after my Lord Edward abdicated in his favour. What do these renegades seek to gain by freeing him?'

For a few weeks I was on tenterhooks, wondering where the former King could possibly be hiding and worse, what he and his supporters might be planning to do?

This was a question to which there was no clear answer, but to my relief Edward was recaptured within a month. Thereafter, the pursuit of those who had set him at liberty continued with a large measure of success. Yet, by early September, to my intense frustration, reports reached me of yet another plot to liberate him, which apparently emanated from Wales, of which Roger was now Justiciar. As such, responsibility for dealing with this latest conspiracy was placed in his hands.

I realised that there would always be the possibility of such plots, while my husband was still alive. Any malcontent could take up his cause in their own interest to justify an attempt on the throne.

Meanwhile, with the ending of the failed campaign against the Scots, Sir John returned to Hainault with his men, but not before presenting a huge account for their services, which it was only possible to meet by raising loans. On a happier note, much to my delight, my son's betrothal to Philippa was confirmed. I was confident, too, that with God's Grace, theirs would be a far happier union than I had ever enjoyed with my Lord Edward.

Then, on the twenty-third of September, whilst staying at Lincoln castle, I received news which really shocked me.

# Chapter 30

## Sad news

I was informed by one of my ladies-in-waiting that a messenger, one of Sir Thomas Gurney's squires, had arrived from Berkeley castle, begging an immediate audience on a matter of great importance.

'By all means. Have him brought to my audience chamber without delay.'

It was clear to me that something ominous was afoot and I felt a growing sense of anxiety until the young man entered my presence and made his obeisance to me.

'Well, what brings you here?' I asked him.

'Gracious Queen, I…' At that moment his voice deserted him, and he looked so tense I wondered if he was about to collapse.'

'Yes, pray continue, please?' I asked him gently.

'I bring sad news. Our former King, the Lord Edward, has died.'

'In God's name, in what circumstances was this?' I expostulated; my voice raw with emotion.

'He developed a terrible sickness. Nothing could be done to save him. He was dead within hours.'

'Have you've seen his body?' I asked.

'…Yes, gracious Queen.'

'He looked down as he spoke these words and though I

stared at him continued to do so. Given his obvious tenseness this didn't really surprise me, though, and with little hesitation I accepted everything he'd just told me as being true.

Overwhelmingly, despite my travails at the hands of my Lord Edward, such momentous news left me with a great sense of sadness. He had never, I believed, been an evil man and he had fathered my four children. Alas, through his own follies, he had tragically lost his throne, and now, sadly, he was dead at the age of forty-three.

At the same time, I was, of course, conscious of the fact that his death relieved me of what was fast becoming a considerable burden. No longer would I have to concern myself with my Lord Edward's security and all that entailed after the attempts to set him free. I must confess before God that for this alone, I gave thanks.

Dismissing the squire from my presence, I was left with the difficult task of having to tell my son the news I had just received. When I did so, he gave me a look of sheer disbelief before his upper lip began to quiver and he shed tears of grief. I immediately embraced him, and he began to sob.

After a short while he calmed down a little but was clearly still distressed. 'Father was always robust and healthy. How do we know that this message isn't a fabrication?'

'What are you suggesting; that your father could have been murdered?'

'I don't know, but it wouldn't surprise me. I just know that I want to be confident that no foul play was responsible for his death.'

'If there has been, I swear to you before God that I've had no knowledge of it.'

'My dearest mother, I wasn't suggesting any such thing.'

'Good. Let me assure you that I will make all due enquiries to fully establish the cause of your father's death. I'll invite Sir Roger Mortimer to carry out a thorough investigation and then report his findings to us...'

My son's face darkened. 'Your lover, you mean. I wouldn't be at all surprised if he isn't responsible for my father's death.'

'Nonsense, he would never stoop so low.'

'Your love for that man blinds you, mother. You do not see him for what he is. I tell you he lusts for power just as much as Hugh Despenser ever did.'

'You malign him terribly. He seeks only to serve you honourably until you come of age.'

At that I broke off our conversation as I found my son's antipathy towards Roger far too painful. Perhaps, he was right that I was blind to Roger's faults, but I simply could not accept that he was anywhere near as avaricious and cruel as Despenser had been. Nor did I want to even contemplate the possibility that he had had my Lord Edward murdered because protecting his security had simply become too burdensome.

In any event, the very same day I prepared and sent a letter to Roger telling him of what I had heard from Sir Thomas. I then asked that he take all necessary steps to investigate the manner of my Lord Edward's death by visiting Berkeley castle and examining his body before reporting his findings to me in person.

The news of Edward's death also saddened me far more than I had ever thought possible. For a few days I was as downcast as my son and could not bring myself to make any public announcement of what had happened until the end of the month. A short while later, when Roger returned to court, I felt thoroughly apprehensive at what he might be about to tell me.

'So, what have you been able to establish?' I asked him as soon as we were alone together.

'I visited the castle as you asked and have conferred with Maltravers. He has given me every assurance that the former King was seized of a fever, which led to his untimely death.'

'And did you inspect my Lord Edward's body?'

'...I saw it, but that was all. You see Sir John has had it fully embalmed, which I think is entirely sensible of him as he realised it might well be some time before any burial can be carried out.'

'I need you to say this to the King. He's been distraught since we learnt of his father's death. What's more, I must tell you, suspicious that foul play was involved.'

'I'll happily reassure him that this was not the case.'

Roger looked me in the eye as we conversed while giving every impression of being his usual forthright, confident self. As such I saw no reason to disbelieve him. Indeed, I felt a considerable sense of reassurance.

Within the hour Roger also spoke to the King, who appeared to accept what he was able to tell him. My hope, therefore, was that after a suitable period of mourning we would be able to put what had happened behind us. Certainly, it was now my intention to give my fullest attention to plans for the arrival of Philippa from Hainault, as well as seeking to secure a lasting peace with the Scots.

Finding a lasting resting place for my Lord Edward's remains also took time. However, on a cold December day, my son and I were finally able to walk in procession behind his coffin through the streets of Gloucester as, draped in the royal standard, it made its way to the Abbey where he was to be laid to rest. As large crowds watched on, Being now a widow, I was once again dressed all in black. Nor could I help but feel deeply moved by the solemnity of the occasion.

Sadness pervaded me, as I reflected on the events which had led to his abdication and overcame me so much that I started to weep a little. Some might say that my tears were not genuine, but I swear before God that they were. I think, too, that these tears would have been all the greater if the embalmed body of my Lord Edward had been allowed to rest upon its bier in accordance with ancient custom. Instead, it had been placed inside the draped coffin after I was informed that the embalming process had not worked properly so the body was already in a state of decay.

This caused me to shun any opportunity to look upon Edward once more, preferring to remember him as he had been in life. I also had little difficulty in discouraging my son from wanting to see his father's face.

It was time, I decided, to put my Lord Edward's death firmly behind me to concentrate on securing my son's future happiness. Philippa had now reached England from Hainault, and towards the end of January, on a cold and blustery day, with snow lying on the ground, we rode out of the gates of York to meet her.

It was immediately apparent to me that since I had last met her, she had continued to blossom into a beautiful young woman, reminding me more than ever of myself, almost twenty years previously. Of course, as intended, the vital difference between her experience and mine was that my son, only a year her senior, was obviously more than pleased to see her again.

Inevitably, this brought back bruising memories of what I had endured, but I quickly dismissed these from my consciousness. Overwhelmingly, I was simply delighted at the prospect of my son and Philippa enjoying a happy relationship, unmarred by the presence of malign favourites akin to the likes of Piers Gaveston and Hugh Despenser. A few days later they were married with all due ceremony in York Minister, followed by an excellent wedding feast. Admittedly, there was heavy snowfall all day long, but I did not see this as an ill omen.

What I could not know, however, was that in France my brother, Charles, was about to die, and when news of this reached me, I was appalled. Yet again, I recalled my godfather's curse, reflecting bitterly not only on the death of my father, but also now in the space of only fourteen years, all three of the sons who had lived to succeed him. As Charles's Queen was pregnant there was then an interregnum while France waited to see if she would give birth to a son.

'Should it be a girl, then as Charles's nearest living male relative, Edward should become King of France,' I asserted firmly to Roger when we discussed the situation.

'But will France be happy to have a Plantagenet King of England take the crown of France as well?'

'Quite possibly not...'

'In which case any dispute over who should be King could spark a war, don't you think?'

'I would rather it did not have to come to that, but I still believe my son has every right to assert his claim to the French throne.'

Meanwhile, as Philippa had reached puberty, the consummation of her marriage was only delayed for a short while by the arrival of Lent. At the same time, I pondered whether to let her be crowned Queen as well as having her own household before deciding that this could wait.

'They may have consummated their marriage, but they are still little more than children, and I think it best that I keep Philippa under my wing while she gets used to life in this country. There is much that I can teach her.'

'Some will say you are jealous of her youth and wish to keep her more under your thumb than your wing,' Roger asserted teasingly.

'Let them say that if they wish to, but it isn't true. All in good time, I say.'

I also saw an opportunity for Roger and me to be together for longer than had been possible since our return to England.

'I thought of spending a few weeks at Leeds Castle in Kent, which I love.' I told him. 'You could join me there, I hope. Of course, as ever, we would need to be discreet.'

'Why yes, I would be delighted to do so.'

Notwithstanding my brother's sad demise, I had good reason to be content with everything that Roger and I had achieved on behalf of my son, since coming to power. Above all, a peace with Scotland, which I had long believed to be in England's best interests, was about to be sealed, whilst at the same time I was exceedingly pleased to have found my son a bride whom he seemed to be very much in love with.

Of course, I understood love matches were a luxury that those of royal blood could never expect to enjoy as the interests of dynasties and nations were of paramount importance.

Nonetheless, that surely served to make any love matches that did exist between those of royal blood even more precious.

Let me also be clear that there was one term of the Peace Treaty that caused me some heart searching. My daughter Joan, at the age of only seven was to be married to the Scottish King's four-year-old son, David. I regarded such a union as an essential part of any lasting peace as it carried with it the expectation of Joan bearing children who would be first cousins to my son's progeny and thus less likely to make war against each other. On the other hand, I felt an inevitable sense of guilt at sending her away to Scotland at such a tender age.

In retrospect, the few weeks that Roger and I spent together at Leeds marked a pinnacle of our happiness before storm clouds began to gather. So long as his wife lived, we could never be man and wife. Yet, away from the eyes of the court, we were free for that short time to fully enjoy each other's company.

The early spring weather was cold with overnight frosts, which were still to be seen on the ground when we woke in the morning. Mostly, though, the days were dry and sunny, with ample evidence of new growth, which I delighted in, especially the appearance of yellow daffodils, my favourite flower.

To make the most of this we went riding every day, unaccompanied by any servants, invariably heading east in the direction of Canterbury. This took us uphill through a dense forest until we reached some exquisitely beautiful valleys, which were always a pleasure to the eye. Reflecting on this I decided to share my hopes for the future with Roger.

'You know, once the King comes of age, it would be wonderful to retire here, I think. I could then visit St Thomas's shrine whenever I wish, whilst it's only two days ride to Westminster.'

'Hm, wouldn't you soon grow bored with its isolation?'

'No, not at all. I know what you mean, of course, but the very point I'm making is that it's not as isolated as it seems. In two days, I could also be in France.'

'And would you still want me to share this Demi-Paradise with you?' he asked me, teasingly.

'Naturally, though it saddens me that we can never be man and wife.'

He shrugged. 'Unless my wife were to die... '

'We cannot wish for that... It is sinful.'

'I agree, but, well, it might still come to pass.'

'One day, perhaps, but then again she might outlive us both.'

'True enough. We can but live for the day and make the most of our happiness together while we can.'

By the time our sojourn came to an end, my late brother's wife had given birth to a girl and my son had announced his claim to the French throne, whilst all too predictably the nobility of France had chosen Philip of Valois as their King. It was the presage to a conflict that continues, even as I write this thirty years later.

What came as the greatest disappointment to me was how poorly the Peace Treaty was received. This was mainly due to it depriving many nobles of their claims to land north of the border. However, I thought that a price worth paying, especially as the terms of the treaty required the Scots to pay compensation for the destruction which their raids on the North had wrought.

My son, Edward, also complained bitterly to me on several occasions about what he called a 'cowardly peace.' When I patiently explained that continuing a war that had dragged on for decades was a fruitless drain on the Kingdom's resources, bringing in its wake nothing more than misery for those living within reach of the border with Scotland, he gave me a sullen look of disagreement.

'You're still too young to appreciate the truth of what I say. Your father was humiliated by the Scots and the campaign you went on last year ended in failure. What's more, how can you hope to fight a war successfully in France if you're still fighting the Scots as well?'

At this he merely scowled. 'I still say it is wrong to have given up what is rightfully mine. When I come of age do not expect me to be bound by what you have signed away.'

'My son, until that day comes, I am simply seeking to act in what I consider to be your best interests, along with that of the Kingdom at large.'

Worse even than this disagreement with my son, was the considerable deterioration in my relationship with Lancaster, who had once been a staunch ally against Despenser. This came about not just because of the terms of the Scottish treaty, of which he disapproved, as well as my acquiring some land to which he claimed title, but also because I had chosen to grant a petition by Sir Robert Holland for the restoration of land, which my Lord Edward had taken away from him. The trouble was that granting this petition went against what had previously been agreed with Lancaster.

All my life I had known men like him; haughty, arrogant, but with brittle egos that were all too easily offended. His late older brother had been such a person and he was much the same. It was nevertheless unwise to make an enemy of him in this way. In my defence, I can only say that I was persuaded by the esteem I had for Sir Robert, who, being handsome and chivalrous, reminded me so much of Roger.

It was also perhaps, inevitable, that we should become rivals sooner or later as he was, after all, my son's official guardian. Yet, I was determined to keep my son close to me in order to rule in his name until he came of age. In a world dominated by men, of course, I realised that I could not do so without Roger's help, and herein lay the seeds of the disaster that was to ultimately befall us both.

I freely admit, too, that I could have allowed Lancaster to become all powerful, but had I done so, I know that he would simply have continued with the disastrous war against Scotland. In short, I had the temerity to believe, even as a woman, that I was more fit to rule. Before God, I must also confess that I had acquired a taste for power. In that capacity, I do not think that women differ so greatly, as may be supposed, from men. As I approached my thirty-third birthday, I had no great wish to relinquish my status before my son came of age.

# Chapter 31

# Growing tensions

At the end of May, at Hereford, I attended the joint wedding of two of Roger's daughters. This had made me somewhat apprehensive as it inevitably brought me into contact with his wife, Joan.

'Afterwards, you must come and stay at my castle at Ludlow,' he'd suggested. 'I've created a substantial modern residence within its walls to match the comforts offered by any royal palace.

'Will your wife be there, too?' I'd asked him.

'Why yes, but she has her own rooms, which are quite separate from what I've had built. As you know, we are to all intents and purposes estranged from one another.'

'And have you ever spoken to her about our relationship?'

'No, not at all, though I imagine she'll be well aware of it.'

'Then my visit will not be easy for her to bear.'

'True enough, but I want you to see what I've had built, especially the chapel dedicated to St Peter. It was on his feast day that I escaped from the Tower.'

'Very well, I'll come, but I've no wish to humiliate her so we must continue to behave discreetly at all times.'

As events transpired, Joan kept her feelings to herself, and behaved with impeccable dignity in my presence. I could sense, though, that she was tense as was I, both of us saying very little to one another. I also found myself unable to look her in the eye, all the while recalling how much I had had to pretend politeness to the likes of Gaveston and Despenser. I did not enjoy the role of being the 'other woman' as there was something undignified about it. It certainly didn't befit a queen, even though our relationship was supposedly secret.

Suffice it to add that I felt like an intruder in her home, so however much I was impressed by what Roger had had built, it was a relief to be able to bring my visit to an end after only two nights as I had an important council meeting to attend at Worcester.

Philip of Valois had by now been crowned King of France, setting our two nations upon a collision course, given that I had already made it publicly clear that I supported my son's claim to the French throne. I now wanted the Council to agree to the raising of an army, which would be sent to Gascony, but to my frustration Lancaster was adamant that too few councillors were present.

'Only the whole council can authorise the sending of an army to make war,' he asserted firmly. 'Otherwise, any decision to do so would be contrary to law.'

'But that will just delay matters unnecessarily,' I responded.

'That is of no consequence. To proceed now would simply be wrong and I will have none of it.'

In the end I decided I had no choice but to accept that he was correct, even though this would involve a delay of about a month. In the meantime, I turned my attention to my daughter's forthcoming wedding, but was bitterly disappointed when my son told me bluntly that he would not attend it on any account.

'Mother, you know I hate the treaty you've agreed with the Scots, and I detest nothing more than your agreeing, to my sister's marriage to the Scottish King's son. She's far too young and I thought after your own experience with father you were opposed to the marriage of infants.'

'I think the situation here is quite different. What's also most important is that the children of their union will be your cousins. It's my hope that the ties of family will then help to prevent war between our two nations in the future.'

'Well, I will still not be seen to give my blessing to this marriage, so Philippa and I will stay away.'

Once again, I was frustrated, but not being able to prevail on him to change his mind, was left with no choice but to set out for Berwick, where the marriage was to take place, without him.

I wish to affirm before God that saying farewell to my daughter when she was still so young was far from easy. Though I believed her marriage was for the greater good of our two nations, I still felt an immense degree of sadness, which for her sake I did my best to disguise.

For her part, she behaved admirably, shedding only a few tears when the time came for us to go our separate ways. The memory of her sweet face as she waved goodbye to me will remain with me to my dying day, whilst I can only thank God that we were destined to meet again in this life.

'I will pray for her every day,' I told Mortimer, who had accompanied me to the wedding. 'I really believe that we've been right to achieve a peace with Scotland. Yet, I would hate to think of my daughter suffering as I did when I first married her father.'

'She'll be treated well, I'm sure.'

'Yes, I do hope so. What also concerns me, though, is the level of hostility to the peace amongst the nobility. It's because of this that I've asked the Scottish King to allow some of our closest supporters to retain their ownership of land north of the border.'

Within days of this conversation, I was pleased to learn that my request had been granted. Unfortunately, those who remained completely disentitled, became, if anything, more disgruntled than ever with the terms of peace. Consequently, several of them, including Kent and Lancaster, failed to appear at the sitting of parliament in York at the end of the month, adding to my concern that the peace with Scotland could have come at too high a price. Furthermore, any discussion of pursuing a war against France had to be postponed once more.

I freely confess before God that I also made a grave error in not passing monies received from the Scots, under the terms of the Peace Treaty, to the Exchequer, as I should have done. The fact of the matter was that since returning to England I had been living far too extravagantly and had let my expenses get out of hand, but this I accept is but a feeble excuse. I had grown to enjoy the trappings of my position; I had grown indulgent over time.

Worst even than this, I was also becoming aware that Roger was beginning to misuse the power he possessed through me to bestow favours on his friends and that this was causing resentment. I realised that I had no choice but to warn him that this was unwise.

'If you overreach yourself, men will say that you're no better than Despenser.'

'Nonsense. I'm simply rewarding those who've been loyal to me for their services."

'Yes, perhaps so, but we must still be careful. Peace with the Scots is making us unpopular, not least with the likes of Lancaster and Kent. Do not, I beg you, give them the excuse to make trouble.'

'Very well, I'll try and be more circumspect in future.'

'Thank you, my love, I believe it is in both our interests that you should be so.' I was trying to be gracious, but I felt that Roger might be less than willing to heed my warning. He had become increasingly keen on having his own way.

—∞—

The following month, to my absolute horror, two of Rogers sons died, one of natural causes and the other because of injuries sustained in a tournament. This left him understandably bereft, so I did my best to offer him as much comfort as I could.

At the same time, I decided to make overtures to Lancaster by inviting him to a meeting at which he would have every opportunity to set out his complaints. However, when he arrived for this, it was at the head of hundreds of armed men, which I found totally unacceptable as did Roger.

'My Lord, I asked you to come here in good faith, hoping that we could discuss your grievances in a spirit of conciliation, 'I told him. 'Yet, you now appear with a small army at your back as if you mean to threaten us. This is intolerable.'

'I've only brought my men to make it clear how angry this wretched peace with the Scots has made me, not to mention your choosing to acquire land that is rightfully mine.'

'But bringing armed men into the King's presence, as well as mine, is still an affront to our persons, surely you understand that? If they don't withdraw immediately, we've nothing to discuss.'

'If you don't hear me out, I'll turn my men on you!'

'So, you are threatening me then!'

'Only if you won't hear me out.'

'No, only if you withdraw your men.'

At this, my son, Edward, held up a hand. 'My Lord, I must make it clear that you've offended me by bringing armed men here in such numbers. If you will not withdraw them then I suggest that you lay your complaints before Parliament when it meets in Salisbury next month.'

'Very well, that's what I'll do then.'

With that he left, taking his men with him. It had been a confrontation that left me feeling upset as well as fearful for the future, although I was impressed by the maturity my son had displayed in diffusing the situation and I told him so.

'But let this be a lesson to you,' I added. 'Men like him think too highly of themselves and are a threat to the peace of the realm.'

Certainly, I was fearful of the possibility of a civil war, as was Roger who went so far as to muster men from the marches of Wales, whilst urging me to ban public assemblies as well as remove from office any sheriffs whose loyalty was in doubt.

'You must act decisively before matters get out of hand,' he insisted. I agreed. By early October, however, news reached me that I found deeply distressing. By now Roger and I were in Gloucester where my son joined us shortly afterwards.

'I must tell you, dear mother, that Lancaster tried to capture me. Fortunately, I received advanced warnings of his intentions so was able to evade him.'

Within a day or two news reached us that Lancaster's supporters had encouraged the city of London to throw its weight behind him. Its mayor was also making a series of demands, including that Sir Roger be banned from court for abusing his position. What's more, that Edward should be allowed his own income and that I should give up most of my own to make that possible.

I was appalled by this news, more than anything because it demonstrated how unpopular both myself and Roger had become in such a short time. Consequently, I couldn't help breaking down in tears in my son's presence.

'But this is utterly unjust,' I said between sobs. 'Lancaster has become our enemy and is spreading falsehoods against both me and Sir Roger.'

'Please don't distress yourself so much, dear mother. I hate to see you so upset.'

I gave him a weak smile. 'That's entirely to your credit. I just can't help but find these accusations and demands upsetting when all I'm trying to do is act in the country's best interests. Perhaps, I have been a little too acquisitive, but think how much was taken from me by that villain, Despenser.' I knew that I was trying to excuse my own sometimes questionable actions and that this might seem somewhat disingenuous, but I was a queen after all.

We soon travelled on to Salisbury to attend Parliament, only to receive the yet more shocking news that Lancaster had had Sir Robert Holland murdered. I knew there had been bad blood between the two men for some time with Sir Robert daring to launch attacks on Lancaster's estates. Nonetheless, I was angry that Lancaster should behave so hypocritically; on the one hand making outrageous allegations against myself and Roger, and yet on the other taking the law into his own hands in such an egregious fashion. I felt that the tide of events was quickly turning, and not in our favour.

I was now concerned that Lancaster would again seek to take my son into his custody, so sent him and Philippa to my castle at Marlborough. Then we waited nervously for Parliament to sit with Roger making it clear that to protect himself he would only attend if his own armed men were also present. In the circumstances I was quite prepared to tolerate this, but I became angry with him when he went so far as to threaten the bishops if they failed to support him rather than Lancaster.

'You go too far. Men will accuse you of being a tyrant,' I told him bluntly.

'Let them do so. You know full well that I am not.'

'Only if you don't behave like one.' His dismissive attitude gave rise to a feeling of alarm, but I tried not to show it. I was afraid for him.

In the event, Lancaster failed to appear, although his spokesperson, the Bishop of Winchester, came in his place, contending that the Earl was fearful of being attacked by Roger if he attended in person.

At this, Roger took hold of the Archbishop of Canterbury's crucifix and, melodramatically, swore by it that he had no such intention. In support of this I then asked my son to send Lancaster a letter guaranteeing his safety but still he failed to attend. Instead, he sent a response reiterating the demands that we'd received from the Mayor of London, and at the same saying that he would appear so long as he was permitted to bring an armed retinue with him.

I appreciated that such a letter could not go unanswered so sat down with my son to craft a suitable response. Meanwhile it became apparent that the Bishop of Winchester was doing his upmost to garner as much support as he could for Lancaster's cause by calling a meeting of bishops. When Roger discovered this, he was furious.

'Wretched man. I'll put a stop to him conspiring behind our backs with his gross falsehoods!'

'Don't harm him, I pray you. It will do our cause no good at all.'

'Have no fear, I'll not do that. I'll merely send some armed men to put a stop to this meeting.'

And so, he did, whilst by the end of the day I was satisfied with what had been written to Lancaster and had it immediately dispatched to him.

'It's short but courteous,' I told Roger that evening. 'Of course, it refutes the allegations that have been made against us and points out that if he fails to attend council meetings the King is entitled to seek advice from others.'

'And what about the demand that you surrender most of your revenues to the King?'

'I've sidestepped that. The letter simply states that this is a matter between the King and me. The letter also offers him safe conduct to attend Parliament.'

'But he deserves to be arrested for having Holland murdered...'

'And I believe he still could be.'

'He's no fool. He'll likely come to the same conclusion and keep his distance.'

As it transpired, Roger's prediction proved to be well founded, and I decided to press on with something that had been on my mind for some time.

With the benefit of hindsight, it is all too easy to say that it was a mistake to raise Roger to the highest ranks of the nobility by making him Earl of March, but I can only make it clear before God that at the time I thought it the right thing to do. Of course, he was my lover with great influence over me. Yet the idea was essentially mine as a reward for his loyal services, without which I do not believe that I would have successfully conquered England and then been able to rule in my son's name for the best part of two years.

What I failed to appreciate was that making Roger an earl, would foment envy and even hatred towards him amongst the ranks of the nobility. Many of them already believed that he had risen too far above his station and enjoyed too much power. I fully admit, too, that I underestimated how much his ennoblement along with a handsome income would exercise his ego along with his taste for extravagance. His elevated status had gone to his head, he had changed, and not for the better.

The trouble was that all my life I had been used to living in the shadow of rich, powerful men, many of them Princes of the royal blood. To a man they were vain and arrogant, with some simply being more so than others. I had also learnt that their monstrous egos needed careful flattering. It was essentially why I wished to flatter Roger's; a man, whatever his faults, whom I had come to love and rely upon.

# CHAPTER 32

# A SENSE OF PRIDE

The sitting of Parliament was adjourned at the end of October with the intention of sitting again at Westminster. However, to my dismay, it was then discovered that Lancaster's forces had occupied Winchester, effectively standing in our path. This meant that we still faced the real prospect of a confrontation and with it, the possibility of civil war. This was just what had dogged my Lord Edward's reign and now, despite all my endeavours, it threatened to dog my regency as well.

'He can't be allowed to get away with this,' Roger insisted. 'I suggest we move on Winchester and at the same time make it clear to Lancaster that if he doesn't lay down his arms he'll be arraigned for high treason.'

I agreed, though not without some trepidation, and in the event, by the time we arrived there, Lancaster had prudently withdrawn his forces. Our continued progress towards London was then a leisurely one with prolonged halts at both Wallingford and Windsor, so November was three weeks gone before we finally arrived there.

At this juncture I received a conciliatory letter from Lancaster, proposing that our differences be debated at a meeting of the full council. As had become my custom, I turned to Roger for advice.

'What should I do? I must say his recent conduct has somewhat hardened my attitude towards him.'

'Does he say anything about whether he intends to bring his soldiers with him?'

'No, he doesn't.'

'Then, I expect nothing's really changed. Tell him that he's offended the King and that as far as you're concerned there's nothing to debate. He may attend full Council but only to submit to the King's will and nor should he bring any armed retinue with him.'

'Are you sure that's wise?'

'Of course, I am. You must be firm with the man, otherwise he'll start demanding that we renege on the treaty with the Scots as well as expecting you to surrender all power to him.'

'Yes, alright, I'll do as you suggest.'

Meanwhile, an emissary arrived from France with a demand from King Philip that my son pay homage to Gascony, the very idea of which considerably displeased me.

'Why should my son, the offspring of a King pay homage to the son of a mere Count?' I declared, scathingly.

However, I had more pressing concerns closer to home. The conflict with Lancaster and his allies was rumbling on, with accusations and counter-accusations going backwards and forwards, until at the close of the year the realm appeared to plunge headlong into a civil war.

'We must stand firm against Lancaster's lies,' Roger insisted 'Furthermore, I propose that your son declare war on Lancaster, but at the same time offer an amnesty to those who submit to him as King.'

I thought this a somewhat dangerous strategy, yet at the

same time could see no real alternative, no matter how much the prospect of a bloody conflict horrified me. In the event, though, it worked, thanks to Roger seizing the initiative by attacking Lancaster's lands before capturing the strategically important city of Leicester.

At this juncture the Earls of Kent and Norfolk decided to submit and realising that he now lacked the support to continue to oppose us, Lancaster finally did the same in mid-January. This took place at Bedford with the occasion being something of a triumph for us when he dismounted from his horse, knelt before us, and swore on the Gospels that he would do nothing to harm the King and Queen, myself, or any members of the Council.

Roger was certainly in a jubilant mood whilst I just felt a huge sense of relief that unnecessary bloodshed had been avoided.

'Lancaster deserves nothing less than execution for his treasonous behaviour,' Roger declared, but I was inclined to be more forgiving.

'But he's submitted freely to our will. I hear, too, that he's losing his sight.'

'He could still cause us more trouble in the future.'

'To kill him might just make a martyr of him. I don't think that would be at all wise.'

'He should still be imprisoned and face a heavy fine.'

This I was more prepared to agree to. Yet, following an intercession on his behalf by the Archbishop of Canterbury, he was allowed to remain at liberty, though fined the equivalent of half the value of his land and stripped of all his offices of state, save one.

There remained the issue of what we should do with Lancaster's supporters, amongst whom was a man I had once considered a friend, Henry de Beaumont, husband of my namesake, Isabella, with whom I had enjoyed a friendship since first becoming Queen. I was upset that he had chosen to oppose me and would have been prepared to see him imprisoned for his disloyalty, but in the event he escaped abroad. Isabella didn't go with him, but her husband's hostility towards me sadly severed our friendship for ever.

Otherwise, I persuaded Roger that it was in our interests to be as lenient as possible and, after a while, this policy even led us to restore most of the lands that Lancaster had forfeited.

'Above all, I do not wish to be accused of being tyrannical as Hugh Despenser was,' I declared firmly.

The issue of paying homage to King Philip of France for Gascony also came to the fore again. I would have liked nothing better than to have continued to reject any such idea, but I was forced to alter my position after being advised by Roger that we totally lacked the resources to be drawn into a full-scale war with any hope of success. Through gritted teeth I therefore agreed to my son visiting France for the purpose of offering homage, an event which took place in June. He was accompanied for this purpose by his uncles, the Earls of Kent and Norfolk, and returned safely to England after successfully completing this task.

He was now a few months short of his seventeenth birthday, a fine young man, and increasingly, I thought, King in the making, who would surely outshine his unfortunate father. It was obvious, too, that his relationship with Philippa was blossoming, and before the year was out, she became pregnant for the first time.

I realised full well that my son might become increasingly impatient to be able to rule in his own right, but I still hoped that this could be a gradual process over the next three to four years as he approached his twenty-first birthday. In the meantime, I allowed him to keep twenty men at arms at his side, commanded by his good friend, Sir William de Montagu, and granted Philippa a generous annual income of a thousand marks for her household expenses.

While my son was in France, it was a pleasure for me to return to Canterbury to worship at the blessed St Thomas's shrine once more, and it was during my stay in this city that I received news that the Scottish King had died. He had been a formidable enemy whom I had come to respect. When my son arrived from France I was able to tell him that his younger sister, Joan, was now Queen of Scotland at the age of only eight.

I was proud for her but also apprehensive, knowing what difficulties I had faced as a Queen of tender years. Equally, I allowed myself a feeling of pride at my own accomplishments. The daughter of a King, despite my struggles, I had lived to see my oldest son become King and a daughter become Queen. As God wills it, my blood and that of France should continue to flow in that of two royal dynasties for centuries to come.

That summer brought more cause for celebration when Roger's daughters, Beatrice, and Agnes, were married to the heirs of the Earls of Norfolk and Pembroke. We both attended their weddings, and I was delighted for him as such marriages raised his status still further. It was an altogether happy occasion save for one act of folly on my part. Having drunk a little too much wine, Roger and I made love, and I allowed him to penetrate me.

It was consummation of the love we had for one another, but I was left dreading the possibility that I might become pregnant. A few weeks later when my normal courses did not flow, I feared the worst. At the first opportunity I told Roger.

'I fear that I am pregnant. In fact, there's no doubt in my mind that that is the case,' I told him as calmly as I could. 'We should not have made love in the way we did after your daughters' weddings.'

'But we both wanted to. You seemed so happy.'

'I had drunk too much wine, but, yes, I was. Now there's a price to be paid. Concealing my pregnancy will not be at all easy. Nonetheless, all possible steps must be taken to try and do so, as well as the birth itself, of course. You can imagine the scandal if this fails.'

'And after that, assuming the child lives?'

'Naturally, the child must be well provided for, but far from court. My identity as its mother must also be concealed.'

'What, for ever?'

'Um…Until after my death, certainly. We also need to consider the possibility that I might die in labour.'

'Heaven forbid: you're a healthy woman and have been safely delivered of four babes.'

'True, but I was much younger then. We must face the fact that at the age I am now there is more risk that I will not survive.'

'I suppose so. But what if the child is more fortunate?'

'Plans for its welfare would still need to be put in place. I suggest the child should be brought up on the understanding that its mother died in labour and when you consider the time is right to do so you could reveal my identity.'

Subsequently to this conversation I decided to make plans for the possibility of my demise by making Roger heir to several of my properties. Then, trying to put my pregnancy to the back of my mind, I was pleased to attend a magnificent tournament in further celebration of Roger's daughters' marriages in which he entered the lists as King Arthur whilst I assumed the role of Queen Guinevere.

Given my love of the stories of this legendary King, I was delighted to play the role of his Queen. It seemed an innocent enough pleasure to me, but I was subsequently to learn that there were those who saw it as just another example of Roger overreaching himself by behaving as if it was he, rather than my son, who was the realm's monarch. Without doubt, I would say that there were those, however unfairly, who were jealous of the power and influence he now enjoyed.

Furthermore, I still did not appreciate how much my son was coming to resent Roger's position. Looking back, I realise it was naive of me, but then I was totally in love with Roger and that state of mind made me blind. Even when my son decided to appoint his own man as treasurer of his household, replacing the person previously appointed by Roger, I thought little of it.

Likewise, I saw no reason to object when he made his former tutor and secretary, keeper of the privy seal. He was, after all, now within weeks of his seventeenth birthday and as I saw it, fully entitled to begin to make his own decisions about who served him.

By the end of October, the court was in residence near Warwick at Kenilworth Castle, with its mighty keep, which until recently had been in Lancaster's possession. I was comfortable there, but increasingly anxious that my pregnancy would begin to show in full view of a host of people including my son and daughter-in-law. When she then announced that she was pregnant, the irony of the situation almost made me titter with laughter. Fortunately, I just managed to restrain myself, before offering her my profuse congratulations.

Within days she began to suffer from severe morning sickness, leaving me to fear that I might do the same. It had not, though, been something from which I had suffered much with my previous pregnancies, so I could but pray that it wouldn't happen on this occasion. Then one morning, I felt a terrible pain in my belly, and within an hour, whilst in the privy, had lost the babe I was carrying.

Only my personal maid was a witness to what occurred, so of course, I had her swear on the gospels that she would never speak to anyone of what she had seen, before also handing her a generously filled pouch of silver coins.

'This is for your devoted services, these last few years, nothing more. You understand?'

She curtseyed to me. 'Of course, your Majesty.'

My overwhelming emotion at this moment was one of relief rather than sadness, much as I would have been happy to present the man I loved with a child, had our circumstances been different. I then hastened to inform Roger of what had happened, hoping that he would not be too upset. To my relief he assured me that he was not.

'It's for the best, I'm sure. And how are you feeling?' he asked me gently.

I was grateful for his solicitude. 'Somewhat tired, but I expect I'll be better after a few days rest.'

It was never my intention to remain at Kenilworth for more than a month, pleasant though it's surroundings might be. Yet, in the event Philippa was too unwell to travel anywhere until Christmas approached, whereupon it was decided that we would remain where we were until the arrival of the new year. It was to prove a thoroughly momentous one.

# Chapter 33

## An extraordinary tale

By early January I was back at one of my favourite places, Eltham Palace, where I remained for almost two months. I was pleased to have come south where the weather was generally milder, although, in the event, it still proved to be quite a harsh winter with frequent snowfalls.

Roger also visited me frequently and without any misgivings I decided to bestow more land on him; this time in Ireland, where he had once ruled on behalf of my Lord Edward. Looking back, it is all too easy to feel that I was over-generous, but I certainly didn't think so at the time.

It was during this period that I agreed that it was in both the best interest of the realm, and most especially that of Gascony, that we achieve a lasting peace with France. To that end the Bishop of Winchester was sent to Paris to negotiate a treaty that would provide for the marriage of my two youngest children, John, and Eleanor, to the daughter and son of the French King. This did not, however, please my son, who was all for war.

'But you've always said that my claim to the French throne is superior to that of Philip's. Why do you now want to make peace with him?'

'Because wars are expensive and we are in no position to defend Gascony, for which you have already paid homage.'

'But by making peace you are denying me my birthright.'

'I believe that I am being realistic in circumstances where a war would be a huge drain on our resources. What's more, if we were to wage war, our defeat could easily result in the loss of Gascony, which would be a terrible blow.'

'Defeat is out of the question. We have our archers and they're capable of destroying any French army.'

I respected my son's total confidence, but I was a realist and I wanted him to learn pragmatism too.

'When you come of age, pursue a costly war if you must, but until then I shall pursue the wisest course I can.'

He still looked very cross, giving me the impression that he would continue the argument, or perhaps just walk away in annoyance. Instead, he abruptly changed the subject.

'So, what about Philippa's coronation? It's not right that this has been deferred for so long.'

I put up a hand to placate him. 'I'm sorry, you're right, I have let other matters take precedence. It's remiss of me, I know. I'll speak to Roger...'

'Why does everything have to be decided by him?'

'He's my faithful adviser, you know that.'

'Oh come, dearest mother, what do you take me for? We both know he's far more than that. He has too much power, thanks to your generosity. Do you not see that?'

'As far as I'm concerned, he deserves what he has in return for his loyal services, both to me and to the Crown.'

'You are blind, dearest mother. He takes advantage of you.'

I confess that this conversation perturbed me. I became flustered, not to say upset. 'Enough, please. I promise you that Philippa will be crowned soon.'

I then spoke to Roger at the earliest opportunity, making it clear to him that it was in no-one's interests to defer the coronation any longer. 'After all, she'll soon be six months pregnant. If we leave it more than a few weeks it will not be possible until after she's recovered from giving birth.'

'Very well, I agree.'

'I must bestow some land on her as well, in recognition of her enhanced status.'

Philippa's coronation took place on the 4th of March in Westminster Abbey with all the due ceremony, although I took care to ensure that its length was curtailed so as not to tire her too much. Outwardly, the Kingdom, was at peace and all seemed to be well, but a few weeks earlier Roger had brought me some news that came as a profound shock. It was late in the evening and we were alone together.

'I believe Kent is plotting against us.'

'You have evidence of this?'

'Most certainly. There has been communication between him and Beaumont using couriers. I had them arrested and put under interrogation...'

'You mean tortured!' I felt that Roger's methods often went too far.

'...So far as that was necessary, yes. It has revealed something that I know will upset you.'

'What is that?'

'Kent believes that your husband, the former King, is still alive...'

'...But how, why? My husband lies buried in Gloucester Cathedral, as you know full well.'

'I have to tell you that it isn't his body that lies at rest there.'

'No, surely not. It must be his. You yourself saw his body.

Don't tell me you failed to look upon his face?'

Roger now became contrite. 'I have to confess that I lied to you…'

'But in heaven's name why?'

'I thought it was in your best interests.'

'Now you're talking in riddles.'

'Allow me to explain.'

'Alright, go on.'

'When I arrived at Berkeley Castle it didn't take me long to establish what had happened. Edward had escaped from there and in so doing killed a man; the same man who presently lies in Gloucester Cathedral. Gurney and Maltravers were so discomforted by his escape, as well as fearful of recriminations that they panicked and tried to conceal the truth. Their duplicity was made easier by the fact that only a privileged few ever set eyes on the King…'

'Even so, they must have realised that such a deception was still likely to be exposed?'

'They thought they could prevent this by having the man's body promptly embalmed and his face covered by a cloth. Had I not insisted on this being removed they would have succeeded.'

'But why did you lie to me?' I exclaimed, I was both confused and angry.

'Because it was clear to me that the King had not escaped with any intention of trying to return to his throne, so posed no real threat. His 'supposed' death left you free of any responsibility for his welfare…'

'But you had no right to endorse this deception without first consulting me. For all you knew, I might have agreed with you…'

'I wanted to save you from having to make such a difficult choice... I realise now that this was wrong of me. I can only ask for your forgiveness.'

'I don't know about that. What you have just confessed to is a grave disappointment to me. Anyway, where do you think my husband is now?'

'That I cannot say, but I've established that he was given a safe haven at Corfe castle for more than a year. Then he left and could be in hiding somewhere else, though I fancy he's gone abroad.'

'So, what's to be done?'

'Kent poses a serious threat. If he's allowed to carry on unchecked, we could end up with everything I've just told you becoming public knowledge. He needs to be stopped as soon as possible. I have devised a plan that I think might work to our advantage...'

'...What's that?' I was still reeling from the revelation that had just been presented to me as well its implications.

'Kent needs to be told that Edward is still at Corfe Castle. I think it might encourage him to try and mount a rescue. If he does that with the express purpose of mounting a rebellion against your son, the King, we will be able to charge him with high treason.'

'...And then have him executed, I suppose?'

'Of course. There's really no alternative. So long as he lives, he'll be a serious thorn in our side, proclaiming that the former King still lives.'

'But he has royal blood and is only being loyal to his half-brother. You'll need my son's authority before you can put Kent to death and what do we do if he refuses to grant it?'

'I'll have to persuade him. Leave that to me.'

'I don't like this. I thought we were agreed that it was wise to be lenient towards our enemies, lest we be accused of being no better than Despenser.'

'But this is on a different scale. It's a threat that could conceivably even see your husband restored to his throne and you made to serve again as his Queen. Do you really want that?'

'Of course, I don't, but remember that my Lord Edward abdicated his throne in favour of my son, who is now close to manhood. I rather doubt if he wants his throne back, even if others think he should have it.'

'He may still be open to persuasion if those who conspire against us succeed. Better to act decisively before we're faced with the threat of another civil war.'

I was not happy with this convoluted plan, but felt I had little choice so did not oppose it.

For all my misgivings, Roger set up his trap for Kent who fell into it all too easily by visiting Corfe castle and handing over a letter, intended for my Lord Edward's eyes only, in which he expressed his desire to restore him to his throne by whatever means were necessary. The letter was then passed immediately to us. Roger, of course, was delighted that his ruse had worked so easily.

'We have him!' he declared and within a day Kent was arrested and soon left with no choice but to confess his crime when he was presented with the damning written evidence we had against him.

All his property was seized, but then came what I had predicted would be a difficult process, namely persuading my son that his uncle needed to be dealt with in the harshest manner.

'What he has done is treasonous and cannot be excused,' I told him firmly.

'But he is my uncle and of royal blood. Surely, we can be merciful and merely imprison him?'

'Not for a crime as heinous as this. He must be executed.'

'I still don't see why. I won't be a party to this. And is it true that my father still lives?'

'...It would appear so but we've no idea where he is now. I just hope he's escaped abroad. For all our sakes, it is best that the world in general never knows the truth of what has happened to him.'

'...Hm, which I expect, dearest mother, is why you want my uncle executed without delay. Isn't that right?'

'I think it's in our best interests, certainly.'

'Yours and Mortimer's, perhaps, but not mine. My father abdicated in my favour, don't forget.'

'I think it would be acutely embarrassing for you as well if he were to, how shall I put it... come back from the grave.'

'No, it wouldn't. I had nothing to do with any of the events that led to his abdication and supposed death. What's more, if he really is still alive, I would like to meet him again. I, bear him no ill will in the way you obviously do.'

'After this length of time, I think he can only want to live in the shadows. Even supposing we could locate him here in England, he might not wish to see you.'

'I accept that would be his decision to make.'

'In any case, I think it best to let sleeping dogs lie.'

When I told Roger how reluctant my son was to see his uncle tried and executed he was exasperated. 'I'll talk to him 'man to man' and get him to see sense.'

'He's old enough to know his own mind. You may not succeed.'

'Perhaps not, but I'll tell him it would be unfair on you to let Kent live, only for him to be a beacon for those who might wish to put his father back on the throne. If that were to happen, we could be facing another civil war, which your son might lose.'

'Very well, do what you think best.'

An hour later Roger told me that he had persuaded my son that it was necessary to proceed against Kent, who was then impeached by Parliament, which happened to be sitting, and condemned to death. Deciding that it was best to act quickly before my son tried to either pardon his uncle, or commute his sentence, I then ordered that the execution be carried out immediately. I knew that this was harsh, but I felt that I had no choice. Sometimes, those in positions of power must take difficult decisions for the sake of expediency and this was one such example. I had grown into my role!

Looking back, I must say before almighty God, that it would have been far better to have let Kent live. Alas, I was simply desperate to silence the man, before the truth about my Lord Edward's fate became widely known. He was not even allowed a proper trial before his peers, as was his birthright, and that, I fully accept, was universally seen as being not just wrong but also tyrannical.

I feared that we might now be seen as being no better than Hugh Despenser. To compound this, it was also becoming clearer to me that Roger was now behaving too arrogantly, which was making our rule more unpopular. I decided to try and persuade him to desist from such behaviour.

'You will become increasingly disliked if you insist on making my son stand in your presence even though he is King, and also walk alongside him as if you were his equal.'

'But he is still only a boy.'

'In your eyes, perhaps, but he will soon be eighteen, and I fear he increasingly resents the power you wield.'

'I endeavour to be no more than a father to him, offering him the benefit of my counsel.'

'Perhaps so, but I would still advise you to be more circumspect. The manner of Kent's death has not gone down well, I fear.'

'We had no choice. Had there been a full trial he would have sought to justify his belief that your husband still lives...'

'That may be so, but there is still, I believe, a perception that our actions are no better than Despenser's. That behoves us to tread with care, especially if you're determined that we try to hold on to the reins of power until my son is twenty-one.'

'Not necessarily that long. A gradual transfer of power once he's twenty would be appropriate, though, don't you think?'

'No, I believe it should be sooner than that. It must begin no later than a year from now, otherwise I know he will become angry and refuse to co-operate with you.'

'Alright, we can discuss this further at a later date.'

'But I will not change my mind. You cannot continue to behave like a king for very much longer, surely you understand that?'

'Yes, of course I do.'

Whatever my misgivings as well as disappointment concerning Roger's conduct, I had no wish for this to come between us. After all, I felt that we were still very much in love. I firmly believed that he was not only devoted to me but also acting in the best interests of both the realm and my son.

To these ends, I was pleased with the progress being made towards achieving a lasting peace with France. Further, we decided that as her pregnancy advanced it was only right to be more generous to Philippa by giving her a household of her own along with an increase in her income. My attention then turned increasingly towards the prospect of becoming a grandmother.

On the nineteenth of June, I was delighted to be present at Woodstock Palace when she gave birth to a healthy boy. Like his father and grandfather before him, he was christened Edward, and from the first time I held him in my arms I felt there was a powerful bond between us. To cap this, my son sealed the peace treaty with France just a few weeks later. Then the skies began to darken once more for me when I realised that I was once again pregnant.

Totally against my better judgement, I had allowed the lust I felt for Roger to get the better of me, so was not really surprised. When I gave Roger the news he was also delighted, making it plain that he wanted a child by me, and that whatever the difficulties this created we would be able to overcome them. I was less confident. Then came the arrival of more bad news.

# CHAPTER 34

# STORM CLOUDS

'Edward, is that you? Is that really you?' There was no response, but I could see his face. There was no doubting that it was him.

'Where have you been all this time?' I asked him, but there was still no reply. Instead, he just seemed to fade away, and with that I woke up.

Ever since I had learnt that my Lord Edward was apparently still alive, I had experienced this recurring dream. It was beginning to annoy me as I really didn't care what had happened to him so long as he never re-entered my life and by so doing destroyed my happiness. But then perhaps that was why I kept having the dream. It was because of an underlying fear that he would do just that, forcing me to reside with him once more against my will.

The previous day we had also received the shocking news that my former friend and ally, Henry Beaumont, was planning an invasion. He was in alliance with the Welsh rebel, Rhys ap Gruffydd, who was apparently ready to attack Roger's lands as a Marcher Lord. This brought home to me just how perilous our position was, making me increasingly anxious. We were living, or rather existing, from one crisis to another, which I found increasingly stressful.

There was an urgent mustering of troops throughout the

country, whilst I would brook no excuses when the Mayor of London at first tried to excuse himself from coming to a meeting. In the end he appeared, swearing his loyalty to my son, the King. Nonetheless, no doubt exacerbated by my pregnancy, I was still so tense that I feared I might fall ill and even die. It made me decide that I needed to speak again to Roger about our future. I felt a sense of despair.

'This development has convinced me that we should surrender the power we enjoy to my son much sooner than we were previously intending to.'

'Oh yes, and how soon is that?'

'Within the year.'

'But he'll still only be eighteen.'

'That is still quite old enough. If we try to cling to power any longer it will just make us even more unpopular.'

'I think you're unduly concerned. Nonetheless, I can see that it would make good sense to surrender power to him by the time he's twenty.'

'I still think that's too long, but would you object to my telling him that we will definitely surrender our powers within the next two years?'

'Very well. Let us deal with this current threat first. But thereafter, tell him this.'

Much to my relief by the end of August it was clear to me the threat of any invasion, or for that matter attack on Roger's lands, had subsided. I was much relieved but was still determined to reassure my son that I would relinquish all the powers I currently enjoyed by the time he was twenty. Alas, when I did so, he was not impressed. He looked at me glumly.

'Two years! No, dearest mother, no! When I am eighteen in

November, I will be more than ready to rule myself. You and your paramour must be ready to step aside then, or, in God's name, I shall be sore angry with both of you.'

I hated him referring to Roger in this fashion and became quite angry. Of course, I had not yet told him about my pregnancy and dreaded having to do so. 'The Earl of March is my faithful adviser.'

'Oh come, come, dearest mother, the whole world and his dog now knows he's your lover.'

'Well, be that as it may, I judge that it would be in your best interests to hand over the reins of power to you on a gradual basis. Perhaps this need not take two years…'

'No, it need not take more than two months. I am perfectly ready to rule in my own right, I tell you! The fact of the matter is that you and your so-called faithful adviser enjoy the fruits of power too much to want to give them up.'

'When the time is right, we will do so, I promise you.'

'Then accept that the time to do so is this November…'

I put up a hand, feeling that our argument was in danger of going round in circles. 'We will talk about this again when I have considered the matter further.'

'Alright but let that be soon.'

My heart sank, I hated being caught in the middle of a power struggle between my beloved son and the man who was the love of my life.

By now we were on our way to Nottingham where the Council was due to hold a meeting. It's impressive castle was set atop a hill with a commanding view over the city. I had only ever stayed there on the odd occasion, finding its keep to be both well decorated and furnished. Upon our arrival, I had my first opportunity to speak to Roger about my son's demand.

'It's out of the question. You should agree to no such thing.'

'In which case life will get much harder for us. There'll be endless arguments as he becomes increasingly discontented. I do not wish to lose the esteem I believe he still has for me, despite everything.'

'What do you mean by that? Have you not striven to always act in his best interests?'

'Why, yes, but he would rather have us fighting the Scots and the French than making peace with them. Added to that, I know the execution of his uncle really upset him.'

'But I tell you, he's still too young to have outright control of everything. He could easily plunge us back into two disastrous wars, which is the last thing you want.'

'Yet, he must be allowed to be his own man, sooner or later, whatever the cost. I'm minded to offer him control of the Great Seal on his nineteenth birthday. That should pacify him, I hope.'

'Very well, you must act as you see fit.'

I then went back to my son with what I hoped was a reasonable proposal, saying to him that I was prepared to agree to a transition of power over the course of the next fourteen months, but still he wasn't satisfied.

'I've waited long enough as it is. I'm perfectly ready to assume what is rightfully mine now, not in a year's time. I will no longer tolerate your paramour strutting around as if he was King!'

'I will restrain him from doing that, I promise you.'

'I doubt he'll listen to your pleas. He controls you; don't you see that?'

'...I have faith in his judgement...'

'Which is precisely the same thing. I am this country's anointed king; I will not be denied the right to rule any longer!'

I was exhausted by this exchange with my much-loved son, not really knowing what to do now for the best. He was pulling me one way while Roger pulled me the other, saying in no uncertain terms that I should not surrender my powers just because my son chose to throw a tantrum.

'He complains, he shouts, but you are still entitled to hold the reins of power for at least another year. Do not be so weak as to give in to him.'

So, in the end I prevaricated with my son, saying that I was still considering his demand and would let him know my position once he enjoyed his eighteenth birthday on the thirteenth of November. At this he still gave me a dark look.

'You're just playing for time, I know it.' With that he just walked away.

To take my mind off the growing sense of concern I felt, I decided to spend as much time as I could in the presence of my grandson, which certainly gave me great joy. At the same time, I was faced with the unfortunate news from France that King Philip was refusing to ratify the peace treaty until my son returned to France to pay him so-called liege homage, which would require him to offer military assistance in a time of war. With a sinking feeling in my stomach, I knew that this was a demand too far, which my son would reject out of hand.

When the Council met on the 15th October the French King's demand was the first matter we discussed and as I expected my son was adamant that he would never agree to this. For all my desire for a lasting peace, I sympathised with him, but Roger was adamant that it was a price worth paying.

'Paying such homage will cost you nothing whereas fighting wars is expensive and costs lives,' he insisted.

'No, it would be totally humiliating to have to pay such homage,' my son retorted. 'I will never do it.'

In the end it was agreed that there was no choice but to refuse the French King's demand and ask him, in the interests of peace, to reconsider.

When we had first come to power, Roger had been careful not to play too prominent a role. In fact, he hadn't even attended Council meetings. Yet, with the passage of time all that had changed, so now he didn't hesitate to not merely attend these meetings but also take command of them. It was just another example of him behaving like a King.

The following day we were informed that Lancaster, though now nearly blind, had arrived in the city. I thought him harmless, but Roger was indignant, demanding that he leave.

'Why are you so concerned?' I asked him.

'It's because I've also now learnt that your son is conspiring against us, in which case it's more than likely that he's in league with Lancaster.'

I was understandably shocked, it seemed that Roger thought everyone was a potential enemy, which was exhausting. 'How can this be?'

'You know that he's on the closest of terms with Sir William Montagu, who commands his men-at-arms?'

'Yes, of course.'

'Well, if the information I've been given is correct, they mean to seize power.'

I gasped. 'I must speak to Edward and confront him with this accusation.'

'He'll only deny it.'

'Even so, I want to hear that from his own lips.'

'In that case I think you should put this accusation to Sir William as well.'

'And should the Council be told?'

'Yes, I think they should. I've done nothing of which I'm ashamed and it's still nearly a month before your son is eighteen.'

I was full of apprehension at this development, even beginning to fear for Roger's safety, although I did not say so. The Council met again the following morning for the specific purpose of hearing Roger's accusation, which he immediately put to my son as well as Sir William.

'I have every reason to believe that you're conspiring against me,' Roger declared. 'Do you deny it?'

'Yes, of course.'

'As do I,' Sir William added. 'My liege Lord, the King, is no traitor. It's preposterous to suggest any such thing as he is our anointed monarch.'

'But he's not yet of age and until that day dawns, if his wishes are in conflict with her Majesty, the Queen Mother's, it is she who should be obeyed.'

'Except that we all know who rules here and it is not my mother, but you,' my son responded.

'I am no more than her trusted adviser, striving always to do what is best for this realm.'

'By which you mean what is best for you and your interests.'

'Not so. Have I not always sought to be a loyal mentor to you, your Majesty?'

'No, you've become self-importance personified, carrying on as if you were King, when that title is mine and mine alone. Sir William and I will not stay here a moment longer to be insulted by you.'

They then immediately stood up, whereupon, feeling very upset, I spoke for the first time. 'My dearest son, I swear before God that I have only sought to do what is in your best interests. Power will be yours soon enough. You simply need to be patient.'

'Dearest mother, your paramour has cast a spell on you, making you blind to the truth. Do you not know that it was he who had my father murdered?'

With that he and Sir William immediately walked out of the chamber, leaving me close to tears. I felt as though the world was crumbling around me, but I knew I must maintain a dignified and strong appearance. I told myself to be true to my royal blood.

# CHAPTER 35

## *COUP D'ÉTAT*

'Is his accusation true?'

Roger and I had retired to bed in our chamber in the castle's keep. It was the first time we had been alone together since my son's abrupt departure from the Council meeting several hours previously.

'No, of course not. Haven't I told you that your husband still lives.'

'Yes, but I have no proof that's true. What's more, though I've told my son that his father's alive, he clearly doesn't believe me.'

'He's simply intent on discrediting me, and what better way can there possibly be of achieving that than by falsely accusing me of murder?'

'Even so, if it becomes widely believed, it could bring us down and place you in mortal danger. We need to make peace with him immediately by offering to hand over the reins of power on his eighteenth birthday.'

'Um, perhaps so.'

'There should be no, 'perhaps', about it. I'll tell him that's the case, whether you agree or not.'

'He could still accuse me of murder?'

'I could make it a condition of surrendering power that he agree to leave you in peace.'

'...Which he might not agree to. It would be better, I think, to arrest the likes of Sir William and in so doing clip your son's wings.'

'Have we really any grounds for doing so?'

'Whether we have or not, it would surely put a stop to the threat we face. But look, let us call a meeting of our closest supporters within the Council to see if we can agree on the best course of action...'

'Very well.'

This took place the following evening, whilst in the meantime I was filled with a sharp sense of foreboding, fearing that this would end badly if we failed to act quickly. I also felt a growing sense of confusion, not knowing what to believe when it came to the fate of my Lord Edward. I had always put my trust in Roger but now I wondered if this had been misplaced. He had already admitted once to lying to me and could just be continuing to do so. This was a reflection I found almost too painful to contemplate so tried as best I could to put it to the back of my mind.

When the meeting got under way in our chamber in the castle's keep, I was feeling some concern for my son as he had retired to bed early, complaining of feeling unwell. It then quickly became apparent that Roger's view had hardened. He was still in favour of arresting Sir William and dismissed my argument that this would just make my son even more resentful.

'If Sir William means to attack us, we must protect ourselves.'

'We're surely safe here, though?'

'Within the walls of this keep, yes, but not once we step outside.'

'We must talk again to my son. As you know I favour relinquishing power to him soon.'

'No, I say he's still too young.'

The other members of the Council who were present; our

Chancellor, Henry Burghersh, Simon de Bereford and Oliver Ingram, all steadfastly loyal to Roger, began to take his side, until I was worn down. The hour was growing late and I was tired.

'Very well, arrest him if you must, but I fear this will end badly for us all.'

As I uttered these words, I had no idea how imminently prophetic they would be, for within a few moments there was the sound of a commotion outside the closed door to our chamber. Then I distinctly heard the cry 'traitors!' followed by the sound of a heavy blow.

'In God's name, what is happening?' I asked. Then the door burst open, revealing a fully armoured Sir William, carrying a drawn sword, who rushed towards us, closely followed by several other armed men.

I screamed in sheer terror, as Roger drew his sword. A brief fight ensued in which he managed to slay one of his assailants before, totally outnumbered, he was overpowered along with Bereford and Ingham. Burghersh, meanwhile, had tried to escape, but was quickly seized as well.

'Is my son, the King, here?' I asked, looking at Sir William, who merely gestured towards the door, whereupon I cried out, 'Fair son! Fair son! Have pity on the good Mortimer.'

This appeal was met by silence and realising that my son preferred not to show his face to me, I turned to Sir William. 'I beg you, do not harm Sir Roger. He's a worthy knight and my dear friend.'

At this he merely looked away before leading Roger and his fellow captives out of my chamber. The door then slammed shut on me, the key was turned, and I realised, in a state of utter misery, that I was a prisoner, too.

# PART 4

# AFTERMATH

# CHAPTER 36

# CONSOLATIONS

I was in despair, fearing that Roger would be summarily executed, so that in this life, at least, we would never set eyes on one another again. At first, I couldn't understand how my son's supporters had been able to enter the keep until it was explained to me by a servant that they had daringly made use of an ancient tunnel, leading them up through the hill on which the keep was built.

I could not stop crying, knowing that in a stroke my world had collapsed around me. Eventually, I must have slept a little out of sheer exhaustion, being woken by the sound of my personal maid, Elisa, entering my chamber. She had served me loyally since my return to England from France, was about twenty years old, and I had grown fond of her.

She curtseyed to me as she always did, her face a picture of nervous anxiety. I looked past her and could make out the back of a man-at-arms guarding the door.

'Close the door,' I groaned at her, which she dutifully did. 'I don't want to get up,' I told her. 'I just wish I was dead.'

At these words she grimaced, I could tell she was trying not to cry. 'I am so sorry, your Majesty. Can I fetch you something to eat and drink?'

'Only fresh water. Then you may leave me.'

She did as I asked, whereupon I told her that she could

return in a couple of hours to help me dress. 'I will eat then as well,' I added.

Once more alone, I was left to reflect on how everything had gone so terribly wrong after the great triumph I had enjoyed by overthrowing Despenser's tyranny. I did not regret falling in love with Roger, far from it, but I realised that he had grown too powerful, and that I had not done anywhere near enough to restrain him. Painful though it was to do so, I also had to contemplate the distinct possibility that he had deceived me over my Lord Edward's fate.

I soon found myself praying that my son would visit me. I knew how painful that would be for both of us, but I was anxious to literally throw myself at his feet and beg for Roger's life. Melodramatically, I even imagined myself offering my own life in exchange for his, although behind that was a deep dread that he now intended to execute us both.

When I felt the baby I was carrying move in my womb, I became even more distraught, wondering what would become of it without Roger's protection. It's very existence also left me with fiercely mixed emotions. Whilst giving birth to the child might offer me some measure of comfort following Roger's demise, the infant would never know its father and would have to bear the stigma of being illegitimate. I might also look to save my life by confessing to my son that I was carrying a child, but I still knew the whole experience would be humiliating.

In the event, he did not come near me, and the following morning after another nearly sleepless night, I was curtly informed by Sir William Montagu that I was to be taken to Berkhamsted Castle.

'I take it I am a prisoner, then?'

'...The King wishes you to remain there at his pleasure for a period. I cannot say more at this time.'

'So, what am I charged with?'

'Nothing... at present.'

'May I speak with my son?'

'That will not be possible, I'm afraid. I must ask that you be ready to leave within the hour. You will be conveyed in your carriage under escort. You may take your personal maid with you together with one lady-in-waiting.'

'Is that all?'

'Yes.'

I recall the journey to Berkhamsted as the most miserable of my life, the wind and persistent rain matching my wretched state of mind. When we arrived at our destination, it was late afternoon, and in the gloom of the dying light, I thought it a grim looking place in which to be confined, its walls surrounded, of all things, by a double moat.

As far as I was concerned, I was now very much a prisoner and as we passed through the castle's gate I wondered, gloomily, if I would ever come out alive. It was some small consolation to me that out of my ladies-in-waiting, Joan, Countess of Surrey, long estranged from her husband, and one of my oldest friends, had willingly agreed to accompany me.

During the journey, I had become calm enough to reason that it was unlikely that Roger would be summarily executed. The last thing I thought my son would want to do upon assuming power, was to behave like a tyrant. It was therefore likely that he would grant Roger a trial by his peers, something which would take time as a Parliament would have to be called. This gave me the opportunity to write a letter to my son, begging him, as I had on the night when Roger was seized, to be merciful. After that, I knew I would have to appeal to the governor of the castle to allow my letter to be dispatched, and I could only pray that he would agree.

Yet, when it came to it, I was not even allowed access to any writing material. Of course, I complained at this, only to be informed by the governor, apologetically, that he had express orders not to allow me to communicate with anyone.

'Not even my own son?' I asked angrily.

'I'm sorry, my instructions are clear. I am not to allow you the means to communicate with anyone and that includes his Majesty, the King.'

I remember that it soon turned yet colder, until in late November there was snow on the ground. Meanwhile, I remained in total isolation, dreading the thought, after so many weeks, that Roger was probably now dead. It was sheer torture, my emotions all at sea, making me tearful, angry, and utterly cast down, both by day and by night. I lost my appetite, too, becoming weak and sickly, and even struggling to find the will to rise from my bed.

Joan did her best to offer me what support she could, exhorting me to eat and to take a little exercise. Then one morning I felt pains in my womb and began to bleed. Within a short while I had lost the babe I was carrying, making me sob in anguish.

For a couple of days after that I didn't rise from my bed, but then from somewhere deep inside me I found the will to survive, I ate a hearty meal for the first time since Roger's arrest, and then went for a short walk in the castle grounds. I was still desperately unhappy but was beginning to find the resolve to endure.

On the last day of the month, I was then informed by the castle's governor that I was to be escorted to Windsor.

'I understand that his Majesty, the King, is to spend Christmas there. I also have a letter for you.'

As he handed this to me, I could see that it bore the royal seal but waited until the governor withdrew before breaking it. As I had expected it was from my son.

Dearest Mother,

It is necessary for me to tell you that Roger Mortimer is dead. I know this will bring you terrible grief, but I am satisfied that he was responsible for my father's murder and for that reason alone he was bound to be executed. However, I spared him the ultimate punishment, which Despenser suffered, and he was merely hung by the neck. Now that all that is rightfully mine has come to me, I also want to assure you that I have no quarrel with you. It is clear to me that Mortimer had too much power over you, making you blind to his faults. Nor do I believe that he would ever have relinquished his power had I not acted as I did. I have now decreed that henceforth you will be known as either Madame, the Queen Mother, or Our Lady, Queen Isabella, and are to be treated with the upmost respect. I expect you to surrender all your land to me immediately but please be assured that in return for that I will make you a handsome annual settlement that will ensure that you are able to continue to live in a manner which befits your rank. On no account will I permit you to play any future role in the government of the realm.

Your loving son.

At first, I barely read the first few lines of what my son had written before bursting into tears, its contents confirming what I had feared to be inevitable. After a while, I managed to control my emotions enough to read the remainder. I realised, as I did so, that despite Roger's execution, I had reason to be grateful to my son for choosing not to blame me in any way for Roger's perceived misdeeds, or, for that matter, the fate of his father. I understood full well that he could very easily have made me languish in prison for the rest of my life, or chosen to confine me to a nunnery, so in essence his letter was, in the sharpest possible way, a double-edged sword.

Having lost one man I loved, whatever his sins, I knew I would be a fool to lose another through anger or bitterness. As far as I was able to do so, I therefore decided to hide my grief, and show my gratitude to my son for behaving mercifully towards me. Accordingly, I willingly did as he had required of me and as a man of his word, the settlement he made me was indeed a generous one. I was pleased, too, for Philippa, as she was the principal beneficiary of the lands that I surrendered to him.

Our first meeting since that fateful night when Roger had been seized, was not an easy one for either of us. Even so, when I started to fall to my knees, thanking him for the mercy he had shown me, he didn't hesitate to take my arm.

'Dearest mother, this is unnecessary. Please, let me help you to your feet. You may be assured of my undying love for you.'

'Thank you, my son, thank you.'

He proceeded to treat me with great kindness as did Philippa, allowing me to join them at the high table throughout the Christmas festivities. As these were ending my son then told me that for the time being he would prefer me to remain at Windsor.

'I think it best that you live as secluded a life as possible. With the allowance I have given you, you'll be able to maintain an adequate household with as many ladies-in-waiting as you desire.'

'So, for how long must I be confined behind castle walls?'

'I haven't yet decided. I don't think you realise how hated Mortimer was and I'm afraid, well…'

'…I am hated, too?'

'To an extent, yes.'

'Can I not at least be allowed to go riding? You know how much I love to do so, and it would lift my mood.'

'Of course, once a day, so long as you don't go too far.'

'Very well, I will be content with that. Thank you.'

In the event, I was not allowed to leave Windsor for more than two years, by which time a third spring since my confinement there was fast approaching. Ever since I had married my Lord Edward, I had lived a life of constant travel, never remaining in the same place for more than a few months, so in many ways I found it quite relaxing to be going no further than a mile from the castle walls and back. But then I grew increasingly bored, especially during the long winter months when the weather was too miserable to even step out of doors.

It was at times like these that I would grow deeply mournful, too dejected even to want to rise from my bed. I found it hard to have to live with the knowledge that the man whom I had loved deeply was remembered as a tyrant, when to me he had been nothing of the kind. I also did my best not to dwell on the manner of his death, which could have been more savage and yet to me was still demeaning and cruel. So much so, in fact, that in the dead of night, the very thought of it would make me tremble as my eyes filled with tears.

As to the fate of my Lord Edward, I simply did not know what to believe. My son was clearly convinced that Roger had had him murdered, but the very men who were supposed to have committed the deed had fled abroad, except for one who had shared Roger's fate. I was left to wonder where the truth lay. Whether I was a widow, or not, I really didn't know.

When, during my third Christmas at Windsor, my son told me that he would allow me to leave with the arrival of spring, I was naturally delighted.

'I thought you would like to spend time with Eleanor before her marriage.'

He was referring to his nearly fourteen-year-old sister, who had been betrothed in marriage to the Duke of Gueldres, whose seat of power was Nijmegen in Holland. I had played no part in this and had reservations about its suitability. She was only a year older than I had been when I married my Lord Edward, whilst the duke, a widower, was all of forty-five. I could only pray on her behalf that he would show her all due kindness.

Despenser's cruelty in taking my children away from me followed by the time I had then spent in France, and the demands upon my time once I returned to England, meant that I had not seen anywhere near as much of either Eleanor or her older brother, John, as I would have wished. Nonetheless, I had been able to enjoy her company on successive Christmases since my fall from power and recognised that she had a personality like my own. Now I looked forward to organising her trousseau and we passed some happy days together before her departure.

After that I turned my full attention to the place that has been my home to this very day, namely Castle Rising, in Norfolk. My son had decided that the time was right to be even more generous to me, with the result that this castle was one of several such places that I once again owned. Ever since, I have been able to live a very comfortable existence, receiving regular visits from my son and oldest grandchild of whom I am especially fond.

Of course, any amount of material comfort cannot make up for the grievous loss of those we loved. Nonetheless, I have enjoyed much consolation and that might have been the end of my story if it was not for events that began to unfold some two years after I first took up residence in my new home.

# CHAPTER 37

# REVELATIONS

'Dearest mother, I must tell you that I have been making every effort to bring father's murderers to justice even though they have fled abroad. Earlier in the year I received a letter from Sir John Maltravers, who I have believed to be one of these, which I want to show you.'

It was a pleasant summer's day, and I was most pleased to have been invited to be with the court at Durham castle for the enthronement of the new Bishop of Durham. I saw it as a mark of favour, indicating that my son no longer saw me as an untrustworthy embarrassment. Enough time had also elapsed since my fall from power, for those amongst the nobility who had become angry with my rule to begin to forgive and forget my supposed misdemeanours.

I was surprised when my son took to me to one side, saying there was a matter upon which he wished to speak to me in private and I was intrigued when he handed me the letter from Sir John, so I began to read it. Its contents referred ambiguously to the honour, estate, and well-being of the realm.

'So, has he revealed any information since writing this?' I asked.

'I decided to send William de Montagu to Flanders to speak to him. He had confessed to having learnt after the event, of a plan to have father murdered, which Mortimer instigated, but insisted that this plan was thwarted when father managed to make good his escape. This was thanks to the help of a servant. While achieving his escape father killed a porter.'

'Then what Maltravers has had to say confirms what Mortimer told me. Not that he ever admitted that he had played any part in a plot to murder your father. Would it not now be worthwhile opening your father's tomb to establish where the truth lies?'

'I'm not sure. I'll have to give this further thought. It would have to be done in the upmost secrecy. Maltravers could also just be spinning the same tale that others have done to try and persuade me of his innocence.'

I did not seek to quarrel with this comment, being grateful that my son had been willing to speak to me at all about such a delicate matter. Even so, it was not lost on me that what had probably prompted his decision to do so was that Maltraver's evidence underlined the point that Roger had been guilty of organising an attempt on my Lord Edward's life and in so doing lied to me. This was a harsh reality that I had already spent the best part of four years trying to come to terms with, and it still had the capacity to torture me.

Following our discussion, I heard nothing more from my son on this matter until the end of the year, at which point he told me that he had decided it was best not to take any further action, and once again I did not demure. Yet, some two years later, there was another development of far greater importance.

It was summertime once more; my life at Castle Rising having settled into a comfortable routine of hunting, reading, and listening to music. My son, accompanied by Philippa, with whom I now enjoyed a very warm relationship, as well as my grandson, had come to visit me as they now did regularly two or three times a year.

From the moment of his arrival my son seemed pensive and ill at ease. 'Is there anything wrong?' I was quick to ask him.

'Not wrong exactly, but there is a matter of considerable importance that I need to speak to you about in private. It concerns father. There has been a development...'

Half an hour later, when we were alone together in my chamber, he then produced a letter. 'Is this from Sir John?' I enquired.

'No, no, it's from a Nicolinus Fieschi.'

This name meant nothing to me. 'Who?'

'He's a Genoese priest who's become a senior notary to the Pope in Rome. This letter says that he has met father and received his confession. He states, too, that father has even met the Pope himself. Whatever my past scepticism, I cannot simply disregard such a revelation.'

'No, indeed not.'

'The letter then goes on to confirm the information that Sir John gave me, so I know I must now give that every credence. To put matters beyond doubt I intend asking Fieschi if it might be possible to meet this man who claims to be my father...'

'Where is he living?'

'It seems in a hermitage in Lombardy.'

'You're surely not prepared to travel that far?'

'No, certainly not. I will ask Fieschi if he can bring father to England. I will offer to pay him handsomely for doing so. Of course, the upmost secrecy will need to be observed, so I will make it clear that father must travel in disguise, as I am sure he would wish, and that once we have met, he will be completely free to return to whence he came. In other words, if he is who he says he is, he need have no fear of me.'

'But he cannot remain in England, surely?'

'No, no, I quite agree. And, nor dearest mother, would I ever expect you to live with him again.'

'Well, I thank you for that. I can't imagine that he would want that, either. But what is to be done about the body in your father's tomb?'

'I think it best that it remains where it is until such time as father dies. When that hour comes, if possible, a substitution will have to be secretly arranged.'

'If he dies in Italy, his body might never be returned.'

'I appreciate that, in which event the body presently lying in the tomb will just have to stay where it is.'

I then read the letter that my son had given me, and by the time I had finished doing so, I was aware satisfied that its contents were more than likely true.

'But what I don't understand is why it's taken so long for this letter to be sent to you?'

'I really don't know. Perhaps it is only very recently that father has given his consent.'

'Well, if that's the case, I expect he wants to see you again, and John, too, of course.'

I was pleased for my son that there was now a real prospect of his being reunited with his father. At the same time, I had no desire at all to ever see my Lord Edward again. Indeed, the very notion made me shudder. Though he was still my husband, it was Roger, above any other, who had been the love of my life, and never a day passed that I did not grieve for him.

Tragically, within months John caught a fever and died at

the age of only twenty. The fact that I had endured so many painful losses before, did not lessen my pain at the loss of a child who I had hoped still had his life before him. I went into deep mourning, once more donning my black gown. I was utterly downcast for several weeks, only finding a small measure of consolation in prayer.

In the meantime, my son, Edward, began correspondence, not only with Fieschi, but also the Pope. During this time, he received a letter from the Holy Father, which he showed me, that not only affirmed Fieschi's credentials but also contained a physical description of the man he had met at the papal court at Avignon.

'From what this says about his height, his age, and more than that, his bearing, there can surely be no doubt that this is my father.'

I could see no reason to disagree. My son was now more anxious than ever to be reunited with his father but to his frustration this took far longer to achieve than he would have wished. Plans were put in place for my Lord Edward to be secretly brought to England the following summer, but these had to be abandoned when the French seized Gascony and my son became totally preoccupied with preparations for war.

Fortuitously, a few months later, my son received an invitation from the Holy Roman Emperor to visit the city of Koblenz in Germany to be made a vicar of the Empire. He was happy to accept and it was decided that this might also afford an opportunity for a meeting with his father to take place in that city.

I am pleased to be able to relate that this finally took place in the late summer with my Lord Edward using the alias William the Welshman. Not only that, but he also remained with the royal party, which included both Philippa and my grandson, until they returned to England in the December.

When I met my son again that Christmas, he was quick to tell me about his reunion with his father.

'He's a changed man, grey-haired, stooped, and rather gaunt in appearance, who now devotes himself entirely to a life of prayer. He was also anxious that I should tell you how much he regrets the way you were treated by him, both when you first married and subsequently whilst Despenser had such a hold over him. He begs your forgiveness for his sins against you.'

'Yes, well, that is all in the past, now. I forgave him long ago. Will you see him again, do you think?'

'I very much doubt it. He departed for Italy a day before we began our journey back to England. I will always remember the time we spent together with pleasure.'

—∾—

My Lord Edward died three years later, though it was to be another two years after that, the year of our Lord thirteen hundred and forty-three, before his body was secretly returned to England and interred in his tomb in Gloucester Cathedral. My son, accompanied by Philippa and my grandson, went on a supposed pilgrimage in order to be present when the interment took place, whilst the body of the man my Lord Edward had killed whilst making his escape was given a Christian burial in an unmarked grave elsewhere. I had been asked by my son if I wished to join them but with little hesitation, I had shaken my head.

'This is all having to be done in secret, which is hard enough to accomplish, I'm sure...'

'All those involved have been sworn to secrecy and received generous gifts.'

'Good, but it would still make it more difficult to maintain this veil of secrecy if I attended along with even a minimal number of people from my household. It would also look very strange if I was to come alone.'

As I write these words, some thirteen years later, the world at large still believes that my Lord Edward died in Berkeley castle in the year of our Lord thirteen hundred and twenty-seven. For all I know it may well continue to do so indefinitely. Yet, it's my hope that in the course of time the true circumstances of his demise will become known. He was not an evil man, simply a foolish one with unnatural affections, which were easily exploited, to their advantage, by Gaveston and Despenser. May he rest in peace.

I have lived a life of comfortable retirement, visiting court only occasionally. About three years ago I did so, for the Christmas festivities at Windsor, where I happened to meet Sir John Maltravers. After years in exile, he had finally had his estates restored to him, and was so much in favour that he had even been made Governor of the Channel Islands. He was now an old man with a white beard, but still carried himself well and was apparently in good health.

The momentous events that had led to my Lord Edward's abdication and then escape from imprisonment were now a distant memory, but I had always remained curious about the extent of Roger's involvement in the attempt to murder him. More than that, too, how much he had lied to me. I was also fully cognisant of the fact that Sir John was the last person still alive who could throw any light on this, so I decided to dispatch one of my squires to his chambers with a request that he attend on me that very evening on a matter of some importance.

When he appeared, I invited him to take wine with me and then I dismissed my servants from our presence, making it clear that I was not to be disturbed.

'What I want to talk to you about will, I promise you, not go beyond these walls. You were a party to the plot to end my Lord Edward's life, weren't you? Yes, I know you've always denied it, but I don't believe that's true.'

'…I confess that I had knowledge of it though I swear I was not at Berkeley castle at the time of his escape.'

'So, when did you first discover that he had escaped?'

'When I returned to the castle a day, or two, later, Gurney told me what had happened. We were unsure what to do for the best so sent a message by fast horse to Sir Roger. He arrived at the castle only four days later…'

'So, it was his decision to pretend that my Lord Edward was dead?'

'…Yes, after we had debated the best course of action. We realised that there was a danger of the King continuing to be a focus for those opposed to the Regency. Nevertheless, the Earl decided that this risk was very slight, especially when I told him how meek the King had become, telling me that he was relieved to have given up the throne and wanting only to be left in peace so he could devote the remainder of his life to prayer.'

'And was it also his idea to ensure that the body wasn't properly embalmed?'

'He was anxious that no one who knew the King well should look upon the dead man's face, so he declared that this was the story he would standby to discourage anyone from wanting to do so. He also insisted that the corpse's face be covered by a cloth.'

'Well, I thank you for being so frank with me.'

'There is one thing more I can tell you... Some while later, the Earl confided in me that he had located the King's whereabouts and was having him watched. It was a precautionary measure, so he said.'

'So, he knew when my Lord Edward left the country?'

'Yes, he told me so.'

'...And after that, was, I expect, even more willing to reveal to me that my Lord Edward still lived. Now everything makes sense to me.'

I thanked him again for what he had told me and shortly afterwards, having exchanged a few pleasantries with me, he withdrew, leaving me to my thoughts. Though Roger lied to me, I no longer feel any vestige of anger towards him. Indeed, I still grieve for him and always will. Perhaps he never intended to surrender power to my son, but I like to think that he would have gradually done so as I still believe that he was an honourable man rather than a villain.

Castle Rising, in the county of Norfolk, December 1356

By God's grace, I Isabella, Dowager Queen of England, having resolved to set down an account of my life, have now faithfully recalled the momentous events in which I have played my part. At the same time I have determined that this testament should not be read until after Sir John Maltravers and I are dead.

For nearly a quarter of a century I have lived in this backwater of a place, growing old in the process, whilst paying only occasional visits to the court of my first-born son, King Edward 111.

The weather here can be bleak in winter; cold, with frequent falls of snow as well as a chilling wind off the Wash, which can penetrate my bones so much that they ache as I recall with nostalgia the warmer climes of my childhood in Paris.

I remember, too, with sadness, those I have loved and lost, yet I must give thanks to the generosity of my beloved son, King Edward, in permitting me to continue to live in the comfort, as befits my status.

The walls of the castle's keep are in good repair and thick as are its doors and shutters, whilst my apartments are adorned with tapestries and rugs of the very finest quality. I also have ample furs, both on my bed and for my person, along with fires, which in winter are kept well-banked by my servants.

Above all, I can enjoy the companionship of my faithful ladies-in-waiting and squires, as well as seek spiritual comfort in the time I devote to prayer and the worship of God.

Nevertheless, my dreams can still turn to nightmares, making me wake in a cold sweat of melancholy and regret as I viscerally recall the tragedies that have beset my existence.

Now, as I have become old and face the prospect of death, like my Lord Edward, I have turned to prayer. Throughout the tempestuous years when I was Queen and then Queen Regent, I was surely more sinned against that sinning. Perhaps, I was too in love with Roger to see his faults, much as my Lord Edward was too in love with Gaveston and later, Despenser.

Yet, I sought, and to an extent achieved, peace with both Scotland and France, though it is a lasting sadness to me that we have since entered into prolonged warfare with both countries.

I now pray for the souls of those whom I have loved and lost and commend myself to my Lord God in the hope that he will have mercy upon my soul.

THE END

# AUTHORS' NOTE

It must have been terrifying for Isabella to be married at the age of twelve to a stranger who was about twice her age. To then discover his relationship with Piers Gaveston would have been shocking, yet she still strove to be a good wife and mother. For a time her circumstances improved, until Hugh Despenser arrived on the scene, making her life intolerable.

Having been granted an opportunity to escape she then made the bold decision to seek happiness with Sir Roger Mortimer, before, with his support, leading an invasion of this country, which was overwhelmingly successful; a real 'game of thrones' on a truly epic scale.

What then followed has become clouded by the mists of time in which she has been cast as a she-wolf, creating her own tyranny, alongside her lover, until her son dramatically seized power, thanks to a surprise attack on Nottingham Castle.

There's sound evidence, though, that Edward wasn't murdered. Instead, he escaped abroad, having killed one of his captors. The body of this man must then have been substituted for his own, as part of a successful 'cover-up.'

Subsequently, the truth was revealed, but only confidentially. Edward had by then, in all probability, become a recluse, living a life of prayer in Italy.

Finally, when he died, after having been reunited with his son, his body was secretly returned to England to be interred in his tomb in Gloucester Cathedral, whilst the body of the man he had killed was interred elsewhere.

It can also be said with confidence that Isabella was a remarkable woman who deserves to be better remembered in the annals of history. Most assuredly, she was more sinned against than sinning.

## ACKNOWLEDGEMENTS

After the first named author completed the first draft of this novel, he came to appreciate, given that it is written through the eyes of Queen Isabella, that it would benefit from a female perspective lending greater credibility to her characterisation. He is therefore very grateful to the second named author for her valuable contribution in providing this. He's grateful, too, for the advice received from friends, Chris McDonnell and Julie Barnes. Further, the source material he relied upon most of all was Alison Weir's outstanding biography entitled Isabella: She-Wolf of France, Queen of England.

## About the Authors

James Walker is a retired author living near Canterbury, Kent. He's married with two sons and five grandchildren. He has a life long love of history.

Francesca Garratt also lives in Canterbury and lectures in creative writing.

## Also by James Walker

*Ellen's Gold* - out of print

*My Enemy my love* - out of print

*I think he was George* - out of print

*Shamila* - out of print

*Aliza, my love*

*Ravishment - The first diary of Lady Jane Tremayne*

*The Hanging Tree - The second diary thereof*

*Falling - The third diary thereof*

*Conspiracy - The fourth diary thereof*

*The Song of Buchenwald*